Advance praise for BLOODLINES

By the end, readers will be hooked on the brother-sister team
and assorted shady characters.
-Kirkus Reviews

Recognition for BLOODLINES

Honorable Mention
Mystery/Suspense Novel Category
Oklahoma Writer's Federation, Inc., 2015

Finalist
Fiction Category
Author U Draft to Dream Book Publishing Competition, 2015

BLOODLINES

Lynn Lipinski

Majestic Content Los Angeles

Cover design by Seven25.
Formatting by Polgarus Studio.

This is a work of fiction. Names, characters, business, organizations, places, events are the product of the author's imagination or used fictitiously. Any resemblance to actual persons, living or dead, or locales is entirely coincidental.

Trade paperback ISBN: 978-0-9964676-1-2
eBook ISBN: 978-0-9964676-0-5
Library of Congress Control Number: 2015910074

http://majesticcontent.la

Publisher's Cataloging-in-Publication
(Provided by Quality Books, Inc.)

Lipinski, Lynn, author.
    Bloodlines / Lynn Lipinski.
    pages cm
    LCCN 2015910074
    ISBN 9780996467612
    ISBN 9780996467605

1. Homicide--Fiction. 2. Fathers and sons--Fiction.
3. Detective and mystery fiction. 4. Suspense fiction.
5. Psychological fiction. I. Title.

PS3612.I634B56 2015   813'.6
                                 QBI15-600146

For my father, who believed I could do anything.

John Lipinski
1936-2012

Acknowledgements

My most sincere thanks to:

Stephen Arakawa, my love of eleven years, for his unwavering support and encouragement throughout the writing, rewriting, rewriting, and rewriting process.

My mother, Rosemary Lipinski, and my sister, Laura Kane, for believing in me and my writing more than I did sometimes.

Editors Marlene Adelstein, Susan Krawitz and Peggy Glenn for helping me find the story and polish the manuscript.

Robert Eversz, author and writing instructor, who taught me many things about writing, and told me perseverance is key. He was right.

Beta readers Shizuka Otake, Priya Kapoor, Michele Jourdan, Liz Satterthwaite and Leo Vegoda, whose encouragement and feedback helped me gain confidence and shape the story.

Barry Downer at the Tulsa Zoo and Misha Body at the California Science Center for their herpetology expertise, Arkansas River Historical Society Museum Curator Allan Avery for background on the Port of Catoosa, and Tracy Mott at Home-Mart for helping me find my protagonist's mobile home.

CHAPTER ONE

His mother was dead. The words that he thought were impossible lies a few moments ago became true in one instant.

Zane stood in the morgue, his mother's charred skin burning his eyes and assaulting his nose with its not quite unpleasant smell of burnt flesh. It was her, and also not her, but he knew the only path out of the room and away from this awful sight was to identify her.

"That's her, Sherri Clearwater," he choked out as tears clouded his vision and a huge gasping sob racked his body.

The white-coated technician handed him a tissue with a well-practiced sympathetic expression on his face. Zane took it and pushed his way through the swinging doors, the detective on his heels.

Back in the waiting room, Zane stood there, his back to the pastel art, his arms wrapped around his chest, unable to figure out what to do next. He rolled the damp tissue into a tight ball as though to destroy the evidence of his grief. Time ground to a halt.

The detective scratched at his notepad with one of those yellow pencils they made kids buy for school. His Old Spice aftershave accompanied by a whiff of stale cigarette smoke drifted through the

1

air toward Zane, briefly erasing the disinfectant smell of the room. The man had introduced himself, but Zane had forgotten the name nearly as soon as the man had said it.

This wasn't his first loss. Zane's father was dead too, but that happened before he was born, so it was different. He didn't remember it, obviously. Twenty-six years ago, he was simply born into a world where his father, Ely Clearwater, was dead. He was a shadowy presence in Zane's life, a black silhouette with no details. His mother parsed out facts about him like they were gold: He was an army veteran. He was full-blood Cherokee. He died in a rafting accident.

If growing up without a father was a dull ache that never went away, then losing his mother suddenly and unexpectedly was a twisting knife to the gut.

High above Zane's head a fluorescent light buzzed like a mosquito on a suicide mission to the bug zapper. His stomach flipped like he needed to eat but he wasn't hungry.

Today was the start of the next part of his life, he thought. Today he was reborn, but it wasn't a sensation that came with any joy or anticipation. Just sorrow as cold and empty as the morgue he just left.

"Take me through what happened last night," Old Spice asked.

Zane wished he could remember.

He knew how the night had started.

He had gone into the QuikTrip with the thought of getting a Slurpee but had found himself by the beer case instead, and without too much hesitation, he had decided to toss a year and a half of hard-won sobriety in the trash can. He had bought a tall beer and then sat in the truck, not even driving out of the parking lot before drinking it. Then he had gone back inside and bought another.

"It was a shitty day," Zane said. "Got fired, got drunk."

"Where did you work?"

"At the zoo." Zane saw a flicker of a smile cross the detective's lips. People were fascinated by the zoo. Hearing that he worked there always made them smile and want to ask about the animals. "I am—I mean, I was—on the maintenance staff. I didn't work with the animals. I cleaned up spilled sodas and stuff," he said before the guy could ask.

"What did you get fired for?"

"Stealing turtle eggs," Zane said. "I didn't do it. And I really needed that job."

"Turtle eggs? What would you do with them?"

"I didn't steal them. I wasn't going to do anything with them. Randy at the zoo said they were worth money and a bunch of them were missing."

Old Spice wrote something down.

"Who's Randy?"

"My boss at the zoo. Randy Womack. Facilities manager."

Zane was pretty sure Randy had wanted him out of the way since he had been hired at the zoo anyway, but losing the job had made things a lot more uncertain. Just as Zane had been turning his life around, halfway through welding school with enough money saved up to pay for his last two semesters, plus move into his own apartment. Getting fired wasn't fair, but the world was a tough place, always ready to bring you back to your knees just when you thought you were getting somewhere. Case in point: Not only had he lost his job, but now he was standing in the county morgue identifying his mother's body.

Old Spice leaned forward and cleared his throat.

"How did you wind up sleeping by the river then? Why didn't you just sleep at home?"

What did he care?

"I do that sometimes," Zane said. "When I need a break. I like the sound of the water."

Zane couldn't piece together why the detective wanted to know where he had slept. Then the realization hit him like a punch to the stomach. He was a suspect. A suspect. They thought he had set fire to his mother's home. This detective was watching him, looking for signs that he was lying.

He suddenly wanted to see his sister, Lettie, who at fourteen years old, was all the family he had now. And his responsibility, he realized with a start.

Was this detective going to arrest him? He'd have to call Emmaline to come and bail him out. She was the closest thing he had to family now, even though his feelings for her had been way more than sisterly for years. She'd either be disappointed he was drinking again, or she'd feel sorry for him, or maybe she'd just give up this time. Her parents certainly thought she should cut Zane loose, but she kept him on as her charity project and her best friend with benefits.

"When was the fire?" Zane asked, hoping to fill in some of the gaps in his mind.

"Call came into 911 around ten thirty," the detective said.

He remembered driving home around seven to the Majestic—a trailer park near Mingo Creek that utterly failed to live up to its name. He remembered walking in and seeing his mother in the brown plaid recliner, reminding him of nothing more than a flabby snail poking out of its shell, her face lit bluish white by the television perpetually tuned to Fox News.

She was drinking as usual. A glass jug of wine with a screw-off cap was on the coffee table in front of her, and cigarette smoke hung in the air despite an open window allowing in gusts of cold

October air.

He told her he had been fired. "And you're off the wagon, huh?" she asked. "You're well shed of those two jerks. Isn't Randy the one who kept calling you Tonto or Chief and asking you to do a rain dance?"

Zane nodded. "Emmaline said I could probably go to human resources and file a complaint. They're not supposed to discriminate against people because they're part Indian."

Sherri slid the jug of white zinfandel toward him. "You can't count on some clerk in human resources to fight your battles, son, you know that. You gotta find your own way out. You learned that in juvie, now didn't you? Go get yourself a cup, son, and sit down with your mama."

He remembered all that, but he didn't remember leaving. This kind of blackout was nothing new to Zane. His entire sophomore year of high school was a blank. Jesus. He left her there alone and she died. His heart twisted with grief and guilt. Thank God, Lettie was okay.

"So, you and your mom were watching the ten o'clock news?" The detective scanned his face like it was filled with lines of text.

"I think it was Fox. Not the news. One of those talking-head shows she likes."

"You remember which talking heads?"

"They're all the same to me."

"Bill O'Reilly, you think?"

"I don't know."

"What were you talking about?"

"I don't remember. You ever black out? It means you don't remember nothing."

"Can't say that I have blacked out, myself, though I know a few buddies who have. Couple of them that found their way to AA like you did. I don't touch the stuff myself."

"Good for you," Zane said. He expected no understanding outside of the AA meetings. The normals never got why drunks just didn't stop drinking.

Old Spice cleared his throat. "So, besides your sister, where is your kin?"

"The three of us are it. Mom didn't have any family. Her mother and father died when she was little. She was an only child. My dad's dead too."

"Where was your mom born?"

"She told me she grew up in Missouri, so I guess she was born there. Somewhere in the Ozarks. She was raised by nuns in a Catholic orphanage."

"Were you and your mom close?"

"What does that mean? Yeah, I guess. I mean, I still lived with her, so she was in my business a lot. Telling me to do chores, or sometimes trying to borrow money if it was close to the end of the month. Look, what about Mom's body? Don't I need to bury her or something?"

"It'll be a little bit before the coroner releases her," he said, not unkindly. "Clearwater is an Indian name, isn't it? You a tribal citizen?"

"No, I mean, yes. Mom said Clearwater was a Cherokee name and my dad had Cherokee in him, but she said it was too much work to go proving it."

"You might want to look into it now that she's gone. You might qualify for some of their assistance programs. And maybe there might be some family out there who can help you and your sister with the funeral part," Old Spice said.

CHAPTER TWO

Zane tapped the brakes lightly as he drove into the gravel driveway leading into the Majestic Trailer Park. He could hear the truck's frame groan and squeak as it rolled over the smaller potholes. He'd had long enough practice to know how to miss the big ones practically without looking.

The sun was already low in the sky and sliding behind a bank of pale clouds thick as shaving cream. Crunchy brown leaves littered the ground like scabs. Proof that the Majestic did not inspire homeowner's pride was everywhere. Propane tanks left outside to rust, leaves clogging rain gutters, cars on cement blocks, and faded Christmas decorations that had been up since four Christmases ago. At least it was finally October and they were almost in season again.

He thought he was prepared, but the sight of the yellow police tape and the charred remains of the mobile home made him hit the brakes hard. The home looked melted, the metal frame of its roof bent and drooping like a tissue box someone had stepped on. The front skin had disintegrated, so he could see through the home, and what was left of its blackened contents, through to where the neighbor had parked his red truck.

He took his foot off the brake and let the truck drift twenty more feet, getting as close to his usual parking space as the crime scene tape allowed. He opened the truck door, and the bitter smell, almost a taste, of melted plastic and burnt wood filled his nostrils and coated his mouth. It felt thick and toxic and oddly cold in his throat and lungs. He wondered if he were responsible for hauling away the remains. He doubted his mother had any kind of insurance.

He stepped over the crime scene tape and pulled himself up into the trailer shell, his boots sinking into the damp, pulpy debris that covered what used to be the kitchen's linoleum. It took a few blinks for his eyes to adjust to the darkness inside. He could make out a metal folding chair and the husk of the refrigerator, but everything else seemed to be charred, in pieces and covered with a cake of ash. The air was still and heavy with a bitter, oily smell. No sign of his mother's beloved recliner.

He moved over to the place where it would have been, his right foot stepping on something brittle that cracked loudly. He didn't look down to see what it was; everything seemed unsalvageable.

It was home, but the familiar became something macabre, like the haunted house at the community theatre Lettie loved to go to every Halloween. He half expected a teenager in a monster mask to jump out at him. However, the reality was that his mother had died here last night. Hot tears ran down his cheeks in single streams that he brushed away roughly.

A circle of white light bounced in the air between the wooden frames of what used to be the wall between the kitchen and Lettie's room. He wondered briefly if it was the cops but immediately dismissed it. No cop cars were outside when he pulled up—the place looked deserted. Probably one of the Majestic's nosy residents.

"Who's there?" he called out. Silence, and then a shuffling noise, like someone was pushing a heavy object.

"Zane?" his sister Lettie's voice answered. He moved toward the sound, and they met in the hallway that led to their bedrooms from the kitchen.

She ran to hug him before he could even see her well enough to make sure she was all right, and buried her face into his chest. Her hands clasped over the small of his back, and he rested his head on her shoulders. He had thought all this time that the grief and the fear and shock would be all he would feel, but her presence brought him relief, even joy. Lettie was alive. He held his breath and closed his eyes, trying to shut out the burnt trailer for a moment before he pulled away from her so he could see her face.

"Mama's gone," he said. The profound weight of the loss hit him again, this time combined with the realization that he was the closest thing Lettie had to a parent right now. He needed to be more than just her big brother looking out for her. He needed to be her guardian. His body felt loaded down with the responsibility.

Lettie's brown eyes filled with tears she tried to blink away. She wore a woman's jacket, probably one of Emmaline's, that was much too large for her skinny fourteen-year-old frame, over a pair of baggy sweat pants and a red thermal henley. She had tied her brown hair in a messy ponytail, and crying had turned her nose and eyes red.

"I know."

Zane took the steel flashlight from her hand and shined it down the hallway to his room.

"Anything left?"

"Some of my clothes are okay but they smell like smoke. My algebra book got burned." She gave a half-laugh. Algebra had been giving her a lot of trouble since school started, so he knew she

9

wouldn't be eager to get a replacement.

Zane gave her the quick rundown he'd gotten from the police.

"Do you think my dad knows?" Lettie's father, Roy Magdite, had been incarcerated at McAlester State Prison for armed robbery and assault for the past five years. Lettie saw him a couple of times a year when Sherri would take her there for a visit on Father's Day and his birthday.

"I don't think so," Zane said. He hadn't spoken to the man since he had been locked up, always declining to make the hour-and-a-half trek to McAlester. He didn't like Roy and was pretty sure Roy didn't like him much either. There was a time, right when Roy started dating his mother, that Zane thought maybe the man could be some kind of father figure to him, but Roy never seemed up to the task. He did all right by Lettie though—a fact that gave Zane mixed feelings of happiness for Lettie tinged with jealousy. Zane's father had died before he was born.

Zane pointed the light back down the hallway and walked to his room, which was just past Lettie's. The white walls and doors had been scorched black. Wire box springs with a few strips of fabric still attached were all that remained of the double bed he had slept in almost his whole life.

His pressed wood dresser was still warm to the touch even in this cold air. He pulled a drawer open and found some T-shirts and socks and underwear, still white but giving off a smoky odor.

He didn't have much of value, so there wasn't much point in going through the room. His most valuable possessions were his truck, his cell phone, and his steel-toed work boots. And the two thousand dollars he had in savings.

"Let's get out of here, Lettie. I don't think it's all that safe," he called out to his sister, who he could hear opening drawers in the other room.

He swung the flashlight inside her bedroom, which was more damaged than his own. Lettie stood by the window, shaking rocks into her hand from a dark fabric bag.

"You find the algebra book?" he asked. As the light hit the rocks, they glistened blue and purple and green. It was her crystal collection, part of her goofy magic fascination and belief that spells and charms could get her a boyfriend or grow her hair out or something.

"Um, no," she said, letting the crystals fall back into the bag and sliding it into a duffle bag next to a black box.

She zipped the bag shut, then straightened up to face him.

"Hey, Emmaline was kind of pissed at you for not showing up last night to celebrate. She got big news. You probably heard by now."

"No, my cell phone battery died. What?"

"I wish I had a cell phone," she said reflexively but without much conviction. She'd been bugging their mom for a phone since she started high school. All her friends had them, of course. But Sherri insisted it didn't fit into the budget afforded them by her disability checks. Certainly not with all the booze and lottery tickets Sherri had to buy every week.

"What was the news, Lettie?"

"She got a call from the producers at that reality show *Pageant Gown Project*. They're flying out here to meet her and see her studio."

"Her studio? You mean the spare bedroom in her parents' home here at the beautiful Majestic? You've got to be kidding me."

In a day of life-changing news, Emmaline's good fortune seemed small and out of place. He knew how much she wanted to be on the show ever since she heard about their open casting call. She thought it was tailor-made for her, and he had to agree. She was certainly pretty and peppy enough to keep a TV viewer's attention, and she could sew. She had a string of happy pageant clients, and even a couple of county fair blue ribbons to prove it.

"Well, it *is* her studio. Anyway, you know TV discovered white trash a few years ago. You've got all these shows like *Make Over My Trailer* and *Redneck Wedding.* Us rednecks are the new celebrities."

"If only they'd make a reality show about welding students," he said. "I'd be in the money."

"Welding students who clean zoo bathrooms at night," Lettie said. "They could call it *Real Stories of the Mop and Broom.*"

"Oh, yeah. I've got another piece of news," he said. "Got fired yesterday." He told her about Randy's accusation, and that he had gotten drunk. He left out the blackout part.

Lettie's forehead creased into worry lines just like their mother's had. She blinked double-quick, her eyes staring as she took in the new information. She looked hopelessly small and young to Zane, her teenage face reverting to one he remembered from her toddler years.

"Where am I going to live?" Her voice was shrill and shaking. "What's going to happen to us?" He could hear the rising panic in her voice as the realization sunk in that their mother was gone, fire had destroyed their home, and her brother had no income.

"Don't worry, Lettie," he said. "You'll stay with me in my new apartment. We can move in two days. That's when the lease starts."

"But it's not big enough for the two of us," she said. "Isn't it only…one bedroom?"

"Yes, but we'll make it work. Tell you what. You can have the bedroom just as long as you share the closet with me. I'll sleep on the couch. And I'll get another job, and we'll get a bigger place as soon as I can afford it."

She closed her eyes and nodded, reaching for his arm as if to steady herself.

"And you thought you were getting away from us," she said, trying to make a joke of the situation. They traded slow, sad smiles.

#

They saw Emmaline standing by his truck before they'd hopped down from the trailer platform. She wore a terry cloth zip-up jacket the color of a robin's egg and matching pants that stretched tight across her hips and butt, lighting up Zane's memories of how her skin felt in his hands, his fingers digging into her flesh. Her thick brown hair spilled over the hood and down her back, looking a little tangled and damp, like she'd just taken a shower.

"Lettie, I told you it wasn't safe to go in there," Emmaline said. "I've been worried sick about where you were, but I could have guessed."

"I just wanted to get some of my stuff," Lettie said, lifting the duffel bag slightly. "There wasn't much left, though."

Emmaline's eyes locked with his and despite everything, he felt the usually goofy grin form on his face. She had always had that effect on him, from the moment he saw her at five years old, her hair, blonde then, shining like a halo around her head as she dug holes in the Majestic's old sandbox. She smiled back, but it melted away to a sadder expression as she approached him with her arms extended for a hug.

"So sorry about your mom, Zane."

Her damp hair smelled like coconut shampoo and was cool on his face. He wanted to hold her for a long time, but she was already pulling away.

"Lettie told me about the television show," he said. "Congratulations."

She dismissed it with a wave of her hand. "I'm just glad you and Lettie are safe," she said, squeezing his arm. "So, where are you going to stay tonight? Mama and Daddy are happy to have you stay with us."

Emmaline still lived at home with her parents at the Majestic, though he knew she hoped that would change soon. Her parents had bought some land out in the country and the plan was that they would move out there and she would get her own place. That day was always a few months away.

"That would be great," he said with some relief. "We can't move into the apartment for another two days."

Emmaline's mother, Glynnis Perryman, opened the door. "Lettie! Do you want to eat some lunch?"

Emmaline gave Lettie a quick squeeze. "You can bunk with me, little sis." Lettie smiled and skipped over to where Emmaline's mother stood in the doorframe of their home. Emmaline and Zane watched as Lettie went inside.

Emmaline turned to face him again.

"You know I saw you leave the Majestic last night. I tried to wave you down but you didn't see me. And it wasn't fifteen minutes after you left that the fire started roaring. If you hadn't left when you did, we'd have probably lost you too."

Fifteen minutes. Couldn't be true. Zane waited for the new information to spark a memory from last night but none came.

"I bet that's why the police pulled me in for questioning today," he said.

"Oh, I didn't tell them that I saw you leaving," she said. "I wouldn't want them to get the wrong idea, 'specially when everyone knows that you and your mama don't get along so good. You get these gossips' tongues wagging and soon everyone's convinced that an accident is something else."

An accident. God, he hoped it was.

CHAPTER THREE

Zane sprawled on the beanbag chair on the floor of Emmaline's sewing room, his cell phone charging on the floor next to him and Emmaline's laptop computer balanced on his knees. Time to ask the mighty internet for information about last night. Maybe it would be more fruitful than trying to dig into his memory had been.

Two pine tables were pushed together in an L shape. The longer one was her main workstation, cluttered with a blue plastic cutting board, glass containers filled with buttons sorted by color, a tan basket filled with bobbins, bottles of fabric paint and two red checked pin cushions.

The smaller table held Emmaline's white sewing machine, a Brother model her parents had bought her for her high school graduation. Scissors, a measuring tape, and pink, purple and blue fabric swatches hung from a cork board on the wall behind the sewing machine. Next to them were photos of her pageant clients dressed in her creations.

Lettie sat next to him on a folding chair, staring intently at the screen of Emmaline's digital camera, reviewing footage she had just shot for Emmaline's sample screen test for the pageant gown show.

Zane gazed at the computer screen, web browser up and search engine loaded, just waiting for him to type in the words "Sherri Clearwater" or "Majestic Trailer Park fire." It seemed too crazy to be true, and he hoped that by seeing some details, something would trigger his memory of what had happened.

He remembered some nature special he watched with his mom a few weeks ago, about the polar bears and how they were running out of ice to hunt on. Something about global warming. In one image they showed a polar bear cub standing on a piece of ice near its mother, then the ice breaking off abruptly into a little ice island that floated away. The little cub, stunned, watching his mother get smaller and smaller. It was as near as Zane could get to how he felt. Adrift on an icy island, floating toward unknown waters.

He typed in her name, took a deep breath, and hit the search key. The internet did its behind-the-scenes magic and produced a string of results, lists of soccer league scores and genealogy sites and some city council member in Boise. He tried "majestic trailer park fire tulsa" and got some hits.

Fire guts trailer at mobile home park in east Tulsa

TULSA — A fire early Wednesday morning destroyed a trailer at the Majestic Trailer Park. The fire was reported shortly after midnight by a resident in the mobile home park who said flames were visible.

When the first fire engine arrived, the structure was engulfed. Firefighters worked quickly to extinguish the fire and stop the threat to nearby property, but the trailer and its contents were destroyed, a spokeswoman for the Tulsa Fire Department stated.

According to residents, a woman lived there with her daughter and son. Their names are being withheld pending family notification. It is not known who was home at the time of the fire or what the cause was.

Zane found a video, shot by a shaky amateur on a cell phone, of what looked like his home in mid-burn. But just as he was ready to hit play, Emmaline's voice jolted him back to the room.

"Lettie! Lettie!" The mobile home's thin walls trembled with her shouting. "Where are you? My model Keysha is here. Can you shoot us coming down the hall?"

Lettie rose and turned the camera back on and looked outside the door. "It might be too dark, but I'll try," she said.

Emmaline's voice went up an octave and got louder. "Keysha, I cannot wait for you to see the dress. I got the crystals yesterday and started placing them for you to see. They look gorgeous with the green satin."

"I'm so excited," a girl's voice said. "If you get your own reality show, you have to promise me that you'll have me on at least one of the episodes. I'll do whatever, you know. If you need drama, I can spice it up. Come running in here with my dress all damaged and you fix it, or something."

Emmaline sighed.

"Keysha, please, just talk about the dress. I want to show the producers what my fittings are like without you yammering on about the show. It's against reality show rules to talk about the show while you're taping the show."

Lettie backed into the room and toward the window as Emmaline entered the room with a slender, pretty black girl who looked a few years older than Lettie. She had an oval face and smooth black hair that curled right at her jawline. She wore a pink T-shirt with the word princess lettered in crystals on the front, dark jeans and black ballet flats. She walked with an unusual grace, like a dancer.

"Let's see it," Keysha said.

Emmaline walked to the dress form and pulled off black fabric draped over it, revealing the dress underneath.

"Ta da!"

Keysha clapped her hands over her mouth as if to stifle a scream. "Oh. My. God. It. Is. So. Beautiful."

Emmaline beamed, her cheeks puffed out with a big grin. Zane wasn't sure what was so different about this dress, other than it was green when usually they were pink or purple. Loads of green shiny fabric gathered into folds so complicated he couldn't see how the girl was going to get into the dress.

Lettie glanced over at him, rolling her eyes at the dramatics as Emmaline and Keysha gushed over all the dress's details.

Zane turned back to the amateur video. The cell phone lens rendered the fire into a yellow and orange blob surrounded by black, as though the fire was draining all the light out of the surrounding scene and into its core. The audio was punctuated by the heavy, shaky breathing of whoever was shooting the camera, who'd apparently run to capture the flames on film.

"Dude, what the fuck?" someone shouted near the microphone, and a thin man in a red and white plaid shirt ran from somewhere behind the fire and toward the trees that lined the northwest end of the Majestic.

The laptop slammed shut and Emmaline waved her hand in front of his face.

"Hey, quit looking at porn or sports scores or whatever has you so engrossed and get out of here so Keysha can try on the dress," Emmaline said.

Zane looked up sheepishly and apologized. He grabbed the laptop and scrambled to his feet. Lettie followed him out.

"What's going on? What did you find?"

"Not anything really," he said. "The local news people don't know who we are or what happened, other than there was a fire."

#

Lettie came out of the Majestic's management office, squinting in the midday sun, and climbed into Zane's truck with a fistful of bills and junk mail. Nothing but stress. He'd just spent a quarter of his savings for his new apartment, hoping to get away from the Majestic and his mother's constant requests for money. Now here he was with double the bills.

He was ready to think about something else. His phone bleeped with a new private message via one of the text and photo messaging services he used. It was from someone he'd never heard of before, a user called "dar_dar."

"Sherri Clearwater doesn't exist," it said.

It was a stomach punch whirling him into a black hole. No, Sherri Clearwater did not exist anymore. He imagined her body in a freezer somewhere, wrapped in plastic, and her soul, whatever that was, had left this earth. Who would say such a thing? The news article he saw didn't mention her name.

He clicked on the link.

Slowly a grainy black and white photograph that looked like it was from a newspaper loaded on the screen. A man and a woman stood holding hands outside of a building. The man was tall and wiry, with a round face and dark, wavy hair like Zane's, his eyes hidden by sunglasses. The woman tilted her head up to look at the man, a half-smile on her lips but a worried look in her eyes. She wore a light-colored coat with huge shoulder pads, and a short, dark skirt.

The caption read "Alleged Elk Grove murder suspect Jeremiah

Doom leaves the Tulsa county courthouse with girlfriend Lily Davis after testifying for six hours."

Lettie craned her neck toward him and stared at the photo from the side.

"What's that?"

"No ideal," he said. Before he could show her the message she hit him on the arm in annoyance at his now-deliberate mispronunciation of the word "idea." It drove Lettie nuts when he and his mom spoke "in hick" as Lettie called it.

"Idea. The word is idea. There is no "L" at the end."

"Okay, okay," Zane said. "Anyway, I don't know what this means. Maybe it's a joke."

"Sick joke. Telling us our mother doesn't exist and what? Linking to an old newspaper photo of someone? What are we supposed to think?"

Lettie's voice was high-pitched and anxious and Zane wished he'd opened it when she wasn't around. She clearly found it upsetting.

She grabbed the phone and zoomed in on the picture of the man. Her lips parted like she was about to say something, but then she shut her mouth with a click of teeth and handed him the phone. She started biting at the skin around her fingernails, her eyes focused at some distant point.

Zane re-read the caption.

"Maybe there's some connection to Mom and this Jeremiah Doom or Lily Davis. I don't know. Or maybe some sick person is playing a joke that's not funny." Zane clicked through a mental list of friends, acquaintances and neighbors from school and from Alcoholics Anonymous, but didn't come up with anybody with that kind of twisted, demented sense of humor. Even Randy Womack wasn't that much of a sicko to send something like that.

He put the phone down and released the truck's parking brake.

"Maybe you could ask one of your psychic friends at Earth Spells."

Lettie nodded as though she was seriously considering the idea. Earth Spells, Tulsa's occult and witchcraft store, was their immediate destination. Lettie had signed up for one of their Saturday classes on crystals or spells or some such silliness. He blamed their mother for encouraging Lettie's interest in the occult. She had taken Lettie along with her for a tarot card reading once or twice and then had been happy as a pig in mud when Lettie had wanted to keep coming back. Lettie had saved up her babysitting money to sign up for classes and crystals and incense.

Zane kept his thoughts about the occult and witchcraft and spirituality to himself. The crystals and spells seemed like someone's idea for how to separate fools from their money, but he definitely did believe in a spiritual realm. His spirituality was more tied to his Cherokee roots. His mother had encouraged that just as she had encouraged Lettie to cast spells.

Zane's mom had taken him to a Cherokee powwow once before Lettie was born. He remembered standing in the sun, watching the men in colorful costumes march in a circle, singing songs he had never heard before. He thought the songs must have come from the earth itself, because they made his blood thrum in time.

His mother had said it was like church but to him it felt more like a joyful party, with the elaborate feather headdresses and the children zig-zagging in and out of the line of dancers. An old man with a face puffy and wrinkled like a walnut shell had talked to him afterwards about how the dance brought the people closer to the earth and the animals.

"All of the earth's living creatures and its elements are strung together like in a giant spider web," the man said in a low voice. "If you touch the spider web in one corner, you make the whole structure tremble. Every action causes another action. That is why balance is important. For example, a hunter may kill a deer to have meat and hide for his family, but after killing it, he is sure to offer his gratitude and respect to the deer."

The man had picked a pebble off the ground and polished it on his jeans. "You share molecules with this pebble. Pieces of it are inside you, and you are inside it."

Zane had taken the rock from him and inspected it closely. It was reddish-brown, and rough to the touch. The man had stood up straight, patted him on the back and walked away. Zane had slipped the stone in his pocket, wanting to take care of this little piece of himself.

That night, nine-year-old Zane had gone home and thanked the chicken who died so that he could eat it for dinner, and his mother had hidden her smile behind the Kentucky Fried Chicken bucket.

Zane took his left hand off the truck's steering wheel to pat the stone in his pocket. He remembered showing it to one of the teachers in elementary school, who had told him it was a sandstone, a common rock found all over Oklahoma and of no particular value, but Zane had kept it anyway. It still meant something to him. Carrying it with him was a habit he never broke, and touching its grainy surface never failed to bring back the idea of the world as that big spiderweb.

Every web began with a single thread that connected everything. He thought about the spider as patient and persistent, picking its way along delicate threads around the world. And he knew well what happened when you tried to forget about that connection or try to inflict your own will too much. You just got tangled in the spiderweb. He'd had his years of fighting the world, and that had landed him in juvie and back to drinking. You think you're punching at the world but all you're doing is knocking yourself out.

He liked the spiritual idea of balance, and that there was a flow and a purpose to the things that happened. But his more vengeful side took comfort that balance also meant there was justice out there. That jerks like Randy Womack would get what was coming to them somewhere down the line. Of course, Zane would like to be the one to give him his due but that wasn't right thinking. He could hear one of those true-believer types in AA telling him that instead of plotting his revenge on Randy, what he should do is pray for good things to happen to him. Some kind of crazy, turn-the-cheek kind of stuff. Maybe he'd try it some day. For now, he'd just take satisfaction in the universe's sense of balance.

Did anyone really feel at peace in the world? Zane couldn't feel further from that today. What kind of world did he live in? Was it one of his own making?

He kept the thoughts and memories to himself. He wanted Lettie to have as much of a normal routine as possible and he didn't want her to know how worried he was. She needed to know she could count on him; he was all she had right now. He was glad she'd been willing to go to her class today. Sitting around Emmaline's parents' trailer wasn't going to do them much good. And this witchcraft stuff seemed to make Lettie happy enough — at least it interested her enough to keep her mind off of things for a little while, he hoped.

He drove past the oil refinery alongside the Arkansas River, remembering how he learned in school that Tulsa — for a couple of decades anyway — was the Oil Capital of the World.

That was ancient history to Zane who was born just as most of the oil companies closed up their Tulsa headquarters and moved south to Houston. Good-paying oil industry jobs were hard to come by unless you moved to Texas or Louisiana or were willing to spend weeks on an offshore oil rig or in Africa. Zane had considered it, though not very seriously; now, with his sister to take care of, it seemed like those kinds of opportunities were closed to him forever.

They found parking in the strip mall lot and took about twenty steps to the glass-front shop, dodging an errant shopping cart from the discount clothing store next door.

Zane pulled the glass door open and they stepped inside.

A short, black-haired woman with an old fashioned feather duster stopped cleaning a set of mini witch cauldrons on a glass shelf and smiled sadly at Lettie.

"Kitten, I'm so sorry to hear about your mother," she said, folding Lettie into a hug, the voluminous sleeves of the woman's paisley peasant blouse nearly drowning the teenager in fabric.

Kitten, Zane thought, wondering what this woman's name was. She looked like an otter, with her sleek black hair and rolls of flesh covered in enough cloth to make a circus tent.

The heavy scent of incense made him sneeze. Like every store in every strip mall, Earth Spells was a long rectangle, its walls lined with pine wood shelves, the kind you buy at the cheap furniture store and have to go home and assemble using an Allen wrench. On the shelves were fat Buddhas and Indian feather dreamcatchers and polished stones and tarot cards.

Lettie introduced him to the other woman, whose name turned out to be nothing more exotic than Brenda. She shook his hand firmly, her silver and turquoise dangle earrings jangling, her bright blue eyes looking deep into his. She was probably in her early fifties, about their mom's age.

Zane was the only man in the store. Even in the Bible Belt, there was a subset of Oklahoma women, young and old and in-between, who had decided on magic and tarot cards instead of prayer or wishful thinking. Or maybe magic didn't rule out prayer, he thought, spotting a crucifix like the Catholics usually had, Jesus Christ with his body stretched in agonizing detail, the tiny nails visible in his hands and feet, his face peaceful but sad.

He stepped around a bony woman with her hair in an elaborate up-do with little ringlets framing her face. She was flipping through a book called "Faeries and Auras."

"Do you want to wait here while Lettie goes to the class?" Brenda said. "You're welcome to sit in the reading area in the back. We have free wireless."

"Maybe you could see what you could find out about Lily Davis," Lettie said.

"Lily Davis?" Brenda asked. "Who's that?"

"Zane just got this weird message on his phone. Show her, Zane," Lettie said.

He took the phone out of his pocket and brought up the message. Brenda took the phone in her hands, clicked on the link and then dropped the phone like it was burning hot. Zane's quick reflexes caught the phone before it clattered to the floor.

Hey! Watch it!" Zane said.

Brenda's face flushed red, and she backed up a few steps.

"What's wrong?" Lettie said.

"Lily Davis. Now I know who that is," Brenda said in a low voice. "And, when I touched it, I got just the *blackest* feeling. Pure hate. Anger."

And then she stared at the air like she could see the molecules dancing in front of her. Zane tried to be polite and suspend disbelief. At least she was a step up from that gypsy psychic their mother had dragged them to at the Tulsa County Fair a few years ago. That woman had smelled like she hadn't showered since the Salem witch trials and her shirt had had dried spaghetti sauce on it that had dripped down her left boob and onto her pot belly. She had tried to sell him a small vial of oil as a love potion "to make the girls fall at your feet." Only twenty bucks. He had declined, preferring to spend his money on one of those big turkey legs instead. He had gnawed the meat off the bone like a medieval knight as they had walked around the fair.

As if she knew he was about to roll his eyes, Lettie gave him a stern look that reminded him of their mother telling him to be nice to one of her boyfriends.

"You ever hear of the Elk Grove murders?" Brenda asked. When their replies were only blank expressions, she seemed to make some kind of decision.

"Let me see if Sahara is okay starting the class by herself, then I can sit and talk with you for a while," she said. "Lettie, you can join late, we're starting with a simple healing spell today and you already know those anyway."

Brenda conferred quietly with two women who were talking over a table of brightly-polished stones and crystals. Both women looked at Lettie and Zane quickly before looking away again. The red-headed one, a skinny girl in a baggy tan sweater, nodded seriously, biting her lip in concentration.

Lettie agreed to skip the class and the three of them went to the reading room in the back to talk. Brenda disappeared into an adjacent storeroom and came back with hot cups of tea and passed them around.

CHAPTER FOUR

A red Persian carpet covered the industrial grey carpet that obviously came with the store, and around it were two overstuffed couches, their seats saggy from overuse. Brass reading lamps beamed hot circles of light over the seats. A long, narrow table was covered in messy stacks of magazines and pamphlets, and a few lit candles.

Still pale and withdrawn from the strong reaction she'd had from seeing the photo, Brenda sat down on one of the couches. She slipped off her black leather clogs and pulled her feet under her, as though she was trying to get as close to the fetal position as she could without actually laying down. She clutched her smart phone with its jeweled case in her right hand, as though ready to call the supernatural police or Ghost Hunters at any minute.

"It was a hot summer night in 1983," Brenda said, pausing for dramatic emphasis and giving Zane the distinct impression she was enjoying her performance as much as any community theatre thespian. He could just imagine her conducting a seance in that same breathy voice.

"These two little Tulsa girls were brutally murdered on their first night at sleepover camp. People said it was the end of

27

innocence for every man, woman and child in Oklahoma. It was a horror film come to life right in our backyard. I was pregnant with my first born. I was terrified, I couldn't imagine someone doing that to a child."

She pushed a button to bring her phone to life and quickly typed something in. Her eyes flickered with recognition at whatever came up on the tiny screen.

"The girls' names were Jennifer Alexander and Amanda Griffin. Jennifer was strangled. Amanda died from head injuries from a heavy, blunt object. She was raped too."

She took a sip of the tea and swallowed with a loud gulp. Zane hated the theatrics but there was something about the way she dropped his phone, almost as soon as she touched it, which had him worried she really had felt something from beyond. He wouldn't have thought she'd had time to even read the caption, though of course she'd lived through the events, so she probably recognized the people from the photo.

"Everyone was on pins and needles waiting for them to find the killer. Summer camps all over the state were cancelled. Finally, the sheriff arrested Jeremiah Doom, a Cherokee Indian with prior felony convictions for burglary and rape. Doom had escaped from county jail and had been on the run for three years when those little girls were killed."

The word Cherokee caught his attention. But there were lots of Cherokees in Oklahoma. That didn't mean there was a connection to him.

"Everyone breathed a sigh of relief. They caught the killer. There were some folks—Cherokee neighbors mainly—that grew up with that Doom man that said he was innocent and that his being accused was a race thing. But most of us considered the case closed. They had the killer. We could go back to our regular lives because this terrible monster was behind bars. Thing was, months and months later, a jury found him not guilty. Not enough evidence. The good ole boy sheriff was sloppy. Ain't that a surprise. I remember seeing in the newspaper pictures of how they kept the evidence from the crime scene in dusty boxes in a jail cell. Stuff disintegrated. Even today, when there are all the TV shows about cold cases being solved with science and DNA, they say that no one can solve the Elk Grove murders because the evidence either disappeared or just turned to dust."

"What did our mom have to do with that?" Lettie asked.

Brenda shook her head. "No idea. I have some vague memory of Doom still living in Sallisaw in the bosom of his tribe, but I don't know about the girlfriend. I remember seeing her in the newspaper like this—she came to the trial every day. People whispered all sorts of stuff about her—that he abused her, that she helped him kill those little girls, that he got her addicted to drugs. It's funny what you remember. I always thought that people were really hard on her because she was a white woman and he was an Indian and she seemed so devoted to him."

Brenda got that faraway look in her eye again. "Well, devoted is not the right word. More like *controlled* by him, if you know what I mean."

Women's laughter erupted from behind the black screens where the witchcraft class was apparently underway. Brenda didn't seem in any hurry to break up the party, but Zane did get the sense she'd shared all that she knew. He was tired of her dramatics and really just wanted to use the store's wireless to look up Lily Davis and Jeremiah Doom and try to figure out what the connection was to his mother.

"Well, thanks for the information, Brenda. Maybe we should join the class," Lettie said.

"You go ahead," Brenda said, collecting her teacup and heading to the back storeroom.

Left alone, Zane looked at dar_dar's user profile. The account was created today, dar_dar had no one in his or her circle of friends, and had sent only one message - the one to Zane.

He looked at the photo, which was posted on a website devoted to the victims of the Elk Grove murders. Whoever ran the site hadn't updated it recently.

He reread the message. "Sherri Clearwater doesn't exist."

He typed her name into a search engine. All he got was a bunch of listings of people with the first name Sherri who lived in some place in Florida called Clearwater. Adding Tulsa to the search string didn't get any hits either. Maybe the person who messaged him was right. Sherri Clearwater didn't exist, at least on the internet where it counted. The closest she got to using technology was her old flip phone with its low-tech card games. He and Lettie had tried to get her to buy a used computer from one of the neighbors once but she didn't see the need and said it was just a trick to get you to spend money you don't have. Which made no sense to him, since he watched her open her wallet many times to buy candles that supposedly would draw money to them that never seemed to work.

He scraped his memory for details about her childhood. There were only a few. She said she'd grown up in an orphanage in Missouri. A Catholic one with nuns who hit her with a yardstick when she was bad. Her parents had died in a car crash. No brothers, no sisters, no kind aunts and uncles to take her in. She didn't talk about it much, swatting off their inquiries like mosquitoes on a summer night. And as far as he knew, she had no baby photos, no school year books and no old report cards. At least none he'd ever seen.

She was just as close-lipped about her past as she was about his father, who she said drowned on a canoeing trip with a bunch of drinking buddies on Little Sugar Creek in Missouri before Zane was born. He had certainly tried to find him often enough, once even paying thirty-five bucks to some website that promised to trace your Cherokee roots. But no luck.

One of the few times she had talked to him about his father was on the day she had dropped him off at the juvenile hall for his sentence. He was sixteen.

"I know you think I'm pretty worthless, Zane, but you got to remember I'm doing double duty for you. I'm your father, and I'm your mother," she had said. "I have two jobs with you and I'm doing the best I can. You may have inherited some bad traits from your father, but I need you to do the best you can to overcome. Do your time like the courts say and spend that time thinking about what you want from life."

He remembered desperately wanting to ask her more about his father—what bad traits??—but she had already gotten out of the car, the conversation over and time for him to start his punishment. Left hungry for more details about his father, a man who apparently left no trace in his mother's life or on the internet.

Kind of like his mom. She had somehow avoided leaving a footprint on the digital stage.

Zane typed in his own name and looked at the results. Mainly a series of links to his profiles on different social networking websites and some old photos of him from parties. No news links to the story of his arrest back in high school—as a juvenile offender, they kept his name out of the papers, though he knew if he searched on Dan Brouse's name, the story would probably still come up. Some things never went away, and that night had left a mark on him and Dan. All the news coverage called Dan the victim, like he was some

LYNN LIPINSKI

sort of helpless pipsqueak that Zane assaulted without provocation, instead of mentioning that just like Zane, Dan had been in his share of fights and the only reason Zane got the better of him that night was because Dan was more drunk than he was. He typed in the name and clicked on the first headline, dated July 15, 2005.

Teenage suspect in aggravated assault may be tried as adult

The teenager accused of beating 16-year-old East Central High School classmate Dan Brouse with a baseball bat may be tried as an adult, the District Attorney's office announced today.

Brouse suffered head injuries after police say he was beaten unconscious with a baseball bat at his mother's apartment during the theft of a PlayStation 2 video game console. Prosecutors and family say it is not known yet if he will recover from his wounds.

District Attorney Chuck Grant said Friday, "It's a case with very serious injuries. We will closely evaluate the case and whatever charges we ultimately decide upon will be determined based on the evidence."

Officers were first notified of the assault by another classmate of Brouse and the suspect, who called the police and initially told them he had been at Brouse's apartment to pick up an item Brouse had borrowed from another friend.

The classmate told police he had left Brouse's apartment when he saw two Hispanic teenagers on the stairs, one carrying a bat and the other a golf club. He said he later heard sounds that led him to believe someone was being beaten with the bat and club.

Police found Brouse lying on the floor of the apartment,

32

severely injured.

The classmate later admitted to the police that he knew who assaulted Brouse, and that he was there during the incident. He said the suspect wanted to steal some of Brouse's property to sell for money to buy a gun.

Was it really that simple, Zane wondered. This happened, then that. The newspaper reporter who wrote this narrative made it seem clean and sequential, but Zane's memories were chaotic fragments and shards of emotion. Those terrifying days after his arrest. His memories of the assault were both vague and stark, like one of those cartoon flip books where you flip the pages and watch a cat move across the page, but one with missing pages. He didn't remember if he'd really told Jason Manner, the unidentified classmate in the article, if he'd wanted to buy a gun or what he would use it for. God knows what had run through his head, but he knew he and Jason had downed a bottle and a half of generic maximum strength cough syrup.

Just like last night. It was a chilling thought.

Brenda came back into the sitting area and sat down, breaking him out of his thoughts and back into the moment.

"I keep thinking about that message and what it means," she said. She reached up with one hand to play with the beads on one of her long earrings.

"You know, no one ever really heard about Lily Davis again after that trial. I hadn't thought about it much, but she really did just disappear. I just tried looking her up, thinking she was probably a mom with three kids living in Jenks and married to a plumber, or something, but nothing came up. Dead end. But you can still find stuff on Jeremiah Doom. Apparently he still lives around here somewhere. Sometimes the local news tries to find him to interview him about that trial but he never talks to anyone about it. He probably never leaves Sallisaw, because everyone there thinks he was falsely accused."

Zane wished she would get to the point of whatever it was she wanted to tell him. Maybe that he was cursed and he needed to pay her money to undo the spell?

"I didn't want to say it in front of Lettie, because I really don't have any evidence of it. Just this gut feeling, you know?"

He nodded like he knew what she meant, hoping that would get her to spill the beans faster and get out of his hair.

"I know this sounds crazy, but I think your mother is Lily Davis. I know I've got nothing concrete to point to, but my intuition is usually spot on."

"What do you mean, my mother is Lily Davis? Like my mother adopted me?" He smiled ruefully, remembering childhood daydreams that he'd been adopted and his real parents, who of course were rich beyond his wildest dreams, would come and scoop him out of the Majestic and into a life of wealth, including guitar lessons with Kirk Hammett of Metallica and a black stallion named Fortune that he would ride around their estate.

Brenda pulled her phone out and brought up a close-up picture of Lily Davis. "Look at the face. The eyes, eyebrows, the lips. Your mom was probably fifty pounds heavier than in this picture, but if you look around the face and the features, don't you see a resemblance?"

Zane tried to imagine his mother skinnier, younger and dressed in something other than stretch pants and a big T-shirt. He squinted at the picture, trying to blur the details of Lily Davis to see if she morphed into his mom. No luck.

"I don't see it," he said. His mother didn't seem anything like this woman. He saw more of a resemblance between himself and the man standing next to her, than he did between Lily Davis and his mother.

"I see it," Brenda said. "I think your mom was Lily Davis. Think about it. She never talked much about her past, and being raised in an orphanage—isn't that a little, well, fictional-sounding? Do you know anyone who was raised in an orphanage besides Little Orphan Annie or Oliver?"

"Who?"

"Just characters from some Broadway plays," Brenda said. "Not important. Look, I'll leave that idea with you. I won't put it into Lettie's head because I don't have any evidence and I don't want to upset her any more than she already is. Might be worth checking out."

"How would I check that out?"

"I don't know, honey," she said. "Maybe the county records office? I think they keep name changes and stuff like that on file."

Zane didn't put a lot of stock in Brenda's intuition, but he didn't have any other ideas either about the meaning of the message and why that person would send a photo of these two people to him. He thought maybe he'd take her advice and see if he could find any evidence that his mother changed her name; or at least maybe he'd mention the theory to the cop and they could do the digging.

The front door bells chimed and a booming male voice reverberated through the store. "Wake up, sinners! The time of reckoning is near!"

"Jesus Christ," Brenda said with exasperation and no trace of irony, hoisting herself off of the couch and walking quickly into the front of the store. Zane followed her.

A tall man in his sixties stood in the entrance, his worn working boots planted in a fighting stance. His face had the weathered look of someone who spent a lot of time outdoors, and what was left of his grey and silver hair was shaved to the shortest buzz cut. Anger and contempt filled his eyes and had etched thick frown lines into his forehead and around his thin lips. Behind him and on either side were two kids who had inherited his lanky frame and unpleasant expression. The boy looked to be about fifteen, with an unstylish and unflattering haircut that had likely been done at home with a pair of kitchen shears. He wore dark green corduroys that were an inch too short and a man's flannel shirt he had yet to grow into. The girl was about Lettie's age, with long straight brown hair that grew past her hips, wearing a long skirt and long-sleeved blouse with a parka on top. White sneakers peeked out from beneath the straight hem of her denim skirt.

The girl reached out to touch one of the Jesus figurines but her father slapped her hand away roughly.

"God calls on you to stop your sinful ways and hear his word," the man said to Brenda and Zane. "John 8:44 says, 'You belong to your father, the devil, and you want to carry out your father's desire… When he lies, he speaks his native language, for he is a liar and the father of lies. Yet because I tell the truth, you do not believe me!'"

"No solicitors, Ebenezer Scrooge," Brenda said. "Don't make me call the police again, old man."

"Exodus 22:18 says, 'Suffer not a witch to live.' Samuel 15 says, 'For rebellion is as the sin of divination, and insubordination is as iniquity and idolatry…'"

"What does that mean, 'suffer not a witch to live?' Are you threatening me?" Brenda said. She took her phone and waved it in the man's face. "I'm calling the police." She punched the numbers in and put the phone to her ear while the girl stepped forward and handed Zane a comic book about the size of a pack of cigarettes. In white block letters on a black background it said "Spells of Blood."

To the left of the words was a picture of the fictional wizard Harry Potter wearing his trademark round glasses and striped scarf but sporting a pair of devil's horns. Zane flipped through the book enough to get the storyline that the Harry Potter book series was the devil's latest recruiting tactic.

Lettie came out of the back with Sahara and some of the other women.

"I know that girl," she whispered in Zane's ear. "She's in my class this year. Her name's Mary."

"Mary gave me this." Zane handed her the comic book and she scanned a few pages.

"She brings books like this to school sometimes. She gave me one about how Catholics weren't really Christians."

"Hello? Operator? Yes, there is a man threatening me in my store," Brenda said.

"As Isaiah says, keep on, then with your magic spells and with your many sorceries, which you have labored at since childhood. Perhaps you will succeed, perhaps you will cause terror. Either way you serve only the devil, not the Lord," the man said as his parting shot. He swung the glass door open wide and left, not even glancing at the boy and girl, who scurried after him and were nearly hit in the face by the door.

Lettie dropped the booklet into a trash can behind the counter.

"Last time they came in, those creepy little kids left comic books hidden all over the place," Sahara said to her. "Whatever happened to 'do not judge lest ye be judged?'"

"They think they are saving us," Lettie said. "That girl Mary is really serious about it, like it's her full time job. I bet I'm going to hear more about it at school."

"Tell her you'll put a spell on her," Brenda said. "Turn her into a toad."

CHAPTER FIVE

Their next stop was the zoo, so Zane could pick up his final paycheck from human resources. Lettie, more than a little oblivious to the fact that Zane might not want to spend time there, relished the visit like a fun field trip. Her excitement about seeing some of the animals made him smile and he agreed they could do a quick tour of the reptile area. Both of them liked the sleek, brightly colored snakes, frogs, geckos and lizards.

They headed for the conservation center, laughing as they usually did about how there was a ceramic plaque of monkeys right under the word REPTILES. As though the zoo was trying to do some kind of bait and switch. "Come see the cute monkeys! Surprise! Only us snakes in here." Lettie and Zane had a running joke about it — when they saw monkeys they would laugh and call them reptiles.

A little boy ran ahead of his parents, pointing at the squat building that housed the zoo's collection of all things slithery. "I want to see the dragon!" the boy yelled.

The Komodo dragon was Zane's favorite too. In fact, it was the zoo's most notorious resident and its biggest attraction. Named Budiman, the ten-foot long monitor lizard weighed as much as a welterweight boxer and was known for its poisonous saliva and its ability to run twenty-five miles an hour—for a short distance anyway. Zane was fascinated by the creature. When he looked in Budiman's eyes, he felt like a caveman staring at a dinosaur.

Doug Grummer, one of the guys who worked in the reptile house, told Zane that in some zoos in Asia, they drew crowds to their Komodo dragon exhibit by feeding the huge lizards a live goat or deer every few weeks. People would stand and watch as the goat sniffed around the pen, until it became aware of another presence in the enclosure and then finally realized it was in the den of a massive killer that saw it as prey. In a flash, the Komodo struck, usually biting into the soft belly and tearing out guts, then leaving the creature to die. It would dine off of its corpse for a few days.

Here in Tulsa, Budiman had to settle for chickens and rabbits and mice—pre-killed of course.

Zane opened the door to the conservation center for Lettie, and they were greeted with a puff of hot and humid air, smelling slightly of chlorine and old moldy wood. He peeled off his coat and draped it over his arm waiting for his eyes to adjust to the cave-like interior, light glowing from heat lamps in every terrarium to keep cold-blooded creatures warm. An aquarium filled with hermit crabs and bright coral drew Lettie to it.

The door opened again and Zane's stomach turned as he heard the barking voice of his former boss and the zoo's facility manager, Randy Womack.

"Clearwater, is that you?"

Up close, Randy looked like a sunburned and grumpy Pillsbury dough boy with his round red face and perpetual grimace. Virgil, the perpetual sidekick, followed a few steps behind.

"Told you it was him," Virgil said. He nodded his head.

"Have you ever heard the term *persona non grata*?"

Either Randy and Virgil hadn't heard the news about the fire at the Majestic, or they didn't care. Zane knew better than to expect any sympathy from these two bozos. Who, by the way, were to blame for his drinking binge. He clenched his fists for a moment until the voice of some former drunk from AA in his head corrected him - they didn't make you take a drink, did they Zane? You did that all by yourself. He let his fists fall open but didn't respond.

"You deaf, Tonto? I asked you a question."

Randy stared at him, his open mouth like a trap for flies. Lettie turned from the hermit crabs and watched them with narrowed eyes.

Zane stared back at Randy, determined not to blink until he did. Randy lasted four seconds before sliding his eyes to the snapping turtle in the tank to the right, and then back.

"It means you are not welcome around here," he said. He put his hands on his hips and shifted them forward in some lame attempt to show he meant business. Zane took a deep breath. *Count to ten*, he thought.

"*Persona non grata* is Latin," Virgil said. From his satisfaction, Zane was pretty sure Virgil had just learned the term and what it meant a few moments ago.

"I came to pick up my check, and my sister wanted to look around. It is a public place, Randy." His throat felt tight, and he could feel a white hot tension spreading through his shoulders. *One. Two. Three. Four.*

"I asked payroll to pay you out in buckets of pennies, but they wouldn't do it," Randy said. Virgil snickered.

Don't respond. Five. Six. Seven.

"Are you guys auditioning for *Dumb and Dumber*? Because I think they already made that movie," Lettie said.

"Lettie, cool it," Zane said. *Eight. Nine. Ten.* He was on enough of a razor's edge as it was, anger clouding his mind and his muscles twitching with rage. If one of these losers insulted Lettie, he wasn't sure he could stay in control. And getting into a fight with them at the zoo wasn't going to help anything and probably would get him kicked out. Right now, he had the high ground and he wanted to keep it.

The radio on Randy's hip squawked, something about lights going out in the Rainforest exhibit. Randy responded with a quick "I'll be right there" and slipped the radio back in its holster.

"If I see you again today, I'm calling security," Randy said.

"To tell them what? That we're looking at the animals?" Zane straightened his spine and squared his shoulders, trying to take full advantage of his height next to these clowns. His voice was calm and low.

Randy pointed a thick index finger at him. "Don't cause me no trouble." He pushed the door open with both hands and marched out. Virgil hitched his wrinkled work pants up and scurried after him.

"Should we take off?" Lettie asked. He could see worry mixed with disappointment on her face.

"No, let's go see the Komodo dragon." Lettie smiled and he put his arm around her as they walked to Budiman's enclosure. Lettie always talked about how the Komodo dragon seemed like a mythical creature, one that might breath fire or hypnotize its prey just with its eyes.

They had the exhibit to themselves. As they entered, Budiman turned his head toward them, his long tongue tasting the air. He rose to his feet, tail twitching, and moved toward the glass. His thick claws made deep impressions in the loose dirt floor that were then wiped clean by his heavy tail. His thick eyelids drooped halfway down yellowish eyes that stayed trained on Lettie and Zane.

"I think he recognizes you," Lettie said.

Zane sat on the bench facing the enclosure, noticing how Budiman's eyes never stopped watching him and Lettie. He was alert and curious—but not in the way a dog or cat might be looking for a belly scratch or treat—but in the way that a predator watches a potential meal. And to the giant Komodo dragon, king of the food chain, everything was a potential meal.

Zane flashed back on Brenda dropping the phone, the dark look on her face as though she'd touched the fires of hell. He heard her voice in his head. *I think your mother is Lily Davis.* Did that mean Jeremiah Doom was his father?

He looked at Budiman, willing him to move, but the monitor lizard only lashed the air again with his yellow forked tongue, watchful and still. He'd read online that Komodo dragons were neglectful parents to their young. They laid the eggs and then left the young ones to fend for themselves against predators, including other Komodo dragons who would happily cannibalize their young. His mother hadn't been so bad. He remembered her saying: *You may have inherited some bad traits from your father, but I need you to do the best you can to overcome.* Had she all this time been protecting him from a father who would harm him? And did he have it in him to harm others?

Well, he knew the answer to that. The question was, what didn't he know? What other secrets were waiting for him?

Lettie hugged her knees to her chest, and Zane's eyes refocused on her reflection in the glass enclosure. She looked like a pale ghost, her face as white as paper. The tears rose from deep inside him and popped out of his eyes. He leaned his head down and wiped them away quickly, not wanting Lettie to see that he was scared.

#

Hours later, Zane laid on the sofa bed in the Perryman's mobile home, the television showing some sit-com rerun with the sound so low only the laugh track was audible. Zane didn't want to disturb Emmaline's parents, who'd welcomed him and Lettie into their home without hesitating. His new apartment would be ready for move-in the next day. A door clicked open softly and he heard the mobile home foundations creak and squeak under someone's light footsteps.

"Zane, you awake?"

Emmaline stood in the doorway in a white tanktop and pink pajama bottoms. Her nipples pushed through the thin white knit fabric.

"Yeah," he said, energized by the sudden rush of blood down south.

"I'm so stirred up about this show and about your mom and this weird message, I can't sleep. I came out to see if you were having the same problem."

"Come on, lay down," he said, holding up one side of the blanket so she could slide in next to him. "We'll have a campout like old times."

"Should I see if Mom and Dad have a bag of marshmallows?" She crossed her arms over her chest and rubbed her upper arms vigorously. "It is cold out here." She smiled and crossed to the sofabed. "Are you sure there's room?"

"Definitely," he said, scooting a few inches to give her more space even though he really wanted to do nothing more than pull her in the bed and hold her tight against him. But he had to wait for her first move. It was the unwritten 'friends with benefits' clause of their relationship. She decided when their friendship could extend into getting naked. If it were up to him, it would be all the time. He'd loved her since, well, forever. But she vascillated between him and a series of boyfriends, never too serious with him or them. Always looking for something better.

He could smell her vanilla body lotion. She lifted up the blanket and folded herself underneath, and he could feel her body heat like a cloud around him. She chose a neutral position with about six inches between them, and laid on her side, her head propped on her hand.

"So, did you figure out who sent that message?"

"No," he said. "It was a new account, just set up today. No friends, no followers, one message sent."

"So basically an anonymous message."

"Basically."

"There's a lot of crazy people out there. They see stuff on the news and want to, I don't know, make a name for themselves or something."

"Mm hmm."

Zane wasn't following what she said. He was thinking more about how close she was and how he would love to run his hands over her, to kiss her lips.

"So, I talked to my boss Avery about why Randy fired you."

That warm feeling he'd been enjoying went cold.

Zane flopped back on the pillow and stared at the ceiling.

"I didn't steal anything like turtle eggs. I didn't steal anything."

"I know that," she said. She squeezed his shoulder lightly, setting his nerves to tingle and warming him all over. "But I just wanted to ask Amory what he'd heard. They had their senior zoo staff meeting today and I thought maybe it came up."

Emmaline's boss Amory Atkinson was in charge of fund-raising for the zoo. Emmaline took a job as his secretary two years ago with a vague promise that it would be on-the-job training for a better-paying position in the communications or marketing departments. So far that hadn't materialized, though he did throw her a bone now and then by letting her write a donor solicitation letter or work with a graphic designer on an event invitation. Her real passion was dress design though, but one or two pageant gowns a month wasn't exactly paying the bills.

She popped up on the sofa bed and stuck her belly out and acted like she was leaning on a cane in her best Amory impression.

"Now, Emmaline, I swear by my nanny's grave that no one is saying to the police, for example, that your darling friend Zane stole anything," she said in a flowery Southern accent. She mimed twirling the cane and stroked her chin.

"We had a good talk with Mr. Womack about what this information might mean to our dear donors who give so much of their valuable money to our cause of conservation and preserving these wonderful, endangered species, and I do not believe you will hear him continuing to tell his story to anyone who will listen about the theft of any tortoise eggs."

She flopped back down on the thin mattress, setting the metal frame of the sofa bed into a series of squeaks and shrieks. The force of her body weight lifted him into the air by a half-inch. He rolled over on his side and propped his head on his hand.

"Amory even said that you could use him as a reference for another job, so you don't have to go through Randy."

Zane laughed. "Well, that's nice, but it will look pretty funny for a maintenance worker to get a reference from the head of fund-raising."

Emmaline shrugged. "He's just trying to help. He likes you. Actually, I think he thinks you're pretty cute…"

Zane half-smiled. "Thanks for that. If I'm looking for a sugar daddy, I know who to call."

"You could move in with him. He lives in a gorgeous house by Swan Lake. You could have dinner parties!"

"Great," he groaned. "That'll be my new plan."

"Beats the Majestic, baby," she said.

"You haven't found your way out yet," he said.

"Give me time," she said.

They laid in silence for a while.

"So what happened that night?" she said.

"Em, I don't remember what happened."

She looked at him for a long time, like she could read his mind just by staring into his eyes long enough.

"That fire was an accident," she said.

"How are you so sure?"

"I know you."

She inched toward him on the mattress, and gravity pulled him closer to her. Her head was on his pillow now, the tip of her nose touching his and her eyes directly on his.

"I've known you nearly my whole life. You're a good person. I know you've gotten in fights and stuff when you've been drunk, but this is different. You wouldn't do something so awful. You just left at the wrong time, that's all. Your mom was probably smoking and fell asleep and the afghan caught on fire."

He wanted to believe her. He wanted to drown in her eyes and in her trust and never wake up again.

She leaned in, pressing her lips on his, and he opened his mouth hungrily and kissed her back. His right hand traced the curve of her waist and hip and then squeezed the soft fleshy place where her butt turned into her thigh.

"We can't, not here, my parents," she said. "They're in the next room."

"I won't make a sound," he said.

"But this cheap old sofabed will," she said. "And the floor's no better."

"I need you so bad."

Emmaline rolled out of bed and onto her feet.

"Come on," she said. She walked down the hallway toward her studio where Lettie slept and turned left into the laundry room. It was dark and smelled like laundry soap and bleach. She shut the door behind him, and even though he wasn't convinced the laundry room offered that much more privacy, his desire for her was so strong he didn't care. It was such a relief to bury his face in her hair, to kiss her neck.

He grabbed her arms and pressed her against the washing machine, his hands on each of her breasts. She hooked her thumbs into the waistband of her pajama pants and panties and let them slide to the linoleum. He slid his gym shorts down his legs until they pooled around his feet, and lifted her onto the machine.

It was over faster than he wanted. She leaned in and rested her cheek against his. Her warm breath on his mouth was intoxicating.

"You turn me on so much," he said by way of excuse.

"It's all right," she said. She jumped lightly to the floor and pulled her underwear and pajamas up over her legs and hips in one motion.

The toilet in the bathroom across the hall flushed. They both stopped moving, eyes locked.

"Lettie," he said.

"We were pretty quiet," she said, not sounding too convinced. They waited silently as they heard the faucet turned on and off, the door opened, and light footsteps down the thin carpet to the studio. Finally they heard the light click of the studio door shut.

"Off to bed with you," Emmaline said, opening the laundry

room door for him. She smacked his bottom playfully as he walked into the hall. He tried not to wonder if she had sex with him because she felt sorry for him or because she wanted a distraction. He knew what his motives were. He loved her. He fell asleep with her smell on his hands.

CHAPTER SIX

Three coyotes stood outside the burnt mobile home, one sniffing the ground and another sniffing the air. The third one, with brownish red and white fur and the attitude of the leader of the pack, stared into Zane's eyes, his ears pointy and erect like he was listening very carefully. Zane stared back, wondering if he should run. A coyote by itself would be scared of him; but in a pack, they had the advantage.

The lead coyote broke the stare and shook his head, then turned and walked toward the woods at the edge of the trailer park. The two other coyotes followed.

After a few paces, the lead turned his head and looked back.

Follow me, he seemed to say.

Zane fell in line with the pack, nodding at the lead canine when he turned his head back occasionally to affirm Zane was still with them. The woods ahead were gold and brown with sunlight falling in bars on the dried grass and dirt at its base.

Something red lay on the exposed roots of a maple. Red plaid fabric stretched over something round. A flannel shirt. The coyotes formed a half circle around the body of a man, his face hidden in shadows. Three sets of eyes watched him approach.

"Who is it?" he asked, feeling like the coyotes would understand him, maybe even answer him.

The smaller one, the one who had sniffed the air before, put a paw on the man's leg, and tilted her head at him. She had a more delicate snout and smaller ears than the other two, and her fur was the color of honey. She put her nose down then raised it, in a sort of canine nod to him.

You need to find out, she told him, somehow making the words float across the air between them.

Zane sat straight up, stifling a scream. Emmlaine was banging on her parents' bedroom door.

"Wake up! They're coming now! Wake up!"

His heart was beating so fast that his body shook.

"Wake up, Zane!" Emmaline stood over him, still wearing the same pajama pants as the night before.

Zane wiped some sleep out of his eyes, not really awake. He wanted to pull her back into the bed and tell her about the dream, but she clearly had something else in mind. Something that involved everyone in the trailer.

"What is it?"

"The producers of *Pageant Gown Project* are on their way here, now."

She stood checking her phone while he tried to make sense of what she was saying. He felt like he was swimming, water distorting every word into hums and indistinguishable patterns.

Lettie came into the living room and sat down on the thin sofa bed mattress next to Zane. She pulled her knees up to her chin and started picking at her blue toenail polish.

"I need you two to get dressed," Emmaline said. "Lettie, did you fold up the sleeping bag?"

Lettie nodded without looking up from her toes.

Emmaline's parents, Cy and Glynnis, filed out of the bedroom and into the kitchen. Glynnis, clad in a lavender robe, headed straight for the coffee maker. Cy stepped around her and to the front door where he plucked the *Tulsa World* newspaper off the stoop.

"Emmaline, you had me reaching for the shotgun with all that banging around."

"Sorry, Daddy, but the producers, they just flew on some overnight flight."

"I guess I'll make some biscuits and gravy then," Glynnis said.

"How did you sleep, Zane?" Lettie asked, her eyebrows raised and a smile playing across her lips. At first he thought she somehow knew about the coyotes, but after a beat he figured she meant his rendezvous with Emmaline. She was usually a heavy sleeper but he guessed she probably didn't sleep too soundly with all the emotion of the day before, and the fact they slept in a strange place last night.

"Fine," he said, trying to put a warning tone in his voice. He didn't need her drawing Em's parents' attention about anything she might have heard or, God forbid, seen last night. Cy might be an old guy but he could probably throw a pretty hard punch; and Glynnis had a rolling pin in her hand that he could envision as a weapon. Not that Emmaline wasn't old enough to make her own choices. What they did last night under her parents' roof was pretty poor judgment, but he never could control himself around her.

"Well, Zane and Lettie, you probably ought to see the paper first," Cy said. "They wrote a story about your mom." He pulled one of the colonial style wooden chairs out for Zane to sit in. "Can I get you a cup of coffee?"

Zane nodded and sat down. He smelled the fresh newsprint, and ran his hands over the picture of his mother's face from her driver's license. Next to it was a photo of the burnt remains of the mobile home.

Lettie, reading over his shoulder, said "Why do they have to point out she was disabled and unemployed in here? That's not anyone's business!"

Emmaline gave Lettie a hug and kissed the top of her head. "Baby, no one reads the newspaper anymore."

Someone was knocking at the door.

"Wow, that was fast! Go get dressed, you two!" Emmaline folded the newspaper and covered the front page with the sports section. Zane and Lettie rushed down the hall to the studio to change clothes.

Emmaline swung the door open, her big smile falling as she saw Kristy Diguchi, reporter from KTUL-TV on the doorstep, her helmet of straight black hair framing an overly sympathetic face. Standing by the white van emblazoned with the Channel 8 logo and slogan "We're Tulsa" was a cameraman, fiddling with some settings on top of the long news camera.

"Is Zane Clearwater here?"

"What makes you think he's here?"

Kristy's friendly expression turned calculating, and she gave Emmaline the once over.

"Well, a few of your neighbors said he was probably staying here with his sister. And isn't that his truck parked right there?"

Emmaline, who had been holding her breath, let out a big sigh. "Right now? It's not even seven in the morning. And we're expecting company."

Sensing an opening, Kristy leaned in with a new smile. "Our viewers want to know about Zane. They want to hear his side of the story. I can help him do that right now."

Emmaline opened the door a little wider. "I'd have to ask him.

I'm not sure he wants to talk."

"Are you Emmaline? Mrs. Ahern over there was telling me that you two are real close."

"Yeah, I'm Emmaline. This is my parents' home. Zane and his sister are staying here for the time being."

"I noticed Mrs. Ahern's Christmas decorations are up pretty early. It's not even Halloween yet." The reporter smiled like she and Emmaline shared an inside joke. Emmaline wasn't going to bite though.

"They're up all year round. They're just coming back into season now. Look, let me talk to Zane and see what he says. Wait a sec."

A white Ford Taurus pulled slowly behind the news van along the gravel road. Emmaline could see two men in the front seat and a woman in the back.

"Shit," she said, smoothing her hair down. Emmaline stepped out on the stoop and shut the front door behind her.

"Your company?" Kristy asked. She snapped the fingers of her left hand at the cameraman and made a rolling motion. He responded by hoisting the camera to his shoulder and aiming it at the bony man getting out of the passenger side of the white car. He had straight, light brown hair and tough skin like he'd spent a lot of time outdoors. Aviator sunglasses covered his eyes.

"Emmaline?" he said.

"Peter Valentine? Nice to meet you. Why don't you come on inside?"

Kristy reached past Emmaline to extend her hand to Peter. "Kristy Diguchi, KTUL. Are you an attorney for Mr. Clearwater? Because we'd love to talk to you."

"Attorney? No. I'm executive producer with Cakewalk Productions from Los Angeles. We're casting a new reality show and Ms. Perryman here is one of our finalists. Did Emmaline call you? Because we asked her to not pursue any publicity at this time."

"I didn't call them, Peter," Emmaline said. "They're here for something else."

Kristy was bouncing from one foot to another, and glanced over at the camera man to make sure he was still filming. Peter followed her eyes and raised a hand up.

"Can we turn the cameras off while we sort this out? Please?"

The camera guy pulled the camera off his shoulder and held it in his hand. The man and woman who had been in the car got out. Both were younger than Peter. The woman wore a red knit cap over curly brown hair and a red puffer jacket over blue jeans and hiking boots. The man, who was a full foot taller than Peter and at least forty pounds heavier, wore a tan barn jacket with a corduroy collar, and grey chinos. All three had a kind of Hollywood vibe—dressed in clothes that a wardrobe department would have selected as a rustic, back-country vibe. They introduced themselves as Shana Burns and James Silk, also with Cakewalk Productions.

Kristy's phone rang and she scooted past Emmaline and Peter to take the call in relative privacy on the other side of the van. Emmaline filled Peter in quickly on the fire and the *Tulsa World* article. He listened intently and nodded, keeping his facial expression neutral.

Zane came out the Perrymans' front door, his brown hair slicked back with water, and the neckband of his white T-shirt was wet in the back. He smelled like the lavender soap that Glynnis kept in the guest bathroom. He wore basically the same outfit as the day before. Only the T-shirt was fresh, if you could call it that, since he'd grabbed it from the burnt mobile home yesterday and it smelled smoky.

The cameraman shouted for Kristy, then hoisted the camera back to his shoulder and aimed at Zane. Kristy rounded the back bumper of the news van and hung up the phone. She pushed past Shana and James and stood in front of Zane on the opposite side of the railing surrounding the raised stoop. Even though she was at a serious height disadvantage, she planted her feet like a fighter and extended her hand up to Zane's.

"Kristy Diguchi. I am so sorry for your loss. We want to help you tell your story to the people of Tulsa. We can do an interview right now that will be on this morning's news."

"I don't know," he said.

One of Tulsa's police cars pulled up and parked on the opposite side of the news van. A male and female cop got out of the white car and walked toward the Perryman's trailer. Zane could see Mrs. Ahern in the trailer next door peeking out of her window. This was more excitement than she'd seen in years, he thought.

"Are you getting this?" Kristy hissed at the cameraman who simply raised his hand at her, his eye still glued to the viewfinder and the camera pointed at the cops.

"Zane Clearwater?" asked the blonde female cop, with that polished veneer of unblinking courtesy he'd seen from the police before. "Will you come with us to the police station? The detective wants to talk to you about your mother's death."

CHAPTER SEVEN

Zane watched from the backseat as the blonde cop pulled into visitor parking at the long red brick police station. Shiny white police cars were parked the length of the building, and two cops, a man and a woman dressed in stiff midnight blue uniforms, paused their conversation to watch him get out of the car and walk to the door. His hands weren't cuffed and they assured him he wasn't under arrest, but it still felt like a perp walk.

The station was lit inside like an operating room. Bright fluorescent lights ricocheted off the shiny white tiled floor. He followed them past the raised fake wood reception desk. The only person who didn't look starched from head to toe was a man in overalls and a grimy camouflage hat, sitting in a black plastic chair along the wall.

The cops led him through one of the white unmarked doors along the room's perimeter and into the hallway and then into a small room, almost the size of a closet, with a square steel table and two chairs.

Blondie flicked on the lights with one hand, then pointed at one of the chairs. The ceiling lights buzzed softly.

Detective Old Spice walked in and with a curt nod dismissed

the two cops.

"Hi Zane. Thanks for coming down."

"I forgot your name," Zane said.

"Angus Pastor, Zane. You can just call me detective, like everyone else does."

He leaned back in the chair and stretched his leg out to rest one black boot on the table. Zane stared blankly at the stains on the worn sole of his boot.

"We've got a little more information about your mom." Sweat ringed the white fabric of his shirt under the arms, and he looked like he hadn't shaved since the day before. A pack of Marlboro reds shone through the thin cotton shirt pocket.

"Do you know if she died from the fire? Or something else?"

Old Spice shook his head. "But it's interesting that you ask that, because that is what I think is at the heart of this matter. Now, she was a smoker, your mother?"

"Yes, pack a day."

"Terrible habit," Old Spice said, patting the pack in his pocket with a rueful smile. "Hard to quit. You smoke?"

Zane shook his head.

"Good, good boy there. Don't start. That's the way to do it. Anyway, see, sometimes these types of fires are real simple to figure out. Someone falls asleep with a lit cigarette, it falls on the sofa cushion and smolders for hours. Some of these cushions, when they burn, they let out some bad fumes. Like hydrogen cyanide. Makes it where your lungs can't use the air you breathe."

"Is that what happened to my mom?"

"That's what I thought, sure enough," Old Spice said. "Those cigarettes, see, the tobacco companies make them so they don't stop burning, even if you're not puffing on them. They do that for the smoker's convenience, if you will, so suckers like me don't have to light and relight our cancer sticks to get our dose of nicotine. So if you fall asleep mid-puff and your lit cigarette falls down it just keeps burning away."

"I've seen her fall asleep with her cigarette before. There's tons of burns all over her chair and table where she always sits."

"You know just about half of residential fires start that way? It sure is something to think about for smokers like myself. But the thing is, that's not how we think this one started."

Zane started thinking that the detective was playing with him. God, he wished he could remember what happened that night. He felt panic moving through his gut like an iceberg as he tried to read between the lines of what the detective was telling him. He told himself that hurting his mother was something he just would not do—could not do. He may have wanted her to change or get out of his business but that didn't translate to taking action to get her permanently out of the way. Or did it? Had he acted out destructively again, fueled by liquor and disappointment and anger and nowhere to go? He remembered seeing Dan's dried blood underneath his fingernails the day after the assault that landed him in juvie all those years ago, and realizing something terrible had happened.

"This fire started in the kitchen area, and it looks like a fire that started fast. Not something that smoldered on for hours. This one looks like maybe somehow a flame lit up right around something very flammable."

"The propane tank."

"Maybe. Now do you remember smelling a propane leak before you left?"

"I told you I don't remember much," Zane said.

"Yeah," Old Spice said. "I sure miss the days when we could smoke in here." He pulled out a roll of peppermints and popped one into his mouth.

"It seems like you got out of that mobile home just in time, Zane. That's what some of your neighbors say. They say they saw you drive off just a few minutes before the fire started. They also say you and your mom fought a lot."

"You're making me feel like I need a lawyer in here with me," Zane said, losing all interest in sharing information with the cop about the message he got yesterday and Brenda's spooky intuition about his mother's identity. He didn't need their help to find out more. Let them figure it out on their own.

"Of course that is your right to have an attorney," Old Spice said, sucking loudly on the candy. "But I'm just having a conversation with you. You know you're not under arrest."

"So I can leave?"

"Sure, anytime you want. But listen, I'm trying to help you, kid. It may not seem like it, but I'm on your side. Arson is a felony, and when someone dies in a fire that someone set, that's first-degree murder. Oklahoma's a death penalty state, son. Let's try to reconstruct what happened that night. You were drunk. We'll take that into account. Your mom, I heard she's said some awful things to you before. Abusive, some of your neighbors say. So she got you riled up. You weren't in your right mind. You turned up the propane, you threw a match, you left."

"That's crazy. I didn't do that."

"But I thought you didn't remember nothing," Old Spice said.

"I don't, but I wouldn't have..." Zane said.

"Is there a chance that you might have? Have you been wondering yourself?"

"No," he said with more conviction than he felt. "I wouldn't do that. Now you said I could leave."

"You can leave anytime you want."

"I pick now," he said.

No one offered him a ride home, and he wasn't about to ask these cops for any favors. He headed west on 11th Street, walking on the gravelly shoulder of the road as cars and trucks whizzed by at forty-five miles an hour. A cold puff of wind whipped his hair around. A thick layer of grey and white clouds covered the sky, as oppressive as a thick net lowering down on him.

If what the detective was saying was true, Zane was lucky to have gotten out of there in time. Too lucky.

He gritted his teeth and shut his eyes. He tilted his face to the sky and prayed.

"Listen to me, please, God. I don't know what to do. You are good and you are forgiving and I need your help here."

Praying felt strange and blank. What made him think that God would listen to someone like him anyway? In AA, all they talk about is turning your life over to God. It's about admitting you have no control over your life. And if the things that happen to you are God's will then what good is there to pray? You weren't supposed to pray to change things — you were to pray instead to accept things and learn from them.

Well, he didn't want to learn from them anymore.

"I DON"T WANT TO DO THIS!" he shouted to God or to anyone who was listening. He stumbled over a water bottle half filled with some gold-colored liquid, and kicked it ten feet into the vacant lot to his left. An SUV blasting rap music whooshed by him. He felt incredibly isolated, outside of the normal world's activities and plans.

What if he set the fire? It was horrible to contemplate, that he could be responsible for her death. What would Lettie think and say? How could she forgive him? How could he forgive himself?

He didn't want to face it. In that moment, he actually wished he were dead instead of here, faced with his mother's death, his sister's care. Nothing but problems and no light at the end of the tunnel.

A semi blew by him and he considered stepping out in front of the next one, letting its ten thousand pounds of metal obliterate him into blood and body parts. What a relief the nothingness would be. He'd never have to arrive at the Majestic, never have to see the burned shell of his home, never have to wonder again if he caused it. Never have to bury his mother.

But Lettie would. And then she'd have to bury him too. He couldn't do that to her. Though she would at least have her dad, even if he was in jail.

Lettie. What was worse? A mother and brother dead? Or brother in jail for killing your mother? It was completely fucked up. And then there was still the weirdo who sent the message that Sherri Clearwater didn't exist. He didn't want Lettie to deal with that. All she wanted to do was go to her homecoming dance and practice her spells and live in a world where magic worked and life was good all the time if you just drew the right energy to you.

He passed one of the historic Route 66 signs and forced himself to think about driving down that road all the way to California. He'd never been out of Oklahoma, but he'd hoped one day at least to see the ocean. How many people had traveled this road looking for the same kind of escape? In Alcoholics Anonymous, they talked a lot about how some people think that by moving locations, you can leave your old problems behind and start a new life. But the grim reality was that "doing a geographical" (as they called it in AA) was that you often just moved your problems with you. You were in a new place with the same issues. So though the idea of leaving Tulsa appealed, he was reasonably sure it wouldn't help.

The QT where he'd bought the beer loomed ahead. If only he

could wind back the clocks and make himself buy a soda instead of that beer and then drive himself to a meeting instead of to the Majestic. It wasn't fair. It wasn't fair. He wanted to stamp his feet like a toddler, to rage at the world for his life and his choices. He was just another one in a long line of criminals, outcasts and losers who were born in the wrong trailer park to the wrong parents with the wrong genes and grew up to do all the wrong things. Probably the best thing he could do for Lettie was to make sure it didn't happen to her.

He shoved his hands in his jeans pocket and his fingertips touched the fine grit of the sandstone given to him at that long ago powwow. Carrying the stone was a habit he'd formed over many years but it had been a long time since he had given it much thought.

In his pre-teen years, before alcohol and drugs numbed out the pain of not knowing his father, he had come to associate the walnut-faced old man from the powwow as a living connection to his father, Ely Clearwater. He'd pictured his father as ruggedly handsome, a man who knew how to start a fire and catch a fish with his bare hands; a man who could live off the land and would have taught Zane how to do the same. Once or twice, Zane had even let his imagination drift so far as to picture the three of them driving together in the car, his father behind the wheel and both his parents singing along to some song on the radio while the flat Oklahoma scenery rushed by the windows.

He swallowed the pain down. The hole of sadness expanded exponentially with his mother gone. He hungered for a connection to something larger than himself. Maybe now was the time to dig into the past and see what he could find out about Ely Clearwater.

CHAPTER EIGHT

The sun was low in the sky and behind enough cloud cover that the trees and houses barely cast shadows. Overhead, birds flew in a V formation, perfectly synchronized. The light wind was crisp and cold, keeping the Majestic's residents indoors and likely in front of their televisions or maybe starting to make dinner. Not even the trailer park's children were out to play.

The rental cars from the production company were parked outside of Emmaline's parents' home.

He instinctively looked to the woods, thinking of the three coyotes in the dream. Was there a man's body out there? The man who had started the fire? He took a few steps toward the trees, calling himself foolish but still compelled to see what was there. Behind him, a door banged open and he heard Lettie saying his name. He stopped and turned to her.

"Is everything OK? Where are you going?"

Her eyes were red and puffy from crying. In response, hot tears surged into his eyes. Thoughts of how precious she was to him, how he was responsible for her, and how she was all he had, overwhelmed him. He wrapped his hand around her thin shoulder and pulled her to him.

"Nowhere. I'm not going anywhere. And yes, everything's all right. They just wanted to talk to me about funeral arrangements."

Lettie looked doubtful, but she let the comment pass.

"Why don't we go look in the trailer and see if we can find her birth certificate or insurance papers or something? They told me I might need that." The lie came out pretty easy, and Lettie looked relieved to have something to do rather than just sit around and worry. No way was he going to lead her into the woods if something like a dead body lay there waiting to be discovered. Anyway, it was just a stupid dream.

The burnt skeleton of their home was still a shock to the eyes, looking blacker and more decrepit than yesterday. The yellow tape still surrounded the perimeter, and some bureaucrat from the city of Tulsa had stopped by to put a sign on the outer wall saying the building was condemned. Well, duh, thought Zane. Even the squirrels knew to look elsewhere for shelter.

Not only did it look terrible, but the unnatural and sharp stench of burnt chemicals and plastic still hung around the place like a cloud.

Zane pulled work gloves out of the Perrymans' tool shed and a flashlight from his truck.

"Just be careful, Lettie, stay near me," he said. He held down the crime scene tape with his boot so they could step over, then lifted Lettie on top of the trailer shell.

"If she had important stuff like that, I bet she would have kept it in her room," Lettie said. "I remember I needed my vaccination records for school and she had them in a metal box in her closet."

Zane was glad to start somewhere other than in the kitchen as it seemed completely ruined. Lettie led the way down the hall past their rooms and into their mother's bedroom.

All that was left of the bed was the metal innards of the mattress and box springs and the frame that held it off the floor. In their efforts to extinguish the fire, the firefighters had thrown items on top of the bed, including a photo album with its plastic cover crackled like alligator skin.

"There's only a few photos in here," Lettie said, opening it to flip through. "One of you eating cotton candy." Zane looked at it over her shoulder.

"I remember that. She took me to the county fair when I was in second grade. I think I threw up later that day on the scrambler."

Lettie didn't see much else to comment on, and laid the album back down on the bed. "I'll do the dresser," she said. "You can have the closet."

The closet still had clothes hanging on the rod and boxes on a shelf above, but all were scorched black. Some of the clothes were in pieces, just a sleeve or part of a leg of fabric, while others had somehow, strangely been completely untouched by the fire. His mom was a big woman and her fashion choices tended toward pants with elastic waists and T-shirts in bright colors.

But it was the boxes on the top shelf that he thought might contain what he was looking for. He'd never seen her bring them down and look through them but Lettie had. He had no idea what was in them, just that Mom had kept them there for years.

He pulled the first one on the left down, brining with it a rain of ash and debris, and set it on the floor. The box was scorched and dusty but intact. Inside were a few melted music cassette tapes from the eighties, some concert tickets, a dried rose and some postcards. It all looked like it hadn't been touched in years, so he set it aside and brought down the second box.

"Look at this," Lettie said. When he turned to face her, she had her arm outstretched toward him with a silver gun with a pearly white handle laying on her open palm.

He took it from her and examined it. It was an old .38 revolver. He spun the cartridge open to see if it was loaded, and found two bullets in the chamber. He dumped them out and slipped them in his jeans pocket. The gun he laid carefully on the floor.

"There's bullets too," Lettie said, holding out a cardboard box.

"Just put them down," he said, gesturing toward the gun on the floor. "We'll take that with us."

"I didn't know Mom had a gun," Lettie said.

"Me neither."

He opened the second box. Like the first, it was relatively intact. On top of an embroidered light green pillowcase was an unsealed envelope from EZ Pawn with a receipt for a Black Hills gold ring with a garnet stone and a turquoise pendant with silver chain, pawned for a total of $120 just the week before.

The rest of the box was just old tablecloths and sheets, nice ones with flowers and swirls embroidered on them. He put it aside to take to his new apartment along with the gun. They looked like they might be very old, like maybe an heirloom.

Lettie ran her hand over the old fabric.

"I wonder what she was saving this for?"

Zane shook his head. "I don't know. Maybe she was going to give it to you when you got married or something. Like something she would pass down to her daughter."

"Oh." Lettie's breath caught in a sob. Zane wrapped his arms around her.

"She was so proud of you, Lettie. She always said you were so smart and kind, and you were going to do great things to help people," he said. "She said you could be anything you wanted to be."

He rested his chin on top of her head and held her tight while her shoulders shook with hiccup-like sobs.

"I miss Mom," Lettie said.

It took a moment for it to sink in. Lettie's simple statement echoed in his ears as he realized he missed her, too.

A week ago, all he did was complain about his mother for getting on his case, wanting money, drinking too much. But now that she was gone, he remembered more good times than bad ones. She had her faults, but didn't everyone? He certainly did.

"I miss Mom, too, Lettie. But it's funny—you have some of her same facial expressions. So sometimes when you look worried or when you are concentrating hard on something, I see her in you."

"You do?"

"I do. You're strong, like she was."

He wasn't sure if he was saying the right things, but he knew it was important to say something—and he was grateful when she finally gave him a smile. He was all she had right now. He felt humbled by the need to protect this girl, to make sure she would be all right.

"Let's finish up here, okay? We'll look a little more to see if there are any blankets or towels or anything like that in the linen cupboard. We can take them to the new apartment. I get the keys today."

"Yes, I can't wait to see the new apartment," she said. She dried her eyes with her shirt sleeve.

They moved in to their new apartment in a sporadic rain, more like a heavy mist that coated their few boxes of possessions with a coat of water droplets. Just last week, Zane had, with a jubilant sense of freedom, put a thousand dollars down as first and last months' rent on a furnished one bedroom on the first-level of a two-story red brick building in east Tulsa. Today, he moved in with a heavy thickness, like a blanket over his heart. But one that still allowed a seed of anxiety to take hold, whispering, how will you pay next month's rent?

They stopped in the office first, where a bored brunette wearing a cheap, shiny blue suit and a nametag that read Irene drew up a new lease adding Lettie as a tenant at no charge, for which he was thankful. She handed him the keys and a welcome kit with a sheet of rules about where to park, where to take the trash and how to pay the rent.

"Welcome to your new home," she said with a brief smile.

They crossed the cracked asphalt of the parking lot back to their unit. It was one of eight identical buildings, placed at equal distances over a rectangular lot. Twenty feet away, he could see a ground floor apartment with its windows wrapped in aluminum foil most likely by some person working the night shift and trying to fool their body into thinking day was night. A small grey and white dog with matted fur sniffed along the brown, crunchy grass, looking for food, with no owner in site.

Holding the cheap metal screen door open with his foot, he unlocked the wooden door and pushed it open for Lettie.

The furniture was mismatched and worn: a brown and orange plaid sofa, a pressed-wood coffee table, a pine kitchen table and three green and white pine chairs. The bedroom's stained beige carpet was partially covered with a full-size mattress on a metal frame and a cardboard dresser with drawers that didn't quite shut right. No television, but electricity and water were included, it was close to the Majestic, the grocery store and Lettie's school, which turned out to be a stroke of luck.

The living room had a large north-facing window that drew little light on this grey fall day; the bedroom looked out on the building's trash dumpster. The kitchen had a relatively new refrigerator and stove and cheap but clean white cabinets. Vinyl linoleum made to mimic granite tiles stretched across the floor.

He checked the refrigerator to make sure it was plugged in. He had no idea how he was going to make this work financially with no job and Lettie to feed. But he had to try to make things as normal for her as he could. He was head of their family now.

Lettie unloaded her trash bag of clothes in the bedroom. If she was disappointed, she didn't show it.

"Maybe we could look at the second hand store for a television," she said. "They also have tons of appliances and stuff like toaster ovens and blenders and crock pots."

"Yeah, that sounds good," Zane said. He liked to hear the excitement in her voice about setting up house, however temporary it might be.

He heard footsteps outside the door and looked up. A petite woman stood outside the screen door. Her black hair was pulled back in a thick braid, and she wore an Earth Wildlife Foundation T-shirt under a red velour hoodie, with matching pants and bright white sneakers. She had on heavy black eyeliner, an orangey-brown eyeshadow and eyelashes like tarantula legs. "Hi, I'm your neighbor. Saw you moving in and thought I'd say hi. My name's Magnolia."

Zane shook her hand and introduced her to Lettie.

"Irene said y'all lost your home in a fire. I'm so sorry to hear that. Let me know if you need anything at all. I'm just next door."

They needed everything, he thought. Much more than she could possibly offer. But still, it was nice of her—and she was cute. She stood in the door for a few seconds, awkwardly, until they both smiled and with a wave, she went on her way.

"I'm really tired, Zane. Maybe I'll take a nap," Lettie said.

"Take the bed—here, I found some old sheets in a box from home. I'll help you make the bed."

He unpacked the sheets and sniffed them. They didn't smell too badly of smoke, just a little musty. He shook them out in one fluid motion over the mattress.

A brown envelope fell out of the folds and onto the floor.

Lettie grabbed it and tore it open before Zane could put the sheet down.

"Petition for change of name in the state of Oklahoma," she read. "Under sealed record."

"Let me see it," Zane said.

About the Person Whose Name is to be Changed:
Lily Davis
421 Checker Street
Okmulgee, OK
Date of birth: March 3, 1964
Place of birth: Edmond, OK
County of birth: Oklahoma County
Name of Hospital of birth: Rosary Heights Hospital
Birth parents: Osbert Davis and Verda Davis

Zane stared at the piece of paper over Lettie's shoulder. He felt rooted to the ground, like he couldn't move. *Sherri Clearwater didn't exist.* And the crazy witch lady was right. His mother was Lily Davis. Born in Oklahoma, not Missouri. An orphanage run by nuns? It sounded silly to him now. How had he ever believed it? How did he not ask her more questions?

And now it was too late. He was out of chances to ask her anything. Why hadn't she told them the truth?

"Listen to this," Lettie said. "Under 'List reasons why you want to change your name.' It says 'Petitioner has been threatened with physical harm and death by her boyfriend and wishes to start a new life.'"

"Her boyfriend is Jeremiah Doom, who was acquitted of the Elk Grove murders in a high-profile trial."

Zane took the papers from her, desperate to see what the date was for the name change. The court papers were filed in January 1987. Seven months before he was born.

He pulled out the phone and clicked on the link that the anonymous dar_dar sent. And looked into the eyes of the man who might be his father.

"Mom must have been real scared," Lettie said. She picked up a pillow and slid it into a pillowcase thoughtlessly, like a robot. "Do you think he tried to kill her because she fell in love with your father?"

Zane wrenched his eyes from the phone, irritated with Lettie. Did he have to explain everything?

"I don't know what to think," Zane said. His brain was flooded with half-formed thoughts. Puzzle pieces falling into place. Did Ely Clearwater even exist?

"Yeah, but...do you think she was scared of this Jeremiah finding her?"

"Stop it," Zane said. "This was a long time ago. Ancient history. There's nothing to be afraid of now."

"But...," Lettie said. "She's dead, now, isn't she?"

CHAPTER NINE

There was an Osbert Davis in Okmulgee listed on Whitepages.com, and after one breathless phone call Zane and Lettie were in the truck on their way to Okmulgee to meet their grandmother for the first time.

She'd chosen a Waffle House as their meeting spot, and Zane spotted its brown and yellow rooftop easily from the highway. He pulled the truck into the parking lot, chasing huge black starlings out of a parking space and sending them fluttering over a jacked-up pick-up and two minivans.

The time-warp waitress in a crisp cotton shirt and bowtie shouted her welcome as Zane and Lettie walked into the nearly full restaurant, and twenty sets of eyes checked them out briefly before settling back on their plates. Long and narrow like a rail car, the Waffle House is one half eating area and one half grill, separated only by a waist-high counter and red vinyl stools bolted to the floor. People from all walks of life came to Waffle House, and the crowd this afternoon was no different. Two women trying to keep three toddlers under control at one table; at another, an elderly couple eating in silence. A couple of guys were sitting at the counter, still in their work uniforms with American flags stitched on the sleeves.

Zane slid into one of the booths by the windows. It was warm and smelled like sauteed onions and steak. He was nervous but didn't want Lettie to pick up on it, so he'd just kept mostly silent for the forty-minute drive from Tulsa to Okmulgee.

A lemon-yellow Cadillac pulled into one of the empty handicapped spaces, its front fender scraping the cement block that marked the end of the space. The driver, a round faced woman with puffy silver blond hair, checked her lipstick in the rearview mirror then opened the door. Black orthopedic shoes emerged and slowly planted on the ground, followed by a three-legged silver cane. A plump hand with bright pink nails grasped the top of the car door, and she lifted herself out of the seat as Lettie and Zane watched.

She swung the door shut with one hand, and shuffled to the Waffle House door. Zane and Lettie exchanged a glance—this had to be her. She was simply an older version of their mother. Same small, determined eyes, same big hair, same hips as thick as saddle bags.

Zane went to the door and held it open for her.

"Verda Davis?" he said.

"Yup, that's me. You must be Lily's boy. I know you told me on the phone, but I forgot your name."

"Zane," he said. "And this is Lettie." Lettie slid out of the booth and put out her right hand. Verda kept her right hand gripped on the cane but used her left hand to squeeze Lettie's.

She smelled like baby powder and lilac, and her bright pink lipstick was a little smeared outside her lip line. A slash of color was on her front tooth as well. Her eyes filled up with tears.

"I told myself not to get emotional," she said. "But seeing you two…my grandbabies…my long lost grandbabies." A thick sob escaped, followed by full waterworks flowing down her cheeks. She threw her head back and said, "Dear Jesus, you take my daughter but you give me two grandbabies. Your will be done."

One of the toddlers, a bald kid with an enormous head and Eskimo Joe's T-shirt a few sizes too large hanging off his bony shoulder, pointed at Verda and screamed. An older woman with short grey hair had turned around to get a better view of the scene, while her husband stared blankly with his mouth open. A waitress with dyed red hair came over with a handful of paper napkins that she tried to give to Verda, who was too overcome to notice. Lettie took them, and Zane guided Verda into the booth, then slid in next to her. Lettie slid the napkins across the table and Verda patted the skin under her eyes, then blew her nose loudly.

"Let me look at you," she said. She cradled Zane's face in her hands and looked deep into his eyes, like she was trying to read his heart or at least use x-ray vision on him. "You're full of love, aren't you? Just like she was."

Lettie let out a kind of laugh snort, and Zane cut her a harsh look.

"And you, pretty girl. You have her good looks. And you're smart too, aren't you? But kind of a dreamer?"

"I don't know," Lettie said. "Maybe."

"So, you bring any pictures of Lily? I ain't seen her in twenty-five years."

Zane and Lettie looked at each other with guilt. They hadn't thought to bring the cracked photo album with its snapshots of their childhoods. We are not a sentimental family, Zane thought.

"I might have one on my phone," Zane said. He scanned through the photo folder and found one he took the day he bought the phone. His mother, sitting in her recliner, the remote control in her lap. He showed it to Verda.

Verda stared at it for some time. The fluorescent lights glistened off of the tears filling her eyes again.

"She put on some pounds, then," Verda said, and slid the phone back across the table. "Course, who am I to comment? I done the same. So you don't have a regular photograph I can keep?"

"Not with us," Zane said.

"We can look through the trailer to see if one's left," Lettie said.

"If it ain't too much trouble," Verda said. "I always hoped she'd come back. Osbert, her papa, he always said she was such a stubborn girl that once she made a decision, she wouldn't change her mind for no one. But me, I thought maybe she would. I had a feeling in my bones that she had children and that someday she'd want to bring them to us. She was our only child."

"Is he still alive?" Lettie asked.

"Osbert died three years ago, massive stroke. We were watching TV and he said, Verda, do you smell burning toast? I didn't smell a thing but I went into the kitchen to make sure I hadn't left something on the stove. By the time I came back out, he done slumped down in his chair and I couldn't wake him. He never came out of it."

"Sorry to hear that," Zane said.

"He would have loved to meet you two. So, Lettie, how old are you?"

"Fourteen."

"And you, Zane? You're about twenty-five, aren't you?"

"Twenty-six."

"So you were growing inside her when she took off," Verda said. "You ever talk to your father?"

"She told me he died before I was born. That his name was Ely Clearwater." But Zane was pretty sure he knew where this line of questioning was going. He'd seen the picture of Jeremiah Doom. There was more than enough resemblance to make the leap. And the timing was right.

"Ely Clearwater? Who's that?"

"Like I said, she told me he died before I was born, I don't know him."

"She never said nothing about Jeremiah?"

Zane felt anger rise up in him. "Look, she never told us we had a grandmother. She said she was an orphan."

Verda looked like he kicked her in the shins, and he was sorry he said it almost immediately. But something in the woman's line of questioning was wearing at him.

"Well, I'm glad she shut him out of her life just as much as she shut us out," Verda said. "He was no good then and I hope he's dead or in jail now. I can almost forgive her for shutting us out since she was trying to make a clean break from him as well. I don't know who this Ely Clearwater is, but it's a blessing if you're his kin instead of Jeremiah's. Though I've got to say you look just like him."

No point in denying it. Zane noticed it the day they got the message but dismissed it. He rat-tat-tatted the fork against the table top. Lettie finally asked the question. "Who?"

"Jeremiah Doom. Your mother's 'one true love' or so she said. Surely you got some of this information off that internet, same as you found my phone number. Now, who's your daddy, Lettie? Do you know?"

The waitress picked this moment to ask for their orders.

"Give us a moment," Verda said with a smile. "We ain't even looked yet." The waitress shrugged and tucked the pen back in her hair and walked away. Zane took three laminated menus from the holder and slid one to each of them.

76

"I didn't mean to sound cruel or nothing," Verda said. "I just wanted to know if you knew him or if you were in the same situation as Zane here. But looking at you two, my guess is different daddies for sure."

Lettie fingered the corner of the menu where the lamination had begun to peel away from the paper.

"My dad's name is Roy Magditc. I have his last name. He's in prison at McAlester but he's going to get out soon."

Zane laughed. "What makes you say that? Last I heard he was serving fifty years."

"You never pay attention to anything I tell you," Lettie said. "He's up for parole next month."

Zane looked skeptical and Verda smiled.

"I guess Lily didn't change her taste in men. What's this one in for?"

"Grand theft and use of deadly force," Lettie said. "He hijacked some trucks for their cargo."

"Well, that ain't the worst I heard," Verda said. "So, you'all got money for the funeral?"

"I've got some money," Zane said. "I got two thousand saved up."

"Your mama leave you any money, any bank accounts?"

"I don't know," Zane said.

"Osbert and me weren't rich," Verda said. "But I know he'd want to put her to rest right. That's a parents' duty if they live past their kids. I'll help out with that. Two thousand ain't enough anyway, and you're going to need that money to find somewhere to live. I'd offer you come stay with me but my house ain't in good shape. Since Osbert died, I ain't kept things up well with the housekeeping or the clutter."

"We didn't come here looking for money," Zane said proudly.

"I've got us an apartment."

"Just like your mama," Verda said, reaching out and patting his hand with hers. "She was so proud like that. I know you didn't come here looking for money, and I'm telling you I don't have much. But I'm going to help out where I can so my little girl can be laid to rest next to her daddy. Take a look at the menu quick now. I'm starving, let's order."

Zane was so grateful that Verda offered to help with the funeral that he couldn't even pretend to protest. He really needed the help. The whole deal was so overwhelming and it seemed like every responsibility and problem was falling on his shoulders. He wanted Lettie to go to school and have her normal life. Before all this happened, she'd been talking nonstop about the homecoming dance next week and he didn't want her to miss it. She had a date and a dress already. She was just a kid, really. She deserved to be one for a little longer. She was handling it well so far, but how much should she have to take?

They ordered T-bone steaks and biscuits and waffles, and before Lettie or Verda could say anything, Zane asked if she knew where Jeremiah was.

"I sure don't," Verda said. "And I don't think your mama would want you to find him. She went to an awful lot of trouble to keep that secret from you."

"I get that," Zane said. "But, I can't help but be curious. I mean, is he still alive?"

"I really don't know," Verda said. "I'd guess he's living with the Cherokees near Sallisaw where he grew up. They always abided by his innocence, just like Lily did." Her tone made it clear that she didn't share their faith in him.

"Want me to do a tarot card reading? See if you should find him?" Lettie started digging through her red cloth tote bag, looking for her deck.

"Lettie, don't start," Zane said under his breath, not sure how Verda would react to Lettie's hobby. Lettie sighed and pulled her hand out of her bag.

"You read tarot cards? I haven't had mine read in years," Verda said.

"Want me to do yours?" Lettie smiled and put her hand back in the bag with renewed energy.

"Food's coming soon," Zane said.

"Maybe another time, Lettie," Verda said.

#

He got in his truck and started it up, rubbing his hands to warm them as the engine heated. Verda pulled away with a wave and Zane checked his phone. It was a little before two, he had a nearly full tank of gas and money in his wallet from a trip to the bank yesterday. He pulled the dog-eared map of Oklahoma out of his glove box and looked for Sallisaw.

Lettie came bounding out of the Waffle House restroom, still shoving an arm into one of Emmaline's parkas. He leaned over and unlocked the passenger door. Lettie hoisted herself onto the bench seat and slammed the door shut.

Lettie eyed the map in his hands. "We going somewhere?"

"Thinking about it."

"You're thinking about going to Sallisaw to find Jeremiah Doom, aren't you?"

Zane nodded.

"Look, I got a bad feeling about this. First of all, she was scared of him. He had threatened her. It said it right there on those court papers. And this morning I did a tarot card reading for you. It didn't sound good. I got five of swords as your future card. The card of surrender, of defeat, of no-win situations. A battle lost to a bad person."

He wished she would stop talking—he didn't want to hear about her tarot card crap right now, and certainly not if it contained bad news.

"Why don't I just kill myself then?"

He regretted snapping at her almost immediately. She was doing her best to help.

"Jesus, Zane, I'm just saying can't it wait?"

"Do you want to go with me or not?"

Lettie didn't say anything. She just put on her seatbelt and stared straight ahead. Zane pressed down on the clutch and shifted the truck into reverse.

They drove east for a little more than hour before hitting the Sallisaw city limits. Zane pulled the truck into the parking lot of the Catfish Pole restaurant, where the teenage cashier at the Hardees where they had eaten lunch had said he should go to ask about Jeremiah Doom. She'd never heard the name but she said the man who owned the Catfish Pole knew just about everybody in town and would be a good place to start.

The restaurant was housed in a pre-fabricated metal barn, painted bright yellow. It looked like someone had just dropped it in the first place they found level land — it only partially faced the main highway and from the street you could only read "Catfi."

A brown dog with black spots stood near the door, trying to lap up the little bit of water left in the bowl. Zane let the dog sniff his hand, then shook the bowl out onto the ground and refilled it using the faucet poking out of the ground a few steps away. The dog sniffed the water then started lapping it up greedily.

A man in his late fifties came around the side of building, wearing a heavy red plaid shirt and jeans.

"We're closed til four thirty," he said, walking by them without stopping toward the restaurant entrance.

"We're not here to eat," Zane said.

The man pivoted on the heel of his worn workboot to face them.

"What's your business here then?"

"Friendly guy," Lettie said under her breath.

"I'm looking for Jeremiah Doom."

The man stared at them for a long time before finally answering.

"You kin of his?"

"Maybe. I just found out that maybe we might be related."

"What makes you think he wants to meet you, boy?"

"I want to meet him. Ain't that good enough?"

The man's slack-jawed expression broke into a joyless laugh, exposing crooked yellow teeth and one black tooth. He reached down and rubbed the dog roughly behind the ears.

"You sure as hell look like him, I'll tell you that. Is this one his long-lost daughter?"

Lettie gave him her best look of teenage disdain. "No relation. I'm just along for the ride, keeping my brother company."

"Well, good for you, little lady. Though you sound like you could give old Jeremiah a run for his money. He ain't got no daughters that I know of."

"Can you tell us where to find him?"

Again, the man stared at Zane for a few moments, as though considering what to do.

"To be honest, I don't right know where to find him. But since you're kin and all, and since it wouldn't be too hard to figure out where his parents live, I'll tell you where to find them. But if you don't need to mention you got the information here, then I'd ask you to leave it out. Just because it's unnecessary."

"Yeah, okay," Zane said.

"Head down 59 here until you see a green tractor with a "For Sale" sign on it. Turn left there, and their house is the fourth one on the right. It's blue."

"What are their names?" Lettie asked.

"Dave and Susie Doom. But Susie's the one you'll talk to. Dave's got that dementia. Half the time he thinks he still running a farm in the drought of '79. But Susie's still sharp, when she's not exhausted from changing his diapers and feeding him lunch."

They thanked him for the information and walked back to the truck.

"Look at us. We got grandparents popping up all over the state. Wouldn't it be nice if they were rich?" Lettie said.

"I bet you they're not, Lettie," Zane said. "Anyway, I wonder why that man didn't want us to say that we found out where they live from him?"

"I don't know. Maybe they hate gossips."

#

White sheets with pink flowers flapped in the wind on the clothesline outside the tiny blue clapboard house where the Dooms lived. Heavy brass wind chimes hanging from the porch light clanked together like an old grandfather clock striking midnight. A white plastic sign read "No Solicitors" in red ink. Zane raised his hand to ring the doorbell but before he could apply the pressure, the door swung open slowly.

"Are you here to sharpen the knives?" An old man wearing grey sweatpants and matching sweatshirt stood on the other side of the screen door. He was slight and frail, barely more than five feet tall if he were to stand straight up. But as it was, he was hunched over so much he had to crane his neck to look into Lettie's eyes.

"No," Lettie said. "We're here to see Susie Doom."

The man munched his lower lip and made a *pfft* sound. "Susie!" He yelled, then turned and shuffled away from them, leaving the carved wooden door open but the screen door shut. He lowered himself slowly into a pine rocking chair then turned back to Zane and Lettie.

"Aren't you coming in?"

Lettie and Zane exchanged glances, then Zane opened the screen door and stepped into the tiny but neat front room. Its walls were covered in shiny brown sheets of fake wood paneling, and thick yellow drapes hung in front of what must have been a sliding door to the backyard. Underneath a long wood shelf holding at least a dozen softball trophies was a green, yellow and white plaid couch, one cushion sunk deep into the frame from years of someone sitting in the same spot. A plastic TV tray next to the rocker held a box of tissues, one of those bright plastic cups that toddlers drink out of and a TV guide folded open to the day's date.

A thin woman with a round, brown face and long grey hair in a braid down her back appeared in their line of vision. She dried her hands on the red-patterned smock covering her T-shirt and sweatpants. Her face was pale and deeply lined with wrinkles, and arthritis had turned her hands into bumpy claws.

"Do I know you?" she said. Her unfriendly tone sent Zane back a few steps, but he kept the screen door propped open with his hand.

"No, you don't know us. But I think we're family."

"Which clan are you?"

A smile played around the lips of the old man, who obviously enjoyed watching his wife take on some strangers. He probably thought it was better than television.

"The man looks like Wolf clan, but the girl is *unega*," he said.

"Dave, hush," she said, exasperated.

"What is *unega*?" Lettie asked. "He said I was *unega*."

"He means you're a white girl. You don't have Indian blood. He doesn't always know what he's saying," Susie said. She turned to Zane. "Now what makes you think we're kin?"

"Our mom is Lily Davis. Was Lily Davis. She died in a fire two days ago. Her mom thinks I'm probably Jeremiah Doom's son."

The women crinkled her eyebrows together and looked them both over slowly. Zane licked his lips and continued.

"My name's Zane Clearwater. This is my sister Lettie. We have the same mom but different dads. I've never known who my dad was. Mom never told me. But now that she's dead we're learning all sorts of stuff about her we didn't know. Like that her name used to be Lily Davis and that she used to be involved with Jeremiah."

"God, I haven't even heard her name in years. She done fell off the face of the earth twenty some years ago. Is this some kind of practical joke or something? I never heard nothing about a son with Lily Davis."

Lettie cleared her throat. "She changed her name to Sherri Clearwater before she had Zane."

"Can I have a pudding?" Dave said.

"Sure, can you wait a minute?"

"Yes," he said.

Susie straightened her arms and let out a breath. Her shoulders sagged like she was a balloon someone let the air out of.

"Clearwater sounds like a Cherokee name," she said.

"Mom said my dad was Cherokee."

Susie gave him a tight smile. "And what makes you want to find Jeremiah?"

"I just want to talk to him. Ain't it natural for a boy to want to know his father?"

"You ever think that maybe your mama didn't tell you who he was for a reason?"

"I can't ask her any more," Zane said.

"I'm sorry you lost your mama," Susie said. "Zane, right? Look, if you want to leave me your phone number I'll tell Jeremiah you came by next time I talk to him. But I can't tell you when that'll be. I don't talk to him regular."

She gestured to a calendar hanging on the wall by the door. "Write your number there." Lettie picked a pencil up from the table and wrote Zane's name and cell phone at the bottom of the month.

"I'm hungry. I want a pudding," Dave said.

"In a minute, Dave," Susie said. "Now you two need to go on home."

"We drove all the way from Tulsa to see him," Zane said. "Can't you call him now? Or tell us where we might find him?"

"People always looking for Jeremiah," Dave said. "But he knows how to live in the hills without nothing but his wits. If he don't want to be found, ain't no one gonna find him."

"Is that where he is? In the hills?"

The old man laughed. "You won't find him, boy. He'll see you coming for miles."

"You all need to go on now. You done taken enough of my time. I gotta feed Dave."

"I want a pudding!"

"Chocolate or vanilla?"

"Chocolate."

Lettie turned to leave but Zane hesitated at the door. Susie crossed the room in four long steps and got right up in his face.

"I said it's time for you to leave," she said.

Lettie tugged on his arm and opened the screen door. "Sorry to be a bother, ma'am. We sure hope to hear from you or Jeremiah."

"Think about what you want, and how you'll feel if you don't get it," Susie said. "Sometimes it's better to let things lie just where someone put 'em."

"I thought blood counted for something," Zane said. His stomach clenched tight, and he felt his fingers curling into fists. Couldn't she see how important this was to him? Why was she trying to throw up road blocks when he'd come so far?

"There's blood, and then there's blood," she said. "I'm telling you, think about what you want from him, and then tell yourself that you're not going to get it. Is it still worth finding him if you can't get what you want?"

"How do you know what I want?"

"It's written all over your face," Susie said. Lettie tugged on his arm again and took a step onto the porch. "You want some father and son reunion, and all Jeremiah's gonna give you is a whole lot of nothing."

"Thank you again, ma'am," Lettie said, as Zane stepped wordlessly out of the house and onto the porch.

CHAPTER TEN

They were back in Tulsa by late afternoon.

"Can you get off at 21st Street?" Lettie asked as they sped down Highway 169 toward the Majestic.

"What for?"

"I need to stop and see Morgan and talk to him about the homecoming dance," she said.

"Can't you call him?"

"Well, first, I don't have a cell phone, brainiac. And two, I think I need to see him face to face."

"You can use my phone."

"Look, let's just go by where he lives. It won't take long."

Lettie gave directions to a red brick house with rust-colored shutters framing the windows. A hollowed-out tree stump was the centerpiece of the dry yellow lawn. An old blue Chevy truck sat on the brick and cement driveway dripping oil. The double garage door was open, with a white Camry parked on one side and a nicked oak work table and bench littered with tools, bicycle parts and hardware running the length of the opposite wall. A lawn mower and weed whacker leaned against the wall next to some snow chains.

The garage was lit with a single bare lightbulb hanging from the ceiling with a ball chain dangling like an earring from it. A boy about Lettie's age sat on an overturned black bucket, fixing the chain on a toddler's pink bicycle.

The boy looked up as they walked up the driveway, pushing his black hair off of his forehead with the back of his hand. His hands were visibly greasy, as were his jeans and work boots. His skin was dark like maybe he had some Indian blood in him. He had baby-faced good looks, but his Adam's apple protruded uncomfortably and made Zane remember puberty with a shudder.

"Hey Lettie," he said, with a warm smile revealing thousands of dollars in orthodontist fees.

"Morgan, this is my brother Zane. We were just driving home from tending to some family stuff and I thought I'd come by to say hey."

He nodded at Zane.

"I'm real sorry about your mom," Morgan said. He looked sincere, seated on the bucket with his eyes focused on Lettie and his hands clasped between his knees. "I would have called but I didn't know where to find you. I was glad to see you online this morning."

"Thanks for writing what you did on Facebook. It was sweet."

"Some of those kids are jerks. They don't know what they're saying."

Zane got interested. "What are they saying?"

"It's just bullshit stuff," Lettie said.

"You know, we don't have to go to that dance on Saturday," Morgan said. "I get it if you don't feel like it or you got to go to the funeral or do family stuff."

"Lettie, you should go," Zane said, surprised to see her hesitate like she was considering it. "Mom would want you to."

"Well, I do have the dress and all. I don't know."

"Funeral isn't going to be this week, the way the cops were talking," Zane said.

He figured it was now his job to make sure Lettie had as normal a life as she could. For as long as he could, anyway. He didn't want her missing the homecoming dance she'd been so excited about just days ago.

"Are you coming to school tomorrow?"

"I don't know," she said, as Zane said "Yes."

"You've got to get back in the routine," he said. "It's the best thing."

"Well, looks like I'll see you tomorrow then," Lettie said.

"I'll look for you before first period to say hi," Morgan said.

A wooden door leading to the inside of the house swung open, and a plump woman with long brown hair stood in the doorway. She wore black yoga pants that had never seen a downward facing dog pose and a hot pink hoodie.

"Morgan, introduce me to your friends," she said.

"Um, yeah, Mom, this is Lettie and her brother Zane," he said.

"Ah," she said, pausing for a moment before clicking her mouth into a half smile. "So sorry to hear about the fire and your mother, terrible thing. Morgan, you know you still have your chores to do, plus your homework. Let's not spend too much time visiting. I'm sure these two have a lot of things to take care of." Her tone made it clear she wanted them to leave.

Zane got the hint. He suspected if they didn't leave quickly she would chase them off the driveway with a broom.

"Yeah, we've gotta go. C'mon Lettie."

Lettie nodded, said goodbye, and started down the driveway without looking back. Zane was amazed at her composure—he'd been a wreck around girls when he was her age but she'd clearly gotten the smooth operator genes from her jailbird papa. He raised his hand and nodded at Morgan and his mom, and followed her to the truck.

Back in the truck, Zane tried to lighten the moment. He put his face close to Lettie's and rolled his eyes while making a simpering face.

"Oh. My. God. It's love," he said, mimicking a lovesick puppy. "Oh, Lettie, I'll wait on bended knee for you to arrive at school tomorrow. Oh Lettie. Let me squire you to the dance."

"Shut up," she said, giving him a goofy smile before punching him lightly in the arm. "He's a nice guy."

"What was all that about defending your honor on Facebook? Are mean girls picking on your dress or something?"

"No, not like that."

"What is it? You can tell your big brother."

"It's just bullshit stuff like I said."

"Do you need me to beat someone up for you? Because I'll do it. I'm a mean fighting machine."

"Zane, look, just let it be. Some of the kids at school are hearing all this stuff about Mom and you and they're just saying shit about how maybe you did it. It's awful and stupid."

He didn't know what to say. How could he tell her he had the same fearsome thoughts running through his head sometimes? And that the cops had those thoughts too? Zane had always been honest with her but he knew it wasn't time for him to share his own uncertainty. It would shake her to the core.

He watched the stop light turn from yellow to red as he slowly approached the intersection. He fidgeted in the seat, trying to think of something comforting to say.

Lettie stared straight ahead, but a few tears spilled down her cheeks. She took a deep breath, like maybe she was trying to swallow a sob, but it caught in her throat instead. He reached over to put his right arm around her and squeeze her slight shoulders. She kept crying all the way through the light change, tears rolling off of her chin and hitting her T-shirt like fat raindrops.

"There's some napkins in the glove box," he said, blinking away his own tears.

She pulled one out and wiped her face.

"They're saying stuff about me, too. Saying I caused the fire with one of my spells. That I worship the devil. All from that stupid girl Mary and her crazy father. I think Morgan's mom heard some of that stuff. Did you see how she looked at me? She was practically willing me off their property."

It was probably just a matter of time before that happened, Zane thought. This was Bible Belt country, with week-long revivals in the summer full of miracle healings and sinners being saved by Jesus. Lettie's spells may be little more than exercises in the power of positive thinking, but they were too weird for a town not known for its high tolerance of the different.

"But you were with a bunch of them that night. So they know firsthand you weren't anywhere near the Majestic."

"Well, that's the thing. See I showed up late to the sleepover. I didn't get there until nine-thirty."

"Where did you go? Didn't you leave home around seven?"

"Yeah, well, I stopped at the thrift store on my way and I was looking at books and stuff and I guess I lost track of time. I got to Becca's house and they were already halfway through the movie and thought I'd decided not to come. Her mom made a big fuss about my riding my bike so late."

Zane suppressed the urge to shake her. Some of the roads around them weren't that well-lit, and she was putting herself in danger riding her bike in the dark. Not only that, but he hoped that someone saw her at the thrift store. He didn't want the police starting to think his sister was a suspect like he was.

But she didn't need the lecture right now. Instead, he reached over and gave her a hug.

His phone rang. Emmaline.

"Zane, you and Lettie have to get over here right now and help me! I've got two hours to make a pageant gown as a surprise audition for this show. No, make that one hour and fifty minutes. Come here now!"

#

The Perryman's trailer was bustling like a movie set when Zane and Lettie walked in. Shana Burns, the production assistant, sat on the couch talking quietly into her cell phone while tapping away at her laptop. Cy and Glynnis sat at the kitchen table gluing sequins to fuchsia satin.

"Some sort of contest the producer fellow set up," Cy said by way of explaining. "Emmaline has two hours to make some little girl's dream dress. We're about an hour in."

"Forty-five minutes left!" Shana called out to no one in particular.

"Em will either put you to work or tell you to leave," Glynnis said. "Could go either way."

"I thought she had the job already."

"So did she," Glynnis said. "But they didn't give her much time to complain about it."

Zane and Lettie walked down the hall to the studio. A blue-haired dude with a spike running through his earlobe followed Emmaline's every move with the camera. A woman Zane had never seen before sat in the blue beanbag chair, playing games on her smart phone and glancing up from time to time at the little girl

92

with strawberry blond hair standing over Emmaline's shoulder.

"Can't you sew faster?" the girl said, one hand on her denim-clad hip with her elbow jutting out. "Did you hear that? Forty-five minutes left?"

The woman sitting on the beanbag looked up, checked Zane and Lettie out, then said, "Nagging doesn't help, Arabella. Let the lady do her work and you wait for when she needs to fit you."

"Zane, Lettie. Thank God you're here. Lettie, can you start pinning these ruffles on the waistband? It's like that dress I did for Maya last month."

"Ooh, that one was so pretty. I know how to do it so I can help." Lettie scooped up a pile of pink and purple organza ruffles from the worktable and brought them over to the dress form, where a waistband was pinned with one pink and purple ruffle, each cascading to the floor.

The little girl extended her hand to Zane. "I'm Arabella. Oklahoma's Best Little Miss."

Zane introduced himself and Lettie.

"So you're the ones that lived in that burned down trailer and lost your mom?"

The woman pushed herself out of the beanbag chair and grabbed Arabella's arm.

"Shush, now, Arabella. That isn't nice to ask about that kind of thing. I apologize. And I'm sorry to hear about your tragedy. I'll keep you all in my prayers." The woman had bright blue eyes and wispy strawberry-blonde hair like her daughter. She was thin and dressed like a teenager, in rhinestone studded jeans with white stitching tucked into black cowboy boots and a slim fitting green and grey checked plaid shirt.

"I'm Julia, Arabella's mom." The bangle bracelets on her arm jangled loudly as she shook hands with Zane, then Lettie.

"Do all of the gown makers in Tulsa live in trailer parks?" Arabella said to no one in particular. Her mother handed her the mobile phone and told her to play a game.

"She channels her stage fright into asking inappropriate questions sometimes," Julia said.

"I don't get stage fright," Arabella said. Zane believed her. The girl was afraid of nothing, born with self-confidence that would take her further than he could ever go. The kind of person who walked into a room and wanted everyone's attention. Where he would rather slink in and sit in the back.

"More pinning, less talking," Emmaline said, glancing at them with eyes that meant business.

Zane and Julia smiled ruefully at each other, then Julia returned to the beanbag chair, tilted her head back and closed her eyes. Lettie settled down in front of the muslin covered dress form, pinning the ribbons until the pile was gone.

Glynnis came in carrying the fuchsia satin bodice, now covered in swirls of sequins. Emmaline inspected closely, with Arabella over her shoulder doing the same, before declaring it good enough.

Emmaline pulled the last of the organza cascades off the sewing machine and bit the thread with her teeth.

"Everyone, out. I've got to put the dress together and do a fitting."

"I'm not leaving," Arabella said, planting her feet like a boxer waiting for a fight.

"I didn't mean for you to leave," Emmaline said. "You're the most important person now."

The little girl beamed at the praise and immediately adopted a more helpful posture.

"Mom, you can go if you want. I think Emmaline just wants me in here for now."

"Oh, OK, Arie." She grabbed her purse and phone and filed out of the room after Glynnis, with Zane and Lettie on her tail.

#

Thirty minutes later, they were in a caravan of cars heading to the Hilton Garden Inn at the airport for a pageant gown showdown with two other competitors for a spot on the reality show.

"How many hoops do I have jump through for these people?" Emmaline said, hand sewing a zipper in the dress bodice. The organza ruffles filled the cab of Zane's truck, spreading over the gearshift and onto his lap. Emmaline looked like she was being eaten by a giant cartoon bird.

"I did videos, I took a two-hour personality test, I let them check my credit and my driver's record, I spent hours on the phone with girls I've sewn for. I had a physical exam, for crissakes. I signed my life away in stupid contracts. Now I'm sitting here making a dress on demand with no notice for some bratty little pageant girl and I'm still competing for a place on the show. Stupid."

"No one's got a gun to your head, Em. If you don't want to do it, don't do it."

"Of course I got to do it, Zane. I mean, this is my big chance. It's just taking so much time. Do you think they're doing this in other cities? Like there's someone like me in Little Rock and St. Louis and Memphis?"

"I can guarantee you that there is no one like you anywhere, Emmy," Zane said, smiling goofily at her.

"Aww, you're so sweet, Zane. But you know what I mean. Is this the semi-finals? The finals? Olympic trials?"

"I don't know, Em. That Peter guy, from what I saw of him, he seems like the dude in charge. So it must be a pretty big deal that he came all the way out here from Hollywood."

"You think so?" She looked so hopeful he knew immediately how badly she wanted to believe him.

CHAPTER ELEVEN

Zane settled into a padded chair toward the back of the meeting room. It was a cavernous room built to hold hundreds, but today it just hosted him and a handful of other friends and family of reality show hopefuls. Emmaline was sewing Arabella into the dress, Glynnis and Lettie were assisting, and Cy was out front talking to an old friend he ran into in the lobby.

The smell of air freshener, cleaning chemicals and the musty uncirculated air of a rarely used room combined to stuff his nose. He'd noticed several times over the last few days that he was breathing shallow and fast. It had to be the stress. He tried to slow down his breathing like they talked about in AA to keep himself in the moment. He really needed to get to a meeting.

It's always the uncertainty that drives me nuts, he thought. It was the waiting and the uncertainty. It made him want to rush into the future as fast as he could. That way he could deal with it, here and now, instead of just stewing in his own juices. It made him think of the saying about how to cook a frog – you put it in water that you slowly heat until it's boiling. The frog's body adjusts to the gradual temperature rise so it never jumps out until it's too late and guess what's for dinner?

He felt so tired. His life had become a series of jumps from incident to incident, solving basic problems like where to sleep and meanwhile, life just happening to him, all around him, out of his control. The police in charge of his freedom, Emmaline in charge of his love life, his father in control of his identity.

He felt as empty as the hole in a doughnut. In some ways, this hadn't changed. He had felt empty all his life. Not knowing your father created one hell of a psychological black hole. In AA they say that you drink to fill up the emptiness. But today's emptiness, in light of all these incredible revelations, was deeper and darker. Edge of the world empty.

Who was he anyway? Why had his mother created this whole new life for herself, shutting out her parents for nearly thirty years? She'd always told him his father was Cherokee, but never taken the time to help him trace his lineage. Could it be that that was the one piece of truth she told him? Doom was Cherokee.

He thought about the things she had wanted for him. She wanted him to go to welding school—she always talked about him learning a good skill, and had at one point tried to talk him into joining the Army. But he didn't want anyone telling him what to wear. When he told her that, she just smiled and said he was like his dad. Which dad, he wondered. His imaginary dad who drowned in a river? Or his real-life dad who was the main suspect in Oklahoma's ugliest murders?

Zane wondered if his blackouts were inherited from his father. And he also wondered what other traits he might have inherited. Maybe that dark rage that overtook him sometimes when he drank? The part of him that itched for a fight or welcomed violence? The part he tried to keep clamped down.

Learning that his life was based on a set of lies was like someone had opened a locked door, but instead of revealing a brightly lit path forward, all he saw was another closed door. He wasn't even sure he had the energy right now to try to open it. The adrenalin of the day had evaporated and he slumped in the chair. There was no fight in him now; all he wanted was a nap.

Peter walked into the room and headed straight for a guy in cargo shorts and hiking boots who was setting up a camera on a tripod in front of the wood parquet dance floor that would undoubtedly be the stage.

"James told you the basics, right? We want to see how the designers do on camera with a live subject next to them. We've told the little girls to ham it up and put on a show, but for shooting purposes your focus is on the women."

The camera guy ran thick fingers through curly orange hair, revealing a half circle of perspiration under the arm of his light blue T-shirt.

"With one camera I'll do my best. I might miss some stuff if you're going to have all of them talking and up at once. Are they going to be performing or anything? Like singing or dancing?"

"No, just talking. And we'll try to do it one duo at a time as much as possible."

A little girl shrieked in the hallway outside the room, causing everyone to whipsaw around to look at her. Her cry was something you would expect out of a deeply wounded animal and Zane expected to see a broken leg or dislocated shoulder.

"I hate this dress!" Two women—by appearance and age he'd guess the mother and grandmother—dragged a little girl who was doing everything she could do be dead weight into the room. Her smooth cheeks, the color of coffee with lots of creamer, were marked with twin streaks of black mascara.

A thin woman about Emmaline's age followed the howling girl and the women into the ballroom, her pale lips pressed together in a thin line. Her everyday clothes and lack of makeup made her seem plain in comparison to the dolled-up pageant princess. Her eyes darted around the room like she was looking for either a new little girl to model her dress or a gag to shut this one up.

The dress looked all right to him, but Zane had to admit he didn't know much about pageant dresses. The top was made of ivory-colored sequins, and the skirt was made of layers of pink and chocolate brown tulle.

"I hate brown! I want yellow!"

Peter intercepted the woman near where Zane was seated.

"Did you ask Lauren what color she wanted, Jessy?"

"I did. But the yellow wasn't an option. This little brat spilled a coffee on it then demanded I get more fabric."

"OK, OK, have a seat, calm down," he said. "Do you want a water?"

She shook her head to the water, and nearly collapsed on the chair next to Zane. She patted her pockets nervously as Peter scurried after the little girl, who was now lying down on the floor with her eyes shut.

"I keep forgetting they took away our cell phones for this part," she said. "I'm about to call in Child Protective Services so I don't kill this child."

"I thought the dress was nice," Zane said. "Reminded me of that Napoleon ice cream, the one that has chocolate, strawberry and vanilla."

"I think it's pronounced Neapolitan," she said. "But yeah, those are kind of the colors. Maybe if I told her it was supposed to be like ice cream, she'd like it better. I need to work on my sales pitch. I tried to appeal to her practical side, then I tried threats. But I need to be selling the fantasy."

"I'm pretty sure that that particular little girl doesn't want to hear about practicality."

She let a few seconds pass before giving him a warm smile along with a flick of her hair.

"You here for one of the little girls, or one of the dressmakers?"

Arabella skipped into the room, watching with great pleasure as the tulle ribbons on her skirt flew in the air. Emmaline trailed behind her, studying the dress as it moved with the girl.

"I'm with her," Zane said. "We're friends, and that's my sister behind her."

"Happy little girl," Jessy said. "And pretty dress." She folded her arms over her chest almost defensively.

"Zane, why are you sitting in the back? Come sit up front with us," Lettie said, giving Jessy the once-over. Jessy met her eyes with a wan smile and stood up.

Emmaline scanned the room like she was looking for someone. Zane waved at her, thinking she was looking for him. But she rushed past him to Peter.

"Maybe I can help with the other little girl, Peter," she purred. "I'm really good with kids."

Zane saw her put her hand on his upper arm and squeeze. She was close to him, really close, and the smile on her face was clearly an invitation to something. And Peter was smiling back. Zane worked his jaw back and forth, sucking in air through clenched teeth. He knew that look. He'd seen it on her face—aimed at him, aimed at other guys. Emmaline had the Hollywood producer in her crosshairs.

"Let's get going," Peter said. "Jessy, Emmaline, Bradley, come on stage with your beauty queens."

A tall guy with a shock of royal blue hair covering one eye stood next to a blonde with curly ringlets and a big blue flower stuck above her left ear. Where the little girl was serene in sky blue satin trimmed with roses, the man was a study in contrasts, with skinny red plaid trousers, black motorcycle boots and a neon green long-sleeved T-shirt with a man's face and the words "Viva la revolucíon!"

"Didn't expect to see a dude in this thing," Zane said to Lettie, who shrugged.

Zane's phone vibrated in his pocket, and both relief and anxiety washed over him like a wave of cool water. The phone said unknown caller, but he was sure it was Jeremiah Doom, and he was ready to start this next chapter. If Zane wanted answers, this man was probably one of the few who could give them to him.

He showed the caller ID to Lettie who whispered, "go, go!" and shooed him into the hallway.

"Hello?" he said, his voice nearly cracking with anxiety like he was a teenager.

"So you're Lily Davis's kid?" The man's voice was clear, self-assured and medium-pitched, with a strong country accent. "Guess you can figure out who this is."

Zane had the vague impression that the man was more amused than curious or shocked. Had he known about Zane this whole time? Or was he convinced Zane wasn't his son?

"Jeremiah Doom, right?"

"That's right," the man said, and Zane heard the clinking of ice on glass in the background. "And you're bringing me a whole mess of trouble, ain't you, Zane?"

Not the warm and friendly reaction he'd hoped for, but Doom's mother had warned him fair enough. Zane reminded himself what he wanted from this man—answers—and swallowed hard.

"What do you mean?"

"I s'pose it ain't your fault that your mother died, but I have the feeling all this noise is going to get me back in the stupid newspaper headlines again."

Zane hadn't given much thought as to how Jeremiah might hate the spotlight being turned back on him again. Zane was so far in the spotlight he couldn't see past it any more.

"And I s'pose we oughta meet so you can take my measure and I can take yours. But you gonna need to come out to Sallisaw again. I haven't set foot in Tulsa since 1987 and I ain't doing it now."

Let's get this over with, Zane thought. A character like this guy might change his mind if he didn't jump on it right now. And, Zane reminded himself, he will have answers. This is how he could start to fill that black hole inside him—with the facts, whatever they were.

"Tonight? I can be there by six or thereabouts. I just got this thing with my friend and my sister I'm at, but we should be done in an hour or so."

"No moss grows on you, does it? I guess I can move a couple of things around in my schedule. Why don't you meet me at JV's bar off of the 4130 byway and you can buy me a beer?"

Zane skipped the "I don't drink" story and agreed. Plenty of time for get-to-know-you stuff later. He didn't want to push his luck.

#

Back in the meeting room, Jessy's little model Lauren was doing a sulky stamp across the dance floor. Someone had cleaned her cheeks of the mascara trails and applied fresh lipgloss, but they couldn't wash the anger out of her face.

Emmaline looked as beautiful as any of the china doll princesses on the makeshift stage. Zane studied her as she watched Jessy

103

stumble through a recitation of the features of the dress. Emmaline kept her face neutral, but he could see a little smile playing there. He knew her competitive spirit well enough to know what she was thinking. One down, one to go.

Arabella whispered something to Lauren that made her press her lips together. Emmaline wasn't the only fierce competitor in the room, Zane thought.

Peter walked behind the tripod and looked through the viewfinder to check the shot. He gave the camera man the thumbs up, then he turned back to Lauren and smiled at the frowning girl. "So what do you think of the dress?"

She narrowed her eyes at him then addressed the camera directly. "I told you. I think it is ugly and I hate it. I'd rather wear a trash bag."

"Remember, Lauren, look at me, not the camera," he said. The little girl smiled and shifted her attention to him.

"This dress is so ugly. I hate it. I'd rather wear a trash bag."

"Isn't that what you wore to the Miss Azalea Festival pageant? Or was it just that everyone thought it was a trash bag?" Arabella said.

"You stupid little crown chaser," Lauren hissed, and crouched into a fighting stance, then leaped across to grab Arabella around the waist and push her over. Zane could hear the sounds of stitches ripping out and the purple and pink tulle they'd spent hours pinning and sewing fell to the ground like leaves from one of Dr. Seuss' trees. The girls rolled onto the carpet, tiny manicured fingers plucking handfuls of tulle and satin and sequins in a crazed attempt to destroy one another's dress. With its many different pieces of fabric, Arabella's gown was easier to rip apart, so Lauren concentrated on pulling down the tulle while Arabella went for Lauren's hair piece.

The cameraman kept the lens trained on the fight while Peter and the mothers rushed in to try to pry them apart. Peter got his arms around Lauren and picked her up as Arabella reached up from the floor and clawed at the satin bodice. A spaghetti strap popped off and Arabella smiled in victory as Lauren kicked the air helplessly. Arabella's hair, once pinned into a clean chignon, now hung in wavy strands around her head. Her mother pulled her up to her feet. Arabella looked like a half-plucked flamingo in the demolished dress, her cheeks pink from exertion and her shoulders heaving as she tried to catch her breath.

"This is your fault," Lauren's mother said, pointing a long, black-tipped fake fingernail at Jessy. "She said she wanted yellow."

Emmaline and Zane exchanged glances and a brief smile. Jessy glared at the women as if calculating whether or not to throw her down on the floor. Zane hoped she didn't try. Lauren's mother easily weighed twice what Jessy seemed to and would probably crush her.

Jessy must have realized the same thing. She took a deep breath and let it out with a sigh.

"I'm out of here," Jessy said. "I don't need to make a fool of myself on reality television this bad." She pivoted on her heel and practically ran out of the room.

"You forgot your phone," Shana, the production assistant, said, chasing after her.

"What happens now?" Lauren's mother asked Peter. She stood with her elbows jutting out like sharp weapons from her hips.

"Well…I think you and Lauren can take the rest of the day off."

"I thought you wanted a show. Because she knows a lot of professional wrestling moves. We watch it all the time. She could get that little girl into a piledriver."

"Ah, yes, well you provided enough of a show. Anyway, I don't think we need to see more from Lauren today. If Jessy had stayed, we would have her try to fix the gown, but she's gone."

Zane had moved next to Emmaline, and was helping her pick up pink and purple strips of tulle. Emmaline straightened up at Peter's words.

"Let me have some time and I can fix both dresses."

The blue-haired man rolled his eyes. "Do Amelia and I get any points for not getting into a brawl? Or are we expected to sew tattered clothing back together too?"

"Of course not," Peter said, shaking his head as if to reset his brain. "Let's regroup in two hours. Emmaline, if you want to try to fix both dresses, more power to you. But I'd recommend you keep Lauren and Arabella apart as much as you can."

Zane whispered to Emmaline, "I think they save their fights for when the camera is rolling anyway."

"I hope you're right," Emmaline whispered back, her eyes on Peter.

"Listen to me," he said to her. He grabbed her arm and she pulled her gaze from Peter to meet his eyes. He quickly filled her in on the call he'd just received.

"This is huge. Zane, you should totally go," she said. "Leave Lettie with me, and see what your dad has to say."

She wrapped her arms around his shoulders and squeezed, and planted a warm kiss on his cheek. He thought about kissing her full on the lips there, in front of Peter and everyone, but he was pretty sure she'd pull away or react badly, and he couldn't handle the rejection. So, he closed his eyes, held her tight and breathed in her slightly sweaty scent, wanting to stay there next to her forever. But she was already pulling away.

CHAPTER TWELVE

JV's bar was in a big barn with a peaked roof, with an ample outdoor seating area left completely vacant in cold October, its empty tables covered in green and white checked oilcloths that flapped softly with the breeze.

Zane opened the wooden door to go inside and was hit by a cloud of cigarette smoke. His eyes adjusted to the dark of the bar. It was big— it could easily hold three hundred people but this afternoon there were only maybe five or ten patrons sitting at the square bar in the center of the building. Model train tracks ran along a shelf stretching the entire perimeter of the wall, in front of a painted village scene. The train raced by on the wall behind him, its cars tricked out with miniature billboards advertising a local bait shop. He sensed a blur of color from above, and looked up to see that hundreds of baseball caps in all different colors were stapled to the ceiling.

It smelled like beer and his boots crunched on peanut shells that had been thrown on the floor like so many autumn leaves.

Two guys paused in their game of pool to size him up. One was built like a linebacker, thick and wide with a low center of gravity and a crooked nose. He made eye contact with Zane as if challenging him to a fight. Zane shifted his gaze to the other one who was just a little bit taller and a little bit leaner but had a strong enough resemblance to the other to make Zane pretty sure the two were brothers.

He walked past them toward the bar, where a man in a black sweater and jeans took a swallow of dark beer and stood up from his barstool to greet Zane. He had wiry long grey hair mixed in with a little brown from younger days, and it had been at least a day or two since he had last shaved. He was just an inch or so taller than Zane, wearing cowboy boots, and probably forty pounds heavier.

"Jeremiah Doom," he said, extending a hand to Zane. Zane shook his hand, hyper aware that his own was clammy and cold. He said his own name, but it came out quiet and raspy instead of confident.

"Sit down with me," Jeremiah said, patting an empty barstool next to him. "Let's get you a drink."

Zane was relieved the bartender was busy at the other end of the bar so he could try to think. The urge to order a beer was strong. It would take the edge off of this meeting. Not ordering a drink might brand him as weak or troubled. And he could handle one drink if he made a commitment right now that it would be one drink. One.

Of course his sponsor would say that he would be showing he was strong if he ordered water. Because he would be owning his weakness, and that was the ultimate in strength. It all sounded like bullshit in his head, though. What this man, his father, would think would be that Zane couldn't handle alcohol, and that would set the tone for the rest of the meeting. Hell, for the rest of their relationship, whatever that might look like. Aren't first impressions all you got?

"Margee!" Jeremiah shouted at the bartender, a short, stout woman with hips like an anvil, who was talking to a customer at the other end. She turned around and waddled over, running a white bar towel over the wooden counter as she made her way to them.

"Hold your horses, there, Jeremiah. No need to go shouting at me."

Jeremiah's lips twitched like he was going to say something mean, but after a pause he smiled at her.

"Just thirsty is all, Margee," he said. "Another one for me, and one for this man."

I won't drink it, Zane thought. I'll just nurse it. I can do that. One sip at the start and then no more.

"So now what did you say Lily was calling herself?"

"Sherri Clearwater."

Jeremiah laughed. "She made herself over as a Cherokee? That's rich. She was the whitest white girl I knew. I bet those parents of hers loved that when they found out. I know they didn't like her being with an "injun" boy like me."

"Her dad's dead, but I met her mom. She didn't say anything about it."

Jeremiah rubbed his chin. "Yeah, I guess she had a lot of other stuff on her mind. So they weren't in touch at all? This whole time?"

"Don't think so."

"Amazing. I mean, I don't blame her for leaving me, but leaving her parents like that to worry she was dead or something. That's wrong."

The beers arrived. Jeremiah drained his first one and Margee wrapped plump fingers around the empty glass.

"Anything else, Jeremiah?"

"Just keep your eye on us now," he said, putting his hand over her wrist and squeezing. It seemed like a veiled threat. "Don't let us go dry, OK?"

"Of course not," she said, backing up a step and waiting for him to release her arm. When he did, she put her waddle into overdrive to get as much distance between her and him as the bar allowed.

Jeremiah raised his glass and Zane did the same.

"Everything that ends is also a new beginning. Us Cherokees believe in harmony and balance," Jeremiah said. "So let's drink to this new beginning."

Zane took a sip. Nothing to it, he thought. I'm nursing this one. I can make it last all night. The taste was bright and refreshing, and the alcohol went straight to his head, making him feel warm and comfortable. He greedily took another drink, this time larger, then set the glass down.

"I've always wanted to know more about being a Cherokee," he said.

"Well, we don't live in teepees and track animals no more," Jeremiah said. "That's for sure. Anyway, we can talk about that shit later. I want to learn all about you. You got a job?"

Zane shook his head and told the story of the stolen turtle eggs and how he got fired.

"You steal 'em, boy?"

"I didn't."

"I wouldn't judge you any way. Lord knows I done my share of shit over time. But I believe you. Cause why would you lie to me? Here I am, a convicted felon that a lot of people think killed those little girls. You want to impress me, you'd probably say, fuck yeah, I stole those turtle eggs and then I beat the shit out of that man—Randy, was his name?"

Zane wondered just how long Jeremiah had been drinking at the bar before he got there. There was a soft slur in his words.

"But you didn't do that, did you, Zane boy? You look like you're a good kid, your mama raised you right."

"I don't know about that. Like you said, I've done my share of shit over time. I spent a couple years in juvie. I'm trying to put it behind me."

Jeremiah laughed loudly, throwing his head back and drawing the attention of the other bar patrons. "You been in juvie? You talk about it like it's McAlester state prison or something. It's kindygarten, boy. What did you do to get yourself in there? Steal another baby's toys?"

"Aggravated assault. Went after a guy with a baseball bat," Zane said. He was surprised that he blurted out the details like that; usually he kept the particulars of that situation close. He couldn't help but wonder if he was trying to impress his father.

"Were you trying to kill him, or just teach him a lesson?"

"I don't really remember. I was drunk."

Jeremiah took a long drink of his beer, looking at their reflection in the mirror behind the bar.

"My mom was right. You do look like me when I was your age."

"Yeah, I saw a picture from the paper and thought the same thing."

"So you got plans to get another job, or what?"

Zane told him about school and his plan to be a welder.

"That's a right respectable vocation," he said, nodding with approval. "You can take that skill and do that anywhere you want. Hell, you might even go into business for yourself or something."

"I guess."

Usually Zane liked to think about the possibilities that would open up to him after welding school. But with the black cloud of his mother's death and the police's suspicion about him being involved, he felt like he didn't even have the right to think about the future beyond today. Being a master welder, graduating from the school, all those positive images he'd been building toward, they felt thin and faded and creased like a leftover flyer from the circus that had left town weeks ago.

"Once you learn a skill, can't nobody take it from you."

Another swallow of beer couldn't hurt none, since he'd already been sitting here five or ten minutes now, Zane thought. He knew his resolve was slipping, but he kept up the fiction in his head that he was still nursing this beer while at the same time telling himself it was okay, now that he'd started drinking, to just go ahead and get drunk. He knew it didn't make sense but he didn't care.

"You want another beer?" Margee said.

"I think something harder," Zane said. Jeremiah hit the bar with his palm and laughed.

"Now I know you're my son," he said, still laughing, and then slapping Zane on the back so hard he felt his lungs move in his rib cage.

#

Zane was buzzed when the two guys from the pool table came over. The husky one spoke to Jeremiah in a low voice, then walked toward the back of the bar and out of sight.

"This is my son, Clyde. Clyde, this is Zane."

From the way Clyde eyed him up now and when he walked in, Zane was pretty sure Jeremiah had told him the full story. Up close, Clyde looked younger than he thought at first. At most he was eighteen or nineteen and Zane wouldn't be surprised if he was still in high school. His shaved head had a thin covering of black new growth, on top of a skinny neck, tattooed with an outline of a wolf, and a bad case of acne on one cheek. He smiled, revealing crooked yellow teeth.

"Can I get a burger?" Clyde asked.

"You got money?"

"Nope, that's why I'm asking."

"We just had sandwiches two hours ago."

"I'm hungry again."

"Teenage boys," Jeremiah said to Zane. "You spend more money feeding them than you do on rent." He reached into his back pocket and brought out a wallet attached to his belt with a silver chain. "Get your brother one too if he wants. Zane, you hungry?"

He nodded, thinking maybe if he ate it would soak up some of the alcohol.

"Get four burgers and fries then," he said. Clyde took a twenty and a five dollar bill from his dad and a set of car keys.

"They don't have food here?" Zane asked.

"The food's shit here," Jeremiah said, loud enough to get Margee's attention. She glanced up from the cutting board where she was slicing fresh limes, an attention to detail Zane wouldn't have expected in such an establishment. Did they get many orders for margaritas or Mexican beer here? He couldn't think what else lime slices would be for.

The other brother came back in as Clyde left. He patted his father on the back with one hand, and with the other, he slipped some folded bills into his dad's open hand.

"Link, your brother's gone to get some burgers. Have a seat here with me and Zane. You want a drink?"

"Naw, I'm good." Link sat on the barstool next to Zane and grinned. "So you're my half brother. Nice to meet you."

"Now all that ain't fully established there, Link, but it's nice of you to be welcoming to Zane."

"You live in Tulsa?"

"Yup."

"I like it there. I've been telling Dad we need to do some mergers and acquisitions into the city, but he likes us being the big fish in this little shit pond."

"What kind of business you in?"

Jeremiah shot Link an angry look. "Aw, Link's just talking about this idea we have for a business is all. It's an idea, is all."

Zane knew it was best to let it drop; he'd heard and seen enough to have a pretty good idea that they were selling meth.

"Zane's going to welding school," Jeremiah said. "He's going to have a career and all."

"If I don't wind up in jail or worse for killing my mom," he said.

"Shit," Link said.

"Now what's this?" Jeremiah said. Zane told him the story, starting with waking up in the truck with no memory. It was a relief to get it off of his chest.

Four drinks and two hours later, Zane was smashed and carefree, shooting pool with Link. The twin pleasures of alcohol and camaraderie forced any lingering thoughts of his mother or Lettie or the police out of his mind. It was a relief.

A skinny guy with loose jeans and a white hoodie with an elaborate gold and silver graphic silkscreened on the front swaggered in, arms swinging and twitching. Meth head, Zane thought, noticing the grey and brown teeth. When he saw Link getting ready to make his shot, the guy jerked himself around and backed out the door at high speed.

"Motherfucker," Link said, leaning the cue against the fake wood edge of the table. "Clyde! Clyde! Come on now!"

Link took off after the tweaker without noticing that Clyde hadn't heard his name over AC/DC's *Back in Black*. Zane threw his pool cue on the floor and ran after him. The cold air was a shock to his lungs, but he ran full out to catch up with Link, who was gaining on the guy. They didn't call them speed freaks for nothing—meth heads can run really fast and if you did catch them, they were likely to be crazy as hell. Unpredictable and violent, he thought, remembering that kid in juvie that they put in a strait-jacket and a padded room.

That's why Zane ran after Link, he told himself, to protect him. He didn't know why Link was chasing the dude, but he instantly knew he was going to back him up. Like a brother should. And yes, the thought of a fight got his blood pumping with excitement. His fists itched for contact almost as much as he wanted to prove himself worthy to this family. His family.

The parking lot was dark and empty, nobody in sight except Link and the tweaker. One streetlight flickered overhead where the driveway met the 4130 byway. The byway itself wasn't lit. The tweaker seemed to be running for the road rather than getting into a car, and Zane was pretty sure they'd catch him at some point on the flat farmland on the other side.

He'd just crossed the 4130 when he saw the guy stumble and fall. Link made a flying leap on him, as good as any Zane had seen on a high school football field. He heard the thud of Link's body hitting the guy. The air rushed out of the tweaker's lungs in a loud bark.

"Why you running from me, Chris? I thought we was friends," Link said, pinning the skinny guy to the ground with both knees. He easily weighed three or four times more than the tweaker.

Chris's mouth was open wide, blood trickling out of the side like a cartoon vampire.

"Don't have the money," he said, out of breath.

"You know, I thought that might be the case when you ran like a little chicken shit out of JV's. No hello, Link, I've been looking for you so I could pay you the thousand dollars I owe you."

Chris was working his hand into his jeans pocket, and before Zane could shout a warning, he pulled out a switchblade and stabbed Link in the leg. Link's tolerance for pain was higher than Zane imagined, because after a moment of surprise, he smiled and sent a crushing right cross to Chris's head. Chris's hand fell off the knife handle and onto the dirt. He was out.

Link pulled the switchblade out of his leg with a grimace and wiped it on his jeans.

"I oughta carve an IOU into him," he said, looking down on Chris who was splayed on the ground like one of Lettie's old dolls.

"How deep did he get you?" Zane said.

"Not too bad." Link spat on the guy's face.

Zane bent over to empty Chris's pockets. He tossed a smart phone with a cracked screen to Link.

"You can sell that for fifty, anyway." He rolled him onto his side and checked the back pockets. "Here's seven bucks and some change."

Zane dropped the money into Link's outstretched hand and he made a fist around it and shoved it in his own pocket.

"It's freezing out here," he said. "Let's head back."

"Going to leave him here?"

"Well, I ain't gonna carry him home, if that's what you're asking."

Zane checked his phone and saw it was nearly eleven.

"You got to get back to Tulsa?"

"I'm kinda fucked up for a two hour drive," Zane said.

"Want a taste to keep you awake?"

"No, I'll just hang here, maybe sleep in the car."

"I'll ask Dad if you can crash with us," Link said.

#

The Doom house was more of a compound, down a long gravel road and surrounded by a cinder block wall and a metal gate that swung into a large yard. Jeremiah's truck triggered motion-sensor lights and a cacophony of barking dogs. Zane could make out a long house covered in metal paneling painted brown to look like wood. Off to the side was a garden shed and a barn at least two times larger than the house. Two garage doors opened in synchronicity and Jeremiah and his sons pulled their trucks in. Zane parked on the compacted dirt driveway. The barking dogs sounded vicious, ready to attack. Zane looked around but didn't see any canines, but he thought it best to check. He rolled down the window and asked Jeremiah if it was okay to get out.

"Dogs are in their kennels," he said. "Come on inside."

Zane followed him onto the porch and into the house. Jeremiah hung his jacket on a wall hook under a mirror, and kicked off his sneakers on the linoleum floor.

"You can crash on the sofa there." He pointed at a red couch directly ahead of the door. A straight hallway extended to their left and right, with doorways leading to dark rooms on either side. "Kitchen's that way if you want some water or something. Bathroom's down that hall."

Link and Clyde filed in, the garage doors rattling their way down outside. They shut and locked the door. It was a more elaborate ritual than Zane expected, with five locks and one door brace that wedged underneath the knob.

"You trying to keep someone outside or someone inside?"

"Welcome to the house of horrors, Zane," Clyde said with a sinister laugh. "Bwa-ha-ha-ha-ha!"

Zane laughed. "You're creeping me out, man."

"Link sleepwalks, so don't freak out if you see him standing in the middle of the room staring at you," Clyde said. "Holding a gun."

"Of course Clyde sleepwalks too, but he'll just try to cuddle with you," Link said.

Clyde smacked him up the side of his head, and Link grabbed his arm and twisted it. They were both laughing.

"Sweet dreams," Link said.

Zane checked his phone and saw a message from Emmaline. "Where r u?" it read. He considered calling her to hear how the rest of the tryout went for the pageant show, but didn't want the other people in the house to hear his conversation. He wanted to keep Emmaline—and Lettie for that matter—separate and private from the Dooms. He typed "staying the night in Sallisaw with my dad" and put the phone on the floor.

He took his coat and shoes off, and looked around the large family room where the red sofa was for a blanket or something to cover himself with. The house was cold and furnished for function not aesthetics. There were no photos or knickknacks like in his mother's home, just clean tabletops and blank walls and a few men's magazines. Zane glanced at the barely dressed starlet on the cover without much interest. A headline over her thighs promised tricks for how to please a woman in bed. A gun safe stood next to a gas fireplace that he would have loved to light for warmth but didn't dare. He tried to fluff up one of the flat pillows squashed down between the arm of the couch and the cushion, and draped his coat over himself like a blanket. It was better than sleeping in the car anyway, or getting pulled over for drunk driving—although driving here was a risk he'd taken without too much thought.

"At least I remember everything that happened," he thought, a final consolation that brought its own wave of sadness about his mother's death before he passed out.

#

"Time to go to work," Jeremiah said, slapping the bottoms of his feet which were propped up on the arm of the sofa. Zane's head hurt. The smell of coffee brewing made him a little nauseous. "We'll get breakfast on the way."

Outside, the sun was rising like a flame behind a sheet of grey and white clouds. Behind the house was a vast winter wheat field, shoots just emerging out of the ground. Towering above narrow, winding rows of hard red wheat were fifteen wind turbines, a few spinning gently in the light breeze. In the far distance was a stand of grey trees alongside a creek.

Jeremiah seemed to have it all. Land, a nice house, sons working with him. Zane hadn't imagined his father—still hard to believe, suddenly he had a father—so successful. Maybe when he was young, he pretended his father would show up one day and drive him and his mom out of the Majestic and onto some beautiful land like this, where they would grow their own food and work together and live off the grid. His mother, though, would have just seen dollar signs everywhere. That John Deere tractor could be sold for seventy-five thousand; that sprayer tank for two grand. She'd be in hog heaven tallying up the money she could spend on cigarettes and alcohol and Waffle House and at the Cherokee Casino. Probably would never cross her mind that it could pay for welding school for Zane or college for Lettie. His sister was plenty smart enough to be thinking about getting into college; Sherri would tell her to cast a spell for money rather than do any work for it. He would figure out a better way. Maybe, just maybe, Jeremiah would help.

Lettie would love it on this land, he knew, but he couldn't picture her with the Dooms. Something told him to protect her from them. He knew how to handle himself around men like Link and Clyde, and maybe Jeremiah, but they lived in a hard world far away from Lettie's world of magical creatures and positive thinking. He remembered her sprinkling pennies and nickels and dimes on shelves and the desk and coffee table, because she'd read a spell book that said laying money out like that would bring more money into the family. Sherri picked it all up the next day and put it in her wallet. That was pretty much what happened to any money that came into the house anyway. Into mama's wallet and then right back out again at the liquor store.

"So is Clearwater just some name Lily picked out of the phone book, or what?" Jeremiah asked as the garage door rattled up. His words were punctuated by puffs of breath made visible by the cold air.

"Well, I don't know," Zane said, and that was true enough. There was a lot to say here and he tried to pick through his thoughts to figure out the best way to do it. He had to acknowledge Ely Clearwater here. He had to tell Jeremiah that this man's name was on his birth certificate. Hell, Zane realized that there was a chance Jeremiah knew Ely. Maybe he could actually shed some light on the stories his mother had told him.

"She told me my father was a man named Ely Clearwater, who died before I was born."

Jeremiah opened the truck door and slid into the seat. Zane did the same. Their breath came out in damp, warm clouds even in the relative warmth of the garage.

"Ely Clearwater, huh? You ever try to find his kin?" Jeremiah put the keys in the ignition and started the truck. His foot must have been pushing down the gas pedal hard, because the engine roared to life with stunning loudness.

"Yeah, a few times but no luck. It's like he never existed." Zane sensed the news was hurting Jeremiah. "I'm not sure he was more than a figment of her imagination."

It was the first time he had ever said such a thing out loud. Really, the first time he had thought it. But here with Jeremiah, seeing the resemblance between them, well, he felt *home*. This flesh and blood person was so much better than the ghost he had been clinging to for twenty-six years.

"Huh," was all Jeremiah said. He backed the truck out of the garage and did a quick three-point turn before heading back down the driveway.

A few beats passed while they both sat in silence, eyes straight ahead.

Jeremiah cleared his throat.

"Unbelievable. I never thought she had that much imagination, but here she created this whole new life. I wish I had some photos to show you of me and her. Lily was a real foxy babe back then. But my ex-wife Caradeen, she made me throw them all out when she was pregnant. Said it would confuse our kids to see me with another woman. Of course, she wasn't too worried about Link and Clyde being confused when she ran off with that bull rider."

"You lived here a long time?" Zane asked, glad for a shift onto less emotionally charged topics.

"Bought it about five years ago from a survivalist family that was convinced we were in biblical end times. They moved off to some bigger compound in New Mexico with other like-minded folks. They gave me a great deal on it because they didn't really think the money mattered too much, what with the world ending and all."

A dirty white Toyota Corolla with a rust spot and a missing fender came through the gate and into the compound. Two women sat in the front seats. The driver had frizzy blond hair and the passenger had red hair tied back in a ponytail. They parked near the garden shed and sat for a few moments talking.

"Friends of yours?"

"Cleaning ladies," Jeremiah said. "Let's go."

CHAPTER THIRTEEN

The yellow sign of the Dollar General store flickered on when they pulled into the parking lot. A tall man in black pants and a black polo shirt swept leaves from the store entrance into the parking lot. He made up for six inches of receding hairline by growing his black hair collar length in the back. The trade-off didn't really work.

"Hey Jeremiah," the man said as they passed.

"How you doing, Heston?" Jeremiah said without waiting for an answer. Heston didn't apparently expect him to either. He didn't reply and resumed sweeping as the automatic doors shut behind them.

The store was bright and crowded and clean with a little bit of everything in stock. Halloween decorations and candy lined the shelves nearest to the doors. A round of brightly colored scrub pants like doctors wore went all the way to size XXL. A rack of red and white University of Oklahoma T-shirts, flags and baseball caps competed with its rival Oklahoma State University for visibility. OSU's orange and black easily won.

Another customer followed them into the store—a solidly built man in denim overalls and a green camouflage zip-up hoodie. He wore an olive green knit cap pulled over his eyebrows and nearly down to the beginnings of his grey beard. He walked straight past them to the soda aisle, and studied a display of RC cola like it might pounce on him.

Zane followed Jeremiah down an aisle of cookies, crackers, soup and nuts to an end display of prepaid phones. He grabbed five of them without hesitation and headed to the register at the front of the store.

Heston must have been keeping an eye on them because he came back into the store as they approached. He grabbed a pack of Marlboro reds off the back wall and put them on the counter.

"Give me two packs today," Jeremiah said. Heston turned to get another pack.

"You need anything, Zane?"

He shook his head, wondering why Jeremiah needed five burner cell phones.

Heston rang up the purchases. The total was close to two hundred dollars, but Jeremiah didn't act like it was any big deal. He just brought out a thick roll of bills and peeled off ten twenties. Zane had never seen so much money in one roll before.

"How's your sister doing, Heston?"

"She's getting out of Warrior next month."

Zane knew the man was referring to Eddie Warrior female correctional center, a minimum security prison in what used to be an all-black town called Taft. He'd been through it before—it was one of those blink-and-you-miss-it towns where you might get gas on your way to somewhere else. He'd remembered hearing about it in school during Black History month, when they talked about these towns where Indians and former slaves lived together in little farming communities because no one wanted them anywhere else. They made the best of it and wound up being so prosperous that black people started coming from all over the South. So then white people said no more and started making laws against leasing land or hiring Negros.

One of Zane's teachers had always said if you want to know why something happened like an invasion or a war, just follow the money and you'll find the cause. At first Zane thought that was pretty cynical, but he'd come to realize it was true. It was even true about small things in his own life. Always follow the money and you'll find the greed at the bottom of it.

"You tell her to come see me when she's out," Jeremiah said. "I want to make sure she knows that I know the value of a woman who can keep her mouth shut."

Heston looked visibly uncomfortable, staring at the counter between them rather than meeting Jeremiah's eyes.

"She's been talking about staying on the straight and narrow when she gets out," Heston said. "I'm working on getting her a job here."

Jeremiah smiled. "Well, that's fantastic. Good for her."

Heston looked relieved, and glanced at both of them with a tentative smile. "Yeah, we're right proud of her."

"You should be. I'm proud of her too. But you still tell her to come by and see me, OK? I want to thank her properly."

In the truck, Jeremiah handed one of the phones to Zane.

"If you need to get in touch with me, this is how we're going to do it," he said. He held up a second phone. "Put this number in your phone there and that's how you call me."

"What's wrong with my regular phone?"

"Government tracks that shit," Jeremiah said. "This is better. Trust me."

Jeremiah took out the wad of bills he'd flashed in the store. He counted off about half of it and handed it to Zane.

"What's this for?"

"It's for rent and whatever you and your sister need," he said. "It's for making things a little easier at this hard time. You have no job and sure as hell no one is going to hire you right now when you're in the news every day."

"I can't take it." He pushed it back, but he knew his reluctance was all over his face. The money would really help, no doubt about it.

"You can pay me back when things settle down."

Jeremiah put the keys in the ignition and started the truck.

"You're a man with a plan and I like that," Jeremiah said. "You're getting your training so you can have a career. You're a bright boy with a lot of potential and I don't want to see that go down the drain."

Zane thought about Link and Clyde and wondered if they got the same speech from him. He liked the idea of having brothers, or step-brothers really. And a father. A father who would have been there for him while he was growing up, had Sherri only seen fit to tell Jeremiah he had a son. Zane had no doubt that Jeremiah would have been a great dad, teaching him how to shoot and hunt and fix cars and talk to girls. Would have raised him alongside his other sons as their big brother. And they would have fought over toys and later girls but would always be there for one another. Anger at his mother boiled up. Why hadn't she told him?

A man with the sunbaked skin of someone who lived on the streets knocked on the truck window. He wore a blue puffy jacket stretched tight over what looked to be at least three layers of shirts, reminding Zane of the Incredible Hulk in mid-transition, right before his clothes tore to shreds over his expanded muscles. His hands were red and shiny, his eyes were a light green so bright they almost glowed.

Jeremiah rolled down the window.

"Mr. Doom, I wish to inquire if you are looking for any of what you call the 'smurfing' to be done today, and if in fact I may do such tasks for you."

"Thought you were done with that, David."

"Well, I find myself in the need of some of the green cash money, sir, and then what do I see but your fine truck parked right next to the dumpster by which I sleep."

"You can talk to Link or Clyde about that, not me," he said.

"Ah, but neither Link nor Clyde is here right now, and next to you is a man I do not know."

"David, this is Zane. I'm helping him with something right now and we need to get on to it."

"Sir Zane, it is a pleasure to meet you. I am glad our paths have crossed, however briefly." He stretched out a hand between Jeremiah and the steering wheel for Zane to shake. His skin was leathery and dry, his hand icy cold in Zane's.

"Yeah, nice to meet you, David."

"Will Link or Clyde be around this fine establishment later today?"

"I'll tell one of them to swing by, David. But if you are going to start up again I need to know that you're going to follow through with it and not just take the money and buy a bottle of Old Crow bourbon and hole up somewhere."

"If the elixir you call Old Crow was good enough for Daniel Webster and Mark Twain, it's good enough for me and should be good enough for you."

"I don't care what you buy to drink, as long as you buy it after you've delivered the pills."

"A man of business. I respect that. Sir Doom, I will wait for one of your fine offspring to visit me." He bowed at the waist, his hands clasped as though in prayer, and backed away from the car.

"For a town of less than ten thousand, we certainly got our share of crazies," Jeremiah said, shaking his head. Zane watched as David lumbered off to the side of the building, out of sight, wondering what kind of bed the man had and hoping to hell he never found himself sleeping next to a dumpster. It seemed a little too close for comfort these days, with no job, money that was getting spent way too fast and the police on his back.

#

"Tell me all about him," Emmaline said. "Was he intimidating?"

"A little bit, at first. He's tough. Kind of ready to fight, but not looking for a fight if you know what I mean. He brought his two sons to the bar with him. They're both younger than me."

"What does he do? What's his house like?"

"I think he's doing some farming—I saw wheat growing on his fields this morning." Zane figured it best to leave out his suspicions that Jeremiah and his sons were making and selling crystal meth. "It seemed he got married not too long after Mom left him."

Lettie came out of the sewing studio hauling a blue backpack and a white trash bag stuffed with clothes.

"Don't forget the homecoming dress, Lettie!" Emmaline said, jumping to her feet to get it. "I finished it this morning."

"Right," Lettie said, still moving toward the door. "I'm just going to put this stuff in the truck."

"You wanted to borrow my silver sandals too, right?" Emmaline called from the back, but Lettie was already out of earshot.

"She probably does," Zane said. He took the dress on its hanger, covered with a white plastic bag, and the sandals, from Emmaline. He leaned in to try to give her a kiss on the lips but she turned her face so he got her cheek.

"Not now, Zane," she said. "So—the big news is that we're taping the pilot of *Pageant Gown Project* tomorrow. Peter really loved my spirit, he said. He wants to have me and that blue-haired guy do another sew-off and make not just the gowns for the beauty part, but also the costumes for the talent portion. Then he's going to shop it around. They're even going to pay me three hundred dollars for my time."

"That's great, Em."

"Of course he wants to use that little monster Lauren with her wrestling moves. I suppose she's going to pin me down if she doesn't like the dress I make for her."

"She'll like your dress, you're amazing."

"You think so, Zane? I hope so."

"I do," he said, reaching out to squeeze her hand. "Hey, do you want to come over and see the apartment? You know, it's the first place I can call my own. Maybe you could give me some decorating tips."

"Oh, Zane, I'd love to see it, I really would, but Peter's coming by to take me to get my hair and nails done today, and buy a new outfit for the taping tomorrow. I'll come by later, okay? Maybe next weekend."

He was disappointed but tried not to show it. It was kind of selfish of him to ask that of her when she had so much on her mind. She was on the cusp of a dream coming true, and he was trying to find the bright spot in a nightmare. Why would she want to come?

#

He woke up an hour later on his freshly made bed to the sound of his cell phone ringing. It was that detective.

"Zane, I'm over here at the Majestic. We were looking at the trailer again and thought maybe we could talk to you."

His stomach dropped like he was on a rollercoaster screaming down its biggest hill.

"My sister and I got an apartment over on Garnett."

"Mind if I come over and ask you a few questions? Won't take but a few minutes."

"I guess not." Like he had a choice. And at least they weren't hauling him down to the station for an interrogation or worse, an arrest. Maybe they'd finally determined the cause of the fire was accidental. He could only hope.

#

Zane opened the screen door to let Detective Old Spice into the apartment. Lettie looked up from Zane's cell phone to say hi, then returned to checking out what her friends were doing on one of the social networking sites.

"Did the Perrymans tell you it was time to go?"

"No," Zane said. "I had this place lined up last week, for me. Now it's me and Lettie."

"Where you getting the money for all this?"

It was an intrusive question, but that was a police specialty, wasn't it, Zane thought.

"I had some money saved up for welding school," he said, not seeing any need to bring the gift from his father into the detective's line of sight.

"Mind if I sit down?"

Zane gestured to the sofa, but Old Spice took one of the dining table chairs and pulled it over. Zane sat on the sofa next to Lettie.

"A couple of things," he said. "First, do you know that your mother changed her name?"

Zane nodded. "Yeah, we found some papers in her stuff."

"The media have that story now. I don't know who tipped

them off, but they've been calling the station, asking for confirmation. I think you can expect to hear from some of them."

"We don't have to talk to them, do we?" Lettie asked.

Both Zane and Old Spice said no, nearly in unison. "They better not start bothering Lettie," Zane said.

"Just keep your cool," Old Spice said. "They got a right to ask you questions but you got a right not to answer. Don't do nothing to lash out at them, even if they're provoking you. You'll just bring on more trouble. Now, here's the other thing I came to talk to you about. You ever hear of a guy named Arno Jackson?"

Zane and Lettie both shook their heads.

"His body was found in the woods behind the Majestic yesterday. From what the medical examiner tells me, it looks like he might have died the same day as your mother."

Zane twitched with recognition. The coyotes in the dream. Walking in the woods. A red plaid shirt. But it was silly to tell the police about dreams of talking coyotes.

Instead, Zane raised his eyebrows and said, "Never heard the name before. He didn't live at the Majestic, did he?" And it was true that he'd never heard the name before.

"From what we can tell so far, he didn't have anywhere in particular he called home. We're still trying to run down more information on him. I thought maybe you two might know him."

"Why's that?" Lettie asked.

"Well, first, he had a second degree burn on his right hand that looked pretty fresh. And since we're investigating a fire, that's just a little too much of a coincidence for us not to take a closer look. Second, he had a photo of your mother saved on his phone that someone sent him from a prepaid cell."

"Why would this guy have a photo of mom?" Lettie asked, her face twisted as though she rejected the idea outright.

"That's what I'm trying to find out," Old Spice said.

Zane felt some relief and more curiosity. Had he walked in the woods that day instead of going with Lettie to look through the burnt-out trailer, would he have stumbled on Arno Jackson? Would he have learned more had he discovered the body?

"I wish we could shed some light on it for you," Zane said. "But I've never heard the name before."

"Maybe you could take a look at the photo of him. It's a little hard to look at, since he's dead in the picture, but that's all I got. Maybe Lettie, you could look at it too, see if you know him?"

He pulled out a folded piece of paper with a color photo printed on it. The man's eyes were shut and his skin a pale grey. He had short brown hair and a tattoo of a cross behind one ear.

Neither Zane nor Lettie recognized him. But he was wearing a red plaid shirt, just like the body in the dream. It freaked Zane out a bit.

Old Spice folded the paper back up and put it in his jacket pocket.

"Now, this is just for elimination purposes," Old Spice said to Lettie. "There's an awful lot of paperwork that detectives like me have to do, you see. So, Lettie, you told me before that you were at a friend's house for a sleepover. Now we had to check that out, and the girl's parents told me that you didn't actually get there until later."

"She stopped at a thrift store," Zane said. "She lost track of time."

"Is that right, Lettie?"

"Yes," she said, looking scared.

"Now which thrift store was that?" Old Spice asked, then wrote down the name she told him in his notebook.

"Did you talk to anyone there? Will anyone remember seeing

you?"

"I don't know," she said, her voice trembling.

"Nothing to be scared of, Lettie. This is all just routine," Old Spice said.

Zane wasn't so sure.

#

After Zane closed the door behind Old Spice, Lettie began crying. Zane crossed to the couch, sat next to her and pulled her in close. She cried into his shoulder for what seemed like hours. His stomach tightened up with worry and fear. Did she know Arno Jackson? Had she seen something on her way to her friend's house that she was scared to tell him? What did she know? He felt an overwhelming desire to lock her in a tower for safekeeping like a princess.

"What's wrong, Lettie?"

She took a deep, shuddering breath. Zane held the air in his lungs, waiting for her news.

"Morgan says he can't take me to the homecoming dance," she said, then started sobbing again. "He says he has to go out of town with his family."

He exhaled. Zane was glad it was just middle school drama and not something bigger. He turned away so she wouldn't see the relieved smile cross his face.

"Well, sometimes things come up with families and stuff. I mean, I understand that," he said, offering what little comfort he could think of. "You could still go with friends, right?"

"Zane, don't be an idiot. Nothing came up with Morgan's family. It's just all these stupid stories that girl Mary is spreading. You saw how his mother was when we went over there. I bet she told him he couldn't go with me."

"What? Why?"

"These girls at school, they're saying I worship the devil. All sorts of crap like that. I told you this. It's only gotten worse over the past two days. Then I get a message from Morgan that says suddenly something came up next weekend and he has to leave town. It's bull!"

"Do you want to go over and talk to him? I'll take you."

"No, I don't want to go over and talk to him. It'll be enough to see him at school. I can already tell nothing is going to change his mind. He's a stupid mama's boy."

"Then you're better off without him," Zane said.

"But I really liked him," she said, and the tears started again.

Their mother would know better than him what to say, he thought. She wasn't the most loving woman in the world but she certainly had had her share of romantic disillusions and Zane bet she would have the perfect words at hand. Or maybe she'd tell Lettie to burn a candle.

Zane, however, had no idea what he should do or say to make Lettie feel better. He just held her in his arms until the tears stopped flowing and her breathing returned to normal.

"Why don't we go to the Old Country Buffet for dinner, then over to the thrift store to look at televisions?"

Lettie smiled at him, but shook her head. "We can't afford that."

"Sure we can," Zane said. "Chicken fried steak, you know you love it."

"Are you sure?"

"Absolutely," he said.

On the way to the restaurant, rain splatted against the truck windshield in big, heavy drops. The Old Country Buffet for the two of them set him back twenty bucks and the fuel gauge on the truck was getting down to the last quarter tank. Zane found himself so much more aware of money that it hurt to think about it. After the big layout of cash for the apartment, every dollar seemed important. And whenever the coroner released his mother's body, then they'd have the funeral to deal with—which reminded him that Verda had called to check in and he needed to call her back, even just to tell her he didn't have any new information.

The thrift store was brightly lit, with high ceilings and racks and racks of clothing, shoes, and household stuff. The front displays were dedicated to a sad collection of Halloween decorations and costumes.

Lettie led him straight to the television aisle, where it seemed nearly every fat, heavy analog television in east Tulsa sat, all outcasts from homes that had made the upgrade to slim flat screen TVs in the past few years.

"Here's one like our old one," Lettie said, pointing to a thirty-two inch screen built into a fake oak cabinet. Zane checked the price tag—even forty-five dollars seemed like too much.

"How about this one?" He pointed to one housed in a black plastic console that was only twenty dollars.

"Zane, Lettie!"

They turned and saw Mrs. Ahern, their snoopy neighbor from the Majestic. She had a clear plastic rain bonnet covering her hair and secured with a tight little bow underneath her chin.

"How are you doing, you poor little ones? I'm so sorry about your mama," she said, giving each one of them a hug and offering her bony chin for them to kiss.

"Did you hear that the police found a dead body in the woods behind the Majestic?" Zane asked, though he was pretty sure she knew all about it already.

"Oh yes, why, they were out there with their crime scene tape and cameras and measuring tapes and what not for hours this morning," she said. "Did you know the man?"

"No, never heard of him before."

Mrs. Ahern leaned in with a conspiratorial smile to Zane and Lettie.

"Now I understand why you might tell the police that, but you don't have to lie to old Mrs. Ahern. And you shouldn't lie to the police either, because they'll find out eventually. Now, I didn't tell them this, not yet, but I know I'd seen that man before—he came around to see your mom once or twice."

Zane was nothing short of shocked.

"This Arno Jackson? Came to see Mom? When?"

"I think it was Wednesday of last week. Let me think, what day was my podiatrist appointment? Yes, Wednesday, because that was the same day that Louella from the church stopped by to pray with me in the afternoon. I guess you and Lettie were at work and school because it was the middle of the day. This loud motorcycle with the mufflers removed comes speeding by when we're doing the Lord's Prayer and makes it so we can't hear ourselves pray. I look out the window to see who it is, and see this same fellow taking off his helmet and knocking at your mama's door. She didn't look none too happy to see him, but she let him in fast enough, so I don't think he was a salesman or nothing. I thought maybe she owed him money or something. He was still there when Louella left and then I had to leave for my doctor's appointment so I didn't see when he came out. He was gone by the time I got back a few hours later."

"Did you ask her about him?"

Mrs. Ahern twisted her mouth into a grimace. "Well, I did, but she told me to mind my own business. Your mother could be very outspoken, bless her heart."

Lettie and Zane suppressed smiles, picturing their mom saying just that to the old gossip. She'd said more than once that Mrs. Ahern had too much time on her hands and was too nosy for her own good.

They talked for a few more moments and then parted ways. Zane carried the big black television to the cash register up front, Lettie trailing behind.

A group of girls about Lettie's age were sifting through the eighties' rack of clothing looking for Halloween costumes.

"Either I'll be Madonna from the eighties in black lace and crosses and fingerless gloves, or an aerobics instructor in neon," said a skinny blonde girl.

"I don't think you should wear the crosses as a joke. I don't think that is respectful to Jesus," a petite girl with freckles and a brown ponytail said. Zane saw she wore a simple gold cross around her neck and a black T-shirt that said "I've got glitter in my veins and Jesus in my heart." The blonde rolled her eyes and sighed, then fixed her gaze on Zane and Lettie.

"Lettie Magdite, imagine meeting you here," the blonde said.

"Hi, Hillary."

"Buying a homecoming dress here?"

The other girls giggled like a pack of hyenas.

"Oh, what am I saying? Of course you're not. I heard Morgan bailed on you. Too bad. Maybe you can cast a spell and conjure up a demon to go with you."

What was it about some of these girls? Beautiful as angels with hearts darker than midnight. Zane fought the desire to punch the pretty little bitch in the face. Lettie just kept moving toward the cash register without acknowledging the girls. Zane followed after her and paid for the television.

It wasn't until Zane pulled out of the parking lot and they were headed back to the apartment that Lettie started to cry again. Eyes on the road, Zane stroked her hair with his right hand, unsure what to say.

He turned the truck's heat up as though that might provide Lettie some comfort he couldn't. At least he could keep her warm on this chilly October night.

"Want to talk about it?" he said.

She shook her head violently.

"I knew girls like that in high school," he said.

"They're not worth my energy," Lettie muttered. She wiped tears away with the rolled up sleeve of brown corduroy jacket she'd borrowed from Emmaline.

"No, they aren't," Zane agreed.

"That girl Hillary? She once got me to pose for a picture on her phone, telling me she really liked my outfit. I totally thought she was sincere, though I kind of should have been suspicious. I was just wearing the same jeans and this T-shirt with an owl on it I wear all the time. Anyway, she put my picture up on this website she called "Trailer trash of Tulsa." I was one of her examples of ugly outfits."

"Ouch," Zane said.

"I threw that T-shirt away. I was so embarrassed. Mom fished it out of the trash and was like, why are you throwing this away? She bought it for me at the start of the school year. I told her the story and she told me I should wear it proudly. That all those celebrities in the back of those gossip magazines love to be picked for worst outfit of the week or whatever. She said I should just be bold about it, keep my head high."

Lettie tucked her hair behind her ears. The tears were drying up.

"What did you do with that T-shirt? Did you wear it again?"

She smiled.

"I did, actually. I took a marker and wrote "tacky trailer trash shirt" on it and wore it the next day. She saw me and laughed, but I just kept my head up, like Mom said.""

He nodded, imagining Lettie walking through the school hallways, proudly wearing the label "trailer trash" and laughing.

Lettie fell silent. For a while, neither spoke, letting the story float between them like a bubble about to pop.

She shifted in her seat.

"It's getting hot in here," she said.

Zane turned the heater down again, wondering if the crisis with the teenage girls had passed. Lettie had this ability—kind of like a baby does—to let out her feelings in a big way, then just...move on. She didn't keep too much inside. He admired that about her, the way she just blew through emotional storms and came out on the other side, ready to move forward. He reminded himself that he should follow her lead.

"Do you know who that guy Arno Jackson is?" she asked.

Zane shook his head. "It's funny that Mom never brought him up, not once."

"Well, she might've," Lettie said with a last sniffle. "Maybe last time we visited Dad at McAlester, she told him she had to talk to him about one of their old friends. But the way she said friends was sarcastic. She sent me off to get a pop right after that so I didn't hear what else they said."

Zane's mind was racing. This Arno Jackson might have actually set the fire, in fact, and if Zane could prove it, he could get Old Spice off his back for good. It was almost too perfect. But what if the police suspected that Zane not just killed his mother, but also killed this guy Arno? What if he had killed them both? What kind of monster was he?

"Did you see anything, anything at all, that night, Lettie? Before you left?"

"I already told you, I saw you and Mom watching TV and drinking wine. You were both pretty drunk. She was outraged by something they were saying on the news. Nothing new."

It was a blank to him still. Zane thought about who his mom might have confided in. She didn't have a lot of friends, really. Maybe the woman who came by to cut and dye her hair every few months. He couldn't even remember the last time his mother had a visitor or talked to anyone on the phone who wasn't with social services or Lettie's school. He didn't see much choice but to make the trek to McAlester to see Lettie's dad and ask him what Sherri told him.

"So, when are visitation days at the penitentiary?" he asked Lettie.

Her eyes grew wide and a smile flew to her lips. "We're going to go see Dad?"

"Yup, when can we do it?"

"Friday, Saturday or Sunday," she rattled off quickly. "Ten to four."

"Tomorrow it is," he said. "We'll go first thing."

CHAPTER FOURTEEN

He pulled the truck into the QuikTrip on Garnett Road overlooking the Crosstown Expressway. The rain had stopped but had left huge puddles in the blacktop pavement.

About half of the gas pumps were occupied with pickup trucks and SUVs and their owners. He pulled into an empty stall and went into the store to spend a few more twenties on gasoline. Inside, the store was throbbing with off-duty afternoon shift workers from the nearby steel fabricator where he had hoped to land a job with his welding certificate. Three cashiers were on duty, and a line of men in work clothes holding six-packs of beer and bags of chips stretched to the ice machine in the corner.

That guy Peter from the pageant show was standing in front of a long counter of fountain drinks, smoothie machines and coffee pots, his fingers folding in the sides of a paper cup. He was staring blankly at a rotating circle of icy blue slush. Indecision at the QuikTrip beverage counter was a common phenomenon. The store was known for its vast fountain drink selections and encouraged customers to play mad chemist by making their own combos. They even posted recipes with names like Kiss the Rooster and Cherries Jubilee.

He heard a woman's deep laugh, the kind of laugh that jumped at you and made you join in even though you aren't privy to the joke. A smile crept across his face and he turned toward the sound, half hoping it was Emmaline. He wanted to tell her about Lettie and the homecoming dance, and get her advice. Maybe she could talk to Lettie. She'd know what to say.

And it was Emmaline. She swooped into the drink aisle without seeing Zane, or noticing how his heart dropped as she playfully kissed Peter on the cheek. Peter, focused on getting just the right amount of white cherry slush, never took his eyes off of the drink dispenser.

Zane turned the corner around the aisle and came face-to-face with Emmaline, who looked surprised to see him.

"Hey," he said.

Peter moved a few feet down and added orange smoothie to his cup.

"Hey, Zane, how's it going?" Peter had a smug half-smile on his face, the self-satisfied grin of a man who knew he was going to get laid in the very near future.

"Peachy," Zane said.

Zane could see Emmaline had a box in her hand that she was trying to conceal from him. *Don't let it be condoms*, he thought.

Emmaline touched his arm.

"I'm sorry, Zane, it's just…"

"I get it, Em," he said. "Be sure to practice safe sex."

He walked back to the counter, where thankfully the line had diminished, so he could just lay the money on the counter. "Pump number five," he said.

The cashier called out "Come back in for your receipt" but he was already out the door.

#

He was trying to tune in some of the local over-the-air channels on their new-to-them television when there was a knock on the door. Magnolia stood on the step holding an armful of clothes. Lettie opened the door.

"I thought maybe some of these things would fit you," she said. "I'm kind of a shopaholic—I can't resist a sale. Some of this stuff I've never worn. It even still has the tags on."

Lettie giggled with excitement. "Wow!" She opened the door wide and gestured to the sofa where Zane sat. "Bring them over here and let's see!"

"Magnolia, this is really generous of you. You don't have to do this," Zane said.

"I know that, of course. I'm happy to. Seriously."

"Zane, look at this!" She held up an airy top that seemed to be made of handkerchiefs, light and pretty and printed with birds.

"It looks so cute with these," Magnolia said, reaching into the pile and pulling out a pair of skinny jeans in dark denim.

Lettie took the jeans and shirt and ran into her bedroom to try them on. She came out in a few minutes with a big grin, spinning around so they could get the full view. She did the same with a few more outfits, then disappeared into the bedroom.

Magnolia and Zane sat on the couch, the pile of clothes taking up so much of the sofa that they were forced to sit so close their legs touched. Up close, Magnolia was pretty, with smooth skin and soft brown eyes sweet as a puppy's. She smelled of a mix of vanilla and flowers, and he felt the sudden urge to kiss her.

She was saying something about her favorite television show when he moved in for the kiss. His lips covered hers mid-sentence, and she gasped with surprise, but then quickly began kissing him back.

Eager to erase the picture of Emmaline and Peter and the box of condoms from his mind, he kissed her harder, his tongue aggressively working its way into her mouth and his hand cupping and fondling her breast. She shook her head and squirmed away from him into the pile of clothes.

"Hey, hey, let's take it slow," she said.

He moved his hand from her breast to her thigh and tried to kiss her again but she pushed him back.

"Like really slow," she said. "First of all, your little sister is in the other room. And second, we just met."

"Sorry, I misread the situation." In his voice was an undertone of frustration and anger. He wanted to punch the sofa cushion, or himself, for being so stupid.

Instead, Zane stood up and walked to the kitchen.

She got up from the couch as well, and began to pile up the remaining clothes to take back to her apartment. The air in the apartment hung heavy with awkwardness and unsaid words. Zane stared at the stove as though it could speak. He was at a complete loss what to say next.

Her voice rang out clear and shattered the heavy air, saving him the effort.

"Maybe ask me out on a date or something sometime," she said. He smiled and turned to her, grateful for her understanding and her offer of a second chance.

"Do you want to go on a date sometime?" he said.

"Maybe," she said with a smile. She picked up the pile of clothes and he opened the door for her and watched her walk down the moonlit sidewalk to her place.

#

The Oklahoma State Penitentiary sat just beyond the McAlester city limits. No street signs pointed to it, but its presence loomed like a mountain over the town. Zane's truck bumped its way down a two lane country road to a line of cars waiting for admittance to the penitentiary grounds. One by one, the cars were ushered in by a lone security guard who manually opened a wooden arm gate. Once through, they passed the warden's house on the left, a two-story cream Colonial style mansion with an orange stucco roof. It looked like it belonged on a college campus rather than a state facility known for housing the mentally unstable and those sent to death row. The rusted razor wire and cement block walls on the right hand side made sure you knew this was no college campus.

Built in 1908, the prison facilities were a patchwork of old and new buildings in various stages of disrepair. Zane found a parking spot. Lettie, who had been quiet for nearly all of the car ride, began singing along to some pop song on the radio. When Zane caught her eye, she just shrugged and said she was trying to get in a good mood for her dad. "It's hard enough on him being in there," she said. "I don't want to visit him and be all sad."

Noble, Zane thought. But it was the man's own damn fault he was serving time. Prison was a punishment and no one said punishments were easy. He caught sight of a bunker-type building built into a low spot on the grounds. Only its entrance and exit were visible; the rest of the building was submerged below a slope of dirt and grass.

"What's that?"

"H-Unit," she said. "That's where you go if you break the rules or if you're on death row."

Death row. His stomach convulsed and his mouth went dry. He didn't want to think that his own fate was still being determined. The cops were treating him and Lettie like victims, but that could change to suspect in a moment. The worst part was the waiting. He knew he should try to focus on this very moment, just today, and not think about the future. But hanging over him was this threat and uncertainty. What happened that night? Did he set the fire that killed his mother? Would he be arrested for it and charged and found guilty? Would he be coming back to McAlester under very different circumstances? Possibly to H-Unit to live? His composure broke into waves of despair and rage and panic. He could only hope that Magdite had some information that could shed light on Arno Jackson and what was going on with his mother in the days leading up to her death.

#

Lettie filled out the paperwork from the corrections officer, who checked Zane's identification and made him fill out another temporary visitor form so he could escort Lettie back. She was on the approved visitors list; he was not. They went through a metal detector and into another waiting room, where after a few moments they were led into the inmate visiting room, a barebones space of white and neutral colors, glass and stainless steel.

They took their seats on stools that were bolted to the jail floor. Each visiting area was divided into a booth with low walls for some semblance of privacy, but a glass window separated inmates from visitors and ensured no hugging or holding hands.

Muted messages erupted from walkie-talkies strapped to the guards' belts, though all sounds, even footsteps, were strangely muffled. For the prisoners, the visitation space represented a respite from the stress of prison life; for the visitors, it was a cold, tense room reeking of disinfectant and misery.

Roy Magdite shuffled in slipper-type shoes with rubber soles and no shoelaces. He wore a bright orange jumpsuit and had a day's worth of stubble on his puffy cheeks. He was as tall as Zane remembered him, but much thicker and older. His eyes lit up when he saw Lettie, and they both reached for the phone on the wall at the same time.

"Hi Daddy!" she said.

"Well, hello, beautiful. Aren't you a sight for sore eyes?" His smile was so wide and so sincere that Zane felt himself opening up to the man he'd long considered a lost cause who only asked for money and pity and gave nothing in return. He could see that the man clearly loved Lettie, something he'd never let himself consider. And that Lettie loved him back. He wondered if maybe he had just been jealous all these years that Lettie had her father in her life, and he didn't. He wondered if maybe it made it easier for him now because he had found his own father, and felt the comfort and warmth of that connection.

"I'm so sad about Sherri," he said. "I bet you are too. How are you holding up?"

"We're okay. Zane got us an apartment on Garnett, and we already met one of our neighbors who's real nice and brought me some clothes."

"Let me talk to Zane for a minute."

Lettie cradled the phone on her shoulder in between them so both she and Zane could hear and speak. Joe had a lot of questions about what happened and the funeral arrangements, and Zane filled him in with short, to-the-point answers.

"They're saying on the news that the fire might not have been accident. I don't mean to hurt your feelings, Zane, but I want to know for Lettie's sake. Are they looking at you for the fire?"

Lettie turned to see Zane's face as he nodded without expression, then told Joe that he didn't remember what happened that night.

"Sounds like you're going to need a lawyer, son," he said.

"Do you know who Arno Jackson is?" Lettie blurted.

"Arno Jackson? That trash dog? Is he bothering you, Lettie?"

"He's not bothering anyone, Joe. He's dead. The police found his body out in the woods behind the Majestic. Think he died the same night Mama did," Zane said.

"Dead, huh? I'm sure there's a long list of suspects for that, from people he's ratted out to those he's blackmailed."

"Who was he?"

"He knew your mother from before. The Lily Davis days. He'd been showing up that past couple of months telling her he knew who she was and threatening to expose her. Not sure if she was more scared of people finding out who she was, or that Jeremiah Doom figuring out where she was. I don't think she had anything to worry about with the police. She never really told me the full story, just that she changed her name and you kids didn't know nothing about it."

"Why didn't you tell me before?" Lettie said.

"Wasn't my place, Lettie-girl," he said. "Your mama was the one who kept the secret and I made a promise to her. Honestly, I didn't think it mattered all that much anyway. I figured she was being kind of dramatic about the whole thing, though I could tell she was scared to death by the idea of this Arno Jackson spilling the beans. She asked me for money if you can imagine. Like I have anything to offer her."

"How much did she ask you for?" Zane said.

"She wanted five hundred but I couldn't have given her even fifteen."

Zane remembered her asking him for money to pay off some debt a few weeks before. He'd blown her off, figuring that she wanted the money for booze and potato chips and smokes.

"How did he get in touch with her?" Zane asked.

"She said he just showed up at the trailer one afternoon. Never said how he found her or nothing, just showed up, said his name and she recognized him right away even though it had been more than twenty years. He called her Lily and she invited him in, and that's when he asked for some money. She gave him what she had which was about twenty-five dollars from what she said, and that she'd try to get more."

Zane raked his hand through his hair and stood up, leaving Lettie holding the phone. He'd met Jeremiah and he seemed all right. No, he was more than all right. Zane felt a connection to him. In fact, he'd never felt at ease like that with any new acquaintance before. And he thought—he hoped it was mutual. Which brought Zane back to the question: what about Jeremiah Doom scared his mother?

Lettie's steps were lighter—as was her mood—on their way back to the car. She hugged Zane tightly and thanking him for taking her to see her dad. His joy at seeing her smile and laugh was tainted a bit by his guilt at not taking her before, and the troubling comment Magdite made about Sherri being scared of Jeremiah.

On the ride home, she didn't ask for his phone like she usually did to go online or play games. Instead she tuned the radio to a country music station and silently watched the flat farmland and little towns roll by outside the window.

He called Verda back as he drove to tell her they still didn't have his mother's remains. The pre-paid phone Jeremiah gave him rang soon after. It was Link, asking if he was going to be in Sallisaw this weekend. Zane hadn't planned to be, and it wasn't like Link was inviting him—more just checking to see if he was coming. Weird.

Zane wanted to see if his mom left any kind of clues about

Arno Jackson and if she knew anything about Jeremiah's current life. The only place he could think to find anything like that was the trailer, which was a burnt, water-sogged mess that probably only got worse in yesterday's rain.

"Mind if we stop by the Majestic?" he asked Lettie.

"To see Emmaline taping her show? Sure! Maybe we can be on it!"

Zane had briefly, happily forgotten about Emmaline and her Hollywood producer and budding reality show career.

"No, to look through the home, see if we can find anything about Arno Jackson."

Lettie looked disappointed. "Can't we at least go over and see what's going on? We'll be right there."

"You can," he said. "Nothing stopping you. But I'm not."

"OK," she said, settling back into the truck seat and resting her head against the window. Was she dreaming of her own reality show too? God, he hoped not.

At the Majestic, Shana and James from the production team were loading up one of the rental cars with camera equipment and laptop bags. Emmaline stood in the door of the mobile home, light streaming behind her into the dark night like she was an angel. Peter stood in front of her on the porch like a dark shadow. His hand gently wrapped her neck and he pulled her toward him slightly. She came up on tiptoes and kissed him on the lips. Zane stopped dead in his tracks, as an angry heat flushed through him.

Lettie leaned in to him, her eyes narrowed in concentration.

"I'm sorry, Zane. I like Emmaline, I really do. She's like a big sister to me. But I've got to say that I think you'd be better off without her, romantically, I mean. She's not looking for anything serious."

"You think I don't know that?" He jerked away from her, flung the door open. He couldn't help but think about his mother's gun, tucked in a kitchen drawer in the apartment on Garnett, and how satisfying it would be to pull the trigger. The only thing he wasn't sure of was who he wanted to point the gun at: himself, Peter or Emmaline.

The burner cell phone vibrated in his pocket. Jeremiah.

"I thought maybe you'd be coming back to Sallisaw this weekend," Jeremiah said.

"No, I didn't plan on it. I've got my sister with me and we're settling in to the new apartment we rented."

"Why don't you bring her on out with you? I was going to grill up some steaks."

Zane considered the offer. It was nice to be asked and he liked hanging out with them, but he had a bad feeling about bringing Lettie into their boys' club. It felt wrong, a little too rough and unpredictable for his little sister.

"Let me talk to Lettie and see what kind of homework she has. I'll call you back," Zane said. He hung up.

"I don't have any homework. I'm on bereavement leave," Lettie said.

"Lettie, I don't think that means you don't have homework, I think that just means you are going to have more make-up work when you get back. Anyway, that was Jeremiah asking if we wanted to come out to eat some steaks."

"Did you tell him yes?" she asked, clearly excited about the idea. "I want to see his farm."

"I told him I'll call him back," he said. "I'm not sure I want to go out there this weekend."

"But after all that we heard today from Dad, shouldn't we at least go and find out if Jeremiah knew this Arno Jackson?"

He had been thinking the same thing, and also wanting to know more about why his mother might have been so afraid of Jeremiah.

CHAPTER FIFTEEN

Lettie did a tarot card reading that morning to see if they should go to Sallisaw. "It's the time for healing, Zane," she said, pointing to a card with an angel in a white robe. "This is a card all about harmony, combining forces with others. And this card, the eight of swords, shows that you have doubts. But the five of wands here, in the third position, is all about joining forces again. Me and you, joining forces. Let's go."

Her enthusiasm for going was what finally won him over, not the silly tarot card reading. He liked seeing her excited about doing something, and really, what harm could come of having a meal with the Doom men?

But first, they'd run a few errands to see if they could get a few more answers.

#

The first stop was to the Wagon Wheel neighborhood to see the woman who cut and died Sherri's hair. Rhoda Jackson lived in a red brick house at the mid-point of a curve on 109th Street that was so deep it made the road almost seem like a cul-de-sac. Her house sat within a line of houses facing an empty lot of dry grass.

In the distance was a brown brick elementary school.

The street was full of cookie cutter homes, but Rhoda's stood out because it had no garage door at the end of the driveway. Instead, this house had a wood paneled wall and a wood and glass door with a white awning and sign that said Beauty Salon. Zane could only guess that they'd converted the garage into a hair salon so customers wouldn't have to traipse through the house to get their haircuts or permanent waves.

Zane rang the doorbell, shivering a little in the damp cold air on her tree-shaded porch.

She opened the door and peered at him through the screen. After a blink of recognition, she pushed the door open and held her arms out in welcome.

"Zane, oh, baby, I've been thinking about you two," she said. "Little Lettie girl, you poor things."

He hugged her, his face pressed against her crispy, teased brown hair. Her kiss left coral lipstick on his cheek that she smudged away with her finger afterward. She kissed Lettie on top of the head and held her close for a few moments.

"How are you doing? Do you want some breakfast? I just made pancakes for Mr. Jackson."

"No, we're okay," Zane said, even though the smell of bacon was making his mouth water. "We just wanted to ask you a few questions about Mom."

With a shake, she tilted her head to the side and reached up to finger her necklace chain.

"Of course," she said, backing up a few feet and waving her hand toward the green and white couch against the wall. "We saw the news yesterday..." She didn't finish the sentence but Zane knew she was referring to the stories all over TV yesterday that rehashed the Lily Davis and Jeremiah Doom connection.

"It won't take long, we won't even sit down," Zane said. "We're trying to learn more about what Mom had going on right before she died. It turns out she had a visitor in the days before the fire and that he might have been blackmailing her about her past."

"Shocking thing. She had a whole other life! I had no idea."

"No, us either," Zane said. "Did she say anything about needing money or a man named Arno Jackson?"

"Well, funny you should ask, because actually I hadn't seen your mom in months and then she called me last week. I figured she was calling because she was overdue for a cut and color, but that wasn't it at all. She actually asked me if she could borrow some money. Three hundred bucks to be exact. I asked her what for and she wouldn't tell me. That made it hard for me to explain to Mr. Jackson why we should give it to her. So I had to tell her no, that it wasn't a good idea for friends to lend money to friends. She got very upset with me, almost verging on hysteria, but she still wouldn't tell me what it was for, just that it was a matter of life and death. Your mama, well, she can be dramatic you know."

Life and death, Zane thought. She sounded really scared.

Rhoda lowered her voice. "I didn't tell Mr. Jackson, but I drove over to her the next day and gave her what I had in my wallet. It was about seventy five dollars. I was worried about her."

"We think that this Arno Jackson asked her for money to keep from telling people about her name being Lily Davis," Lettie said.

"And he's the man they found dead in the woods, isn't he?"

Zane nodded.

"What was your mother up to? My Lord," Rhoda said. "I wish I'd given her what she'd asked for. I didn't know."

"You had no way of knowing," Zane said, but he wished she had been more generous just the same. "How was she when you brought the money by?"

"She wasn't there, actually. I slipped it under the door with a note, and left her a message to call me, but I didn't hear back from her."

Just more proof that his mother needed money, but not much more information about why. A dead end.

"Do you know anyone else she might have asked for money?" Lettie asked. "Cause we're out of ideas."

"Well, you're going to want to be careful how you approach this one," Rhoda said. "But you might want to check with Cap Fager, the owner of the Nowhere Bar. Just maybe check with him at the bar, not home, since I'm not sure his wife was aware of their friendship, if you know what I mean."

Lettie and Zane exchanged glances, even though they should have learned by now to be surprised by nothing when it came to their mother. It seemed they hardly knew her.

#

The next stop was EZ Pawn on Admiral. It was a clean, bright store with smiling employees in red polo shirts and rows of glass showcases full of jewelry and watches.

"How can I help you?" asked a skinny black girl with bright pink lipstick and long straight black hair. Her name tag read Jasmine.

Zane produced the envelope and receipt for the two pieces of jewelry.

"Are you here to claim these?"

"Not right now," he said, not wanting to spend any more money than he had to. "We just wondered if we could ask a few questions to whoever did the paperwork with our mom. She passed away in a fire last week and we found this in her stuff."

Jasmine scanned the form quickly.

"Looks like Alan did the transaction. He's the manager. Let me see if he's free."

She folded the paper and handed it back to Zane with a smile, and headed for the back. Lettie leaned into one of jewelry counters, studying the shiny gems in every color of the rainbow.

Two men in camouflage stood in the back with their arms folded, looking at rifles hanging in a display case. Wall speakers blared a guitar solo from some nineties hit song, the high notes bouncing off the soft tile floor.

A tall Hispanic man came out of the back with Jasmine, speaking in low voices. He wore the same red polo shirt and khakis as the rest of the staff, but without the name tag as some kind of manager's prerogative. His hair was close-cropped and shiny with some kind of hair product; his eyes were alert and brown and curious, trained on Lettie and Zane as he listened to Jasmine.

He approached them with a big smile and his right hand outstretched.

"I'm Alan," he said.

Zane shook his hand and introduced himself and Lettie, quickly explaining the situation.

"I'm so sorry for your loss," he said. "I remember your mother, but I don't have much information to share with you other than that. She came in stressed and in a hurry, I remember. But honestly, a lot of our customers come in here in some kind of distress. There's usually some urgency around their need for money. She bargained with me pretty hard, but I gave her the best price I could for the two pieces she brought in."

"Did she say anything about why she needed the money or anything like that?" Lettie asked.

Alan shook his head. "No, but not everyone does. I mean, some people come in and want to tell their story, but others, like your mom, just want to get in and out fast. Now that I remember, I think someone was waiting for her in the car. I remember she kept looking toward the door."

"A man or a woman?"

"A man, I think. He was driving a blue Ford truck. I didn't get a good look at him though."

Zane rocked back and forth on his heels, wondering if that man was Cap Fager.

Alan cleared his throat. "Do you want to get these two pieces of jewelry out today? Considering the circumstances, I can see if I can give you a little discount."

"I love that Black Hills gold ring," Lettie said. "Mom said she would give it to me some day."

Zane smiled. "We're going to get it out, I promise, Lettie. But I can't do it today. How long do we have, Alan?"

Alan looked at the paperwork. "Due date is in three weeks, but if you need longer, just give me a call and we'll work out an extension."

They shook hands again and Zane wrapped his arm around Lettie as they walked to his truck.

The sky was blue with high wisps of thin white clouds as they headed east on the Muskogee Turnpike to Sallisaw. It was cold and crisp, a beautiful late fall day, and the road had little traffic. Zane kept to the speed limit; no need to court any more trouble than he already had by getting a speeding ticket.

"None of us are very lucky in love," Lettie said. "I mean Mom sure wasn't...and you and me..."

"Lettie, you're only fourteen. You're way too young to be deciding if you're lucky in love or not."

"It just seems like things work out for other people and they don't work out for us, that's all."

"Oh, Lettie, I think every human who walks this earth has times when things don't work out. We're just in one of those times, me and you."

"Mom's whole life practically didn't work out."

Zane felt sad for his mom and regretted that she'd never told them her secrets. And yes, he felt angry at her for hiding so much from them. But he didn't want Lettie to think that she was fated to have a terrible life. In AA, they use this phrase about "letting go and letting God." The idea behind it is that God has a plan for us, and we may not know what it is, but we have to trust. He was pretty sure if he tried to talk to her about God, though, Lettie would brush him off.

"Well, I don't know about that," Zane said. "In some ways she feels like a stranger to me, when I hear about this married man she was seeing and her visits from Arno Jackson and this whole other life she left behind. But don't you think that life is about drawing, I don't know, the right energy to you or something? Like with your spells?"

"It's probably a bunch of nonsense," she said.

"You don't think that."

"I should. Everyone else does. Or they think something worse."

"Lettie, I look at you and I think you can do anything you set your mind to. I think the only way you would get stuck is if you decided you wanted to be. And this Morgan. So you don't get to go with him to homecoming. Right now, that hurts. But looking back on this, you're going to be stronger from it. He's obviously not the right guy for you if he gave you up that easily. So in the long run, you're better off."

They were both quiet for a while after that, watching the empty road unwrap in front of them and listening to a country song. Both thinking that Zane's advice probably applied to him and Emmaline as well, but neither one needed to say it out loud.

#

Though it wasn't raining, the roads in Sallisaw were still wet from a very recent storm. The yellow and brown grass looked soggy and bright against the bright white sky. They pulled up to the gate and Zane punched in the four-digit access code Jeremiah had given him. With a screech, the metal gate swung open.

Zane parked the truck at the end of a line of SUVs and trucks. Apparently Jeremiah had invited most of Sallisaw to the barbecue as well. The wind carried the sound of a high-pitched girl's voice from around the side of the house.

"Let me go! Let me go!"

A teenage girl just a year or two older than Lettie, with long blonde braids capped by a dark blue bandanna, shook her thin arm free of the grip of the tall woman in her thirties who was trying to pull her toward the cars parked in front.

The woman grabbed the girl's arm again as she tried to run back where they'd come from.

"No one wants you here!"

Jeremiah appeared around the corner, a bottle of beer wrapped in one of those yellow foam cozies people used to keep their beer cool.

"That's not right, Breanna," Jeremiah said, catching her with his left arm and pulling her in tight to him. "I invited your mom here. Now Susan, why can't Breanna stay just a little while?"

The woman hesitated, putting her hands on her hips. She was pretty, with her cheeks flushed from the cold and her hair blowing in the light wind. She wore a waxed cotton puffer vest over a dark fleece pullover and jeans.

"That wasn't Monopoly she was playing with Link in his bedroom. She's sixteen, Jeremiah. And he's twenty-one."

Jeremiah laughed. "You never let your hormones get hold of you when you were her age, did you, Susan?"

"We could stand here all day and count up the things I done wrong and still have work to do the next morning. I want this girl to do better than me. And for one, to not get pregnant in high school."

Jeremiah turned to Breanna, who stood under his protective arm glaring furiously at her mother.

"Maybe you need to go on and do what your mama says," he said.

Zane didn't expect the girl to be subdued so fast, but she went to her mother without another word. Susan looked at Jeremiah suspiciously but said thank you.

Jeremiah pulled out a wad of cash similar to what he had had in the Dollar General. Lettie took in a sharp breath, surprised as Zane had been at the amount of cash the older man was carrying

"Maybe you two can get a nice dinner after Breanna does her homework," he said, peeling off several twenties and handing to Susan. "Look, I told Heston to have you come over here so I could thank you. I know it's tough to do the re-entry thing back into the world after being locked up."

"I told you I don't want your money," she said. "We'll be all right." She shoved her hands into the pockets of her puffer vest.

"It's for Breanna too," he said.

Breanna's eyes darted from her mother to the money in Jeremiah's hand. She looked like she wanted to grab the money herself.

Susan paused for a moment. Then with a weak smile she nodded.

"OK," she said. "I appreciate it." She took the money, turned around and almost marched into Zane and Lettie.

"Oh," she said, obviously unaware they were standing so near. Her footsteps crunched on the gravel driveway as she walked to a small silver car. Breanna watched her mom's back, then quickly leaned over and kissed Jeremiah on the cheek. Zane saw Jeremiah's hand snake around her back to cup her rear. It was not the kind of fatherly pat you might expect a forty-year-old man to give a teenage girl, but she seemed to like it. She smiled as she ran after her mother.

Jeremiah put the rest of the money away. He watched Breanna get into the car, then turned his smile onto Zane and Lettie. Zane wished he had not brought Lettie—what was he thinking? Lettie was just two years younger than Breanna.

"Zane, good to see you," he said. "And this must be Lettie. Come on back."

They stepped into the backyard, where Jeremiah led them to an outdoor kitchen, covered with a roof but without walls. About twenty people, mainly men, milled about the space in various states of inebriation. Classic rock blared from speakers mounted to the house.

A woman in a very short pink skirt writhed in perfect rhythm to the music on top of a man in jeans on a lounge chair, her bright yellow underwear peeking out. Zane didn't like the way some of the men were looking at Lettie. She'd worn the jeans and top from Magnolia with a tan corduroy jacket, and Zane had to admit that she looked older than her age. He put his arm around her shoulders and pulled her in tight. "You stick by me, okay?" She nodded as though reading his mind, but most likely, he thought, she was uncomfortable with Jeremiah's behavior with Breanna as well as the attention from the men.

Jeremiah shouted for everyone's attention, and they quieted down. "This here's my son, Zane, and his sister, Lettie." He gestured to the crowd with a sweeping arm motion. "You treat 'em real nice now."

A round man in a leather vest who stood closest to them nodded and introduced himself as Brazz. The rest of the men in the crowd let their eyes slide off of Lettie and focused back on their conversations.

#

Two hours passed. "You see where Lettie went?" Zane asked Link, interrupting their conversation about University of Oklahoma football. She'd left to go find the bathroom more than ten minutes ago, and though nothing bad had happened so far, Zane still felt like he needed to keep his eyes on her. He'd resisted all offers of a drink because some instinct inside him told him to stay sober.

Link shrugged. "Girls take a long time in the bathroom, man, I don't know why."

Zane stood up, a strange sense of uneasiness growing in the pit of his stomach. He scanned the crowd but no sign of her. He noticed Jeremiah was gone too.

He slid the glass door open and found himself in the room he'd slept in. A welcome mat of yellow-white light poured out one of three doors down the otherwise dark hallway opposite the kitchen. He turned down the hallway, steps muffled by a worn carpet that looked more like a scruffy bed of moss. The first room had a bed low on the floor and a plain navy comforter stretched over the top. Two limp pillows covered in tan cases leaned against the white wall at one end of the bed. A blue and white electric guitar was propped up on a black wire stand in the corner.

His foot hit the light on the carpet and he turned to peer inside what must be Jeremiah's office, now empty. Two off-white metal filing cabinets stood like soldiers on either side of a scratched up wood desk. Stacks of papers, magazines, CDs, DVDs, and books sat on bookshelves mounted to the wall with metal brackets. The desk faced a window onto the backyard, and soft autumn light streamed in.

In detective shows, Zane thought, this is where the amateur detective would step into the room, look at the papers on the desk or the files on the computer, uncover the big clue and solve the case. He would love to find out more about Jeremiah and maybe learn why his mother had been so scared of him—the idea intrigued him enough that he took a step toward the room. But fear and guilt were banging away at his nervous system and he could hear his blood pumping like it was flowing straight through his ears. First, he wanted to make sure Lettie was okay; second, he didn't like the idea of Jeremiah finding him snooping around.

"Lettie?" he called out, deciding to make his presence in the hallway known.

"In here, Zane," she responded from behind a closed door. Zane twisted the brass doorknob and swung the door open to see Lettie and Jeremiah seated on a round bed covered in a spread. Between them was a wooden case with a glass cover.

"Jeremiah was showing me his arrowhead collection," she said.

"Yes, I've collected them from the caves around here," Jeremiah said, carefully placing one back in the box and closing the top.

All Zane could think was to get Lettie out of there as fast as he could. What kind of grown man showed teenage girls his arrowhead collection in his bedroom? It just didn't feel right. But he didn't want to offend Jeremiah.

"Lettie, I, uh, just got a call from the coroner. They, uh, might release Mom's body today."

"On a Saturday?" Jeremiah said.

"Yeah, funny, isn't it? I guess they work weekends. Anyway, we should head back."

Once he'd driven the truck off of Jeremiah's property and onto the highway, he turned to Lettie.

"How did you wind up in his bedroom? Did he touch you?"

"Ick! You think I'm crazy?"

"What happened exactly?"

"After I went to the bathroom, I thought I'd have a quick look around, see if I could find out anything about him. He caught me in the room, so I pretended I was interested in his arrowheads. He'd been telling me about it before, so I think he believed me. Anyway, I was a little creeped out when he shut the door but I heard your voice pretty soon after. It was like you knew to come and get me."

"Lettie, you shouldn't have done that. I don't—we don't know him that well. We don't know what he's like. I think he might be involved in some illegal stuff, so he's not going to want anyone snooping around."

"You mean because he sells meth?"

"How do you know that?"

"I heard that guy Brazz talking about some tweaker who owed them money."

Zane sighed.

"So nothing happened, right? And he thought you were interested in the arrowheads?"

"Yeah, I think so. But Zane?"

"What?"

"He had a picture of me and you and Mom in the dresser drawer."

CHAPTER SIXTEEN

"If I had a smart phone, I would have taken a picture of it," Lettie said when Zane asked her how old the picture was. "It was the three of us at the Thanksgiving dinner at the community church. I think it was from either last year or the year before. It was cut out from a newsletter or something like that, but it didn't have our names printed or anything."

"I don't even remember that picture being taken," Zane said.

"Me neither, really. I don't think we ever had a copy."

He tried to think of a rational reason why Jeremiah would have this picture of them. And where he would have gotten it? Zane took a deep breath. Did Jeremiah actually know who they were before Zane had reached out to him? Had he been watching them this whole time, playing them along for some reason Zane didn't understand? Was he dar_dar, the source of that mysterious message that Sherri Clearwater didn't exist?

Zane felt a ripple of nausea as he pictured Jeremiah sitting outside the trailer, watching them, following them. Waiting for something. But what?

And then—the glimmer of hope that maybe Jeremiah was looking for him. That he was waiting for the right moment to confront Sherri and ask if Zane was his son. He knew it had to be wishful thinking. He'd wanted a father his whole life and here was one, and wouldn't it be wonderful to think that that man was looking for him too?

Lettie's voice was low and hushed. "Remember that card reading I did before you met with him? Five of swords. It said you would be defeated by bad person. Someone waiting to stab you in the back. It can also mean tricks and lies, someone trying to cheat you. I shouldn't have let you go after him."

"It was something I had to do," Zane said. He knew that Lettie's premonitions and fortune-telling would never have held him back, no matter how much she believed in them. "And remember the one you did the other day? A time for healing and all that."

She shook her head dismissively.

"Anyway, Lettie, did he see you with the picture?"

"No, I heard footsteps in the hallway and put it away before he turned the corner. He gives me the creeps, Zane. I know he's your dad and all but he's creepy. And so are his gross friends."

Zane had to admit, just to himself, that he was a little uncomfortable, too. Was there a game being played here? Could he trust his father to have good intentions? Had this Arno Jackson been in touch with Jeremiah to tell him what happened to Lily Davis? Or someone else? If one person had figured out who Sherri Clearwater really was, didn't it follow that maybe there were others who knew, too? He wasn't even sure he trusted Roy Magdite enough to keep the secret.

#

The grey and white cloud bank hid the sun as it dipped below the horizon. The sunset as they pulled into the Tulsa city limits was about as visually stunning as shutting off a light switch.

The Nowhere Bar was in a strip mall across Lewis Avenue from the entrance of Oral Roberts University, with a good view of the college's famous giant bronze sculpture of disembodied praying hands with protruding veins and tendons the size of power lines. The location was an odd one, as ORU didn't allow its student body to drink alcohol. Zane wondered who exactly enjoyed tying one on in view of the Prayer Tower where Oral Roberts had asked Jesus to bring him "home" if he didn't raise enough money.

The bar was tucked into the corner next to a Christian bookstore and a submarine sandwich shop filled with clean-cut college students. There was a very noticeable modesty and decorum in the way the students were dressed on a Saturday afternoon. No ripped jeans, piercings, bold hair color, or tattoos on this student body.

The bar front had windows that stretched from the floor to the ceiling, but inside it was as sunless and stuffy as a cave. Cheap window tinting film reflected their faces like a funhouse mirror as Zane closed the door behind them.

A tall, grey-haired man stood up behind the bar, a clean white apron tied over his shirt. Behind him, the evening news played on a television screen with KTUL reporter Kristy Diguchi behind the desk.

"What can I do for you?" he said with a warm smile that over the years had dug deep creases along the sides of his mouth.

"I'm looking for Cap Fager," Zane said.

"You found him. And you are…?"

"Sherri Clearwater's son, Zane. And this is my sister, Lettie."

Cap braced himself with both hands against the bar and leaned forward.

"Ah," was all he said.

The text "Trailer Park Tragedy" flashed on the television screen and Kristy arranged her face into a serious expression. "And now, to the story we've been following since it happened, tonight we've gone into the KTUL video archives to find an interview we did in 1985 with Jeremiah Doom after he was acquitted."

Three sets of eyes fixated on the screen.

Jeremiah's round face was punctuated with a bushy mustache, and his dark hair was grown long enough to cover his ears in front. He looked comfortable on camera, sitting easily in a gold upholstered armchair. He wore a dark green corduroy jacket and a black T-shirt underneath.

Cap reached for the remote controller to turn up the volume. "I'm guessing y'all want to see this," he said.

A male reporter in a blazer and striped tie sat in an identical chair facing Jeremiah.

"You were acquitted of the murder of two Campfire girls two weeks ago. How does it feel to be a free man?"

"Going to that courthouse every day and sitting through that trial, hearing all those terrible things that happened, all the while fighting for my life. It was an awful experience. But I did not kill those girls; and I am so thankful that the jury believed in me and acquitted me so that an innocent man did not go to jail," Jeremiah said, the camera tight on his face.

"You say that jurors believed in your innocence, but those we talked to said it was more that the prosecution didn't have enough evidence to prove you did it."

"Same difference," Jeremiah said.

"What do you hope to do next?"

"Maybe do a little hunting, spend time with my friends, the people who supported me through all this. I've got a lot of debts to repay so maybe I need to find a job," Jeremiah said.

Kristy appeared back on the screen. "We have more of that

interview to play for you later in this show. But now, let me turn
things over to our meteorologist who will tell us if this cooling
trend is going to continue."

"That man's a hustler, plain and simple," Cap said. "Innocent
my ass. He told your mother he was stoned out of his mind in
some cave in the hills that night and didn't remember a thing that
happened. But then he told her lots of stuff so she was never sure
what was true or not."

"Yeah, we came to talk to you about her," Zane said. "We're
trying to figure out what happened. Sounds like you already knew
a lot more of the story than we did."

"She didn't tell you nothing, huh? Well, I'd be happy to tell
you what I told the police when I heard about the fire. But my wife
is on the way over here to work the Saturday night shift with me
and I hope you understand why that wouldn't be a good time for
me to be talking to you."

"It won't take too long," Lettie said.

"It's just not the right time. She'll be here any minute now.
Look, come back here tomorrow morning and—"

The door swung open and in walked a plump woman with
bright red hair carrying a commuter's coffee mug in one hand and
a bright floral quilted tote bag in the other. Zane could smell the
scotch in the coffee mug as she passed by them to go behind the
bar. Cap changed the channel to a college football game.

"You get an ID for that one, Cap?" she said, pointing at Lettie.

"We didn't come in for a drink," Zane said. Lettie shifted her
weight from one foot to another. She twirled a piece of her hair
around her finger like she did when she was thinking.

"They're, uh, selling ads for the school newsletter, Celeste,"
Cap said.

The woman laid her tote bag on the bar and said only "huh," as though she didn't quite buy the story. She took a sip from the commuter mug.

"Well, we should be going," Zane said. "Thank you for your time."

"Did you buy an ad, Cap? Which school?"

"I already forgot the school name, which one was it, now?" Cap asked them. His eyes went from Zane to Lettie, encouraging them to add on to the story he'd created.

"Reed Elementary," Lettie said. Zane was astonished how quick she was on her feet; he felt like he was running behind a train while she waved to him from one of the cars speeding away. "My little brother goes there. Anyway, we understand that the school newsletter isn't a good place for a bar to advertise. We'll be going now."

"Reed Elementary? That's all the way on the other side of town," Celeste said, still puzzling it out.

"Bye now," Zane said with a wave, holding the door open for Lettie as the lights of the parking lot blinked on.

#

The next morning, the burner cell phone rang.

"I'm coming to Tulsa tomorrow," Jeremiah said. "Wondering if you could help me out with some business."

"During the day?" Zane asked, thinking that he still wanted to keep Lettie away from Jeremiah as much as possible, and this was best achieved if he dealt with Jeremiah while she was at school.

"Yeah, afternoon probably. Why, you got class or something?"

"Just some stuff I have to do," Zane lied.

They arranged to meet at the Reasor's supermarket parking lot on Monday in the afternoon.

As he hung up, his regular cell rang. Emmaline.

He let it go to voicemail, but couldn't resist listening to the message immediately.

"Zane, it's Emmaline. I just wanted to let you know that the producers want me to go to Oklahoma City next week for a pageant. I wanted to tell you because I know that you are going to be planning your mother's funeral sometime soon, and I know I said I'd help with that. Do you have a date when that will be? Let me know. I'm at work because we have a fundraiser today. Call me. Okay, bye."

He threw the phone on the floor next to the bed and rolled over onto his side, grinding his head into the pillow. Not even an apology. How is it possible that he could care so much about her but she could turn her feelings on and off like a faucet? Or maybe she didn't even have feelings strong enough for him that she needed to turn them on or off. It was heartbreaking to consider and just not fair.

He woke Lettie up so they could return to the Nowhere Bar. The Tulsa streets were empty but for some early Sunday morning church traffic. The bar looked dingy and tired in the morning light.

Zane parked the truck in the empty parking lot, and soon after, a white Toyota Corolla pulled in next to them. Cap got out, and they followed him to the door, which he opened with a key plucked from what seemed like dozens on a large round keychain. The bar smell of cigarette smoke and sour beer made him want a drink, but he pushed the thought out of his mind.

Cap gestured to a high-backed booth along the nearest wall.

"So how did you find about your mother and me?" he asked, rearranging the salt and pepper shakers around the ketchup bottle on the wooden table.

"Rhoda told us we should come talk to you. She said Mom was

being blackmailed and asked her for money but she didn't have much to give her. Said maybe you helped her out."

"Well, I'm not going to be asking you kids to pay me back or nothing," he said. "So don't worry about that. Not with all that's happened, you've got enough to worry about it."

It hadn't even crossed Zane's mind that this man would expect to be paid back. Whatever arrangements Cap had come to with his mother, well, that was separate business as far as he was concerned. He ignored the comment and said what was really on his mind.

"The police don't think the fire was an accident."

"Related to the blackmailer?"

"Maybe," Zane said.

Cap took a deep breath then exhaled slowly. "I think I need a drink," he said. "Can I offer you one?"

Zane shook his head but Lettie asked for a soda. Cap went to the bar and poured himself a big shot of whiskey and drank it down in one gulp, then poured another. Still deep in thought, he filled a tall glass with ice then shot soda into it from the soda gun and returned to the table with both drinks.

"I didn't actually believe her about the blackmailer," he said. "I'd just been seeing her maybe a month or so. I thought it was something she cooked up to get money from me."

"Can't blame you there," Zane said.

"She could be a lot of fun, your mom," he said wistfully. "The cancer diagnosis deflated her like a balloon, though."

"The what?" Lettie and Zane said, nearly in unison.

Cap refocused his eyes on them. "The cancer diagnosis. Some kind of blood cancer, like leukemia. She didn't tell you?"

They both shook their heads. "This is getting ridiculous," Lettie said.

"It was about two weeks ago," he said. "I remember because it was the University of Oklahoma-Oklahoma State football game the next day and I was expecting a big beer delivery from the distributor. She came over to the bar crying, saying she'd just thought she had a flu that wouldn't go away but the doctor at the clinic said it was cancer. Some kind of fairly rare cancer that attacks your blood somehow. I didn't really understand it all. But she was upset. She probably wanted to protect you kids."

Zane had his doubts. He wasn't sure that his mother would have necessarily 'protected' them from news like that. Or Roy or even Rhoda. I mean, no one else had mentioned this at all. Knowing her, it didn't make sense.

Zane's phone vibrated on the table. He glanced down and read a text from Randy Womack that said "CODE ORANGE." Stupid shit boss hadn't even bothered to take him off of the emergency contact list for the zoo's maintenance crew after he fired him.

Code orange meant someone was being attacked in an animal enclosure.

Another text buzzed the phone.

"ITS EMMALINE."

Zane pulled Lettie's arm. "We've got to go now," he said.

#

Zane took Interstate 44 to the zoo, keeping the truck's pedal nearly rammed to the floor despite the orange cones and signs to reduce speed in construction zones. He wasn't inclined to follow speed limits in the best of times, and certainly not with Emmaline in danger.

He felt like he'd swallowed concrete, his stomach rock hard and adrenalin pumping through his veins. Images of Emmaline terrified, cornered by some animal. Which one? One of the big cats, ready to tear into her with its sharp claws and long teeth? A bear, tossing her like a toy? The images came too quickly to even process.

They arrived at the main zoo parking lot just twenty minutes later. It was fairly empty and no sign of emergency vehicles anywhere. They ran across the wooden plank bridge that connected the parking lot with the zoo entrance. The wind was snapping the American and Oklahoma flags from draped to straight and back again. No one was in line at the ticket booth.

"Where's Emmaline?" he barked at the ticket taker, a teenage girl with a nose ring he did not recognize.

"Emmaline?" she parroted back as though he'd said something in another language. Incomprehension was all over her face. And she had absolutely no sense of urgency. He half expected her to pick up a nail file and start doing her nails.

"The code orange? Randy Womack just texted me!"

"Code orange?" Her eyes widened in surprise. "You mean someone's in with the animals? No one tells me anything up here." Now, she showed some energy. She got up from her seat and walked to the door leading to the administrative offices behind the ticket booth.

"Terry, you know anything about Randy Womack saying there was a code orange?"

A thin man in a wheelchair rolled into the ticketing area, wearing a plaid shirt with the sleeves rolled up to his elbows, showing muscular forearms with the veins popping out. Terry ran customer service and was one of the good guys at the zoo who always treated Zane, and everyone, with respect.

"Zane, good to see you," he said. "Let me call Emmaline for you on the radio. She's down at the event pavilion getting ready for the fundraiser."

"Terry, I got this message from Randy Womack…it said code

orange, and it's Emmaline."

"You got this on your cell phone? But that's not protocol. I haven't heard anything on the radio."

Terry brought the radio up to his mouth and pressed the red button on the side. "Emmaline Perryman, you on the radio? Over." He released the button and the four of them waited. Zane held his breath.

"Terry, this is Emmaline. What's up?" She didn't sound at all like someone being eaten by a lion or polar bear.

Zane released the air from his lungs in a huge sigh.

"Zane's up front. He got a weird message you were in danger," Terry said. "I'm going to send him back."

"All right," she said.

#

Adrenalin still spiking through his nervous system, Zane forced himself to walk instead of run down the empty footpath along the lake to the zoo's event pavilion. It was one of those dark October days, stark trees against a sky blanketed in grey clouds, wind whipping up dried leaves into clattering funnels. The kind of day mothers keep their toddlers inside and the polar bears and snow leopards stretch on rocks outside to enjoy. A duck swam across the rippled water, flapping its wings. It was so quiet and empty it seemed like after hours instead of mid-morning on a weekend.

"What's going on?" Lettie asked. "I don't like this."

Zane shook his head. "I don't like it either. But let's talk to Emmaline. Maybe we'll find Randy and ask him what's going on. If this is some kind of practical joke I swear to God I'll punch him in the face. I don't care."

"Well, he can't fire you," Lettie said with a smile. "He already did that."

Emmaline met them on the path by one of the zoo's whimsical drinking water fountains built into the open mouth of a brightly painted resin lion's head.

Lettie ran to her and nearly knocked her over with a bear hug around the waist. Zane hung back, smiling with relief at seeing her in one piece. She wore a dark pantsuit with black pumps and a strand of fake pearls around her neck. Her hair was tied up in a loose bun, and wisps of hair curled lightly around her face.

"What's going on?" she said, her brows scrunched together.

Zane showed her the texts from Randy.

"I don't understand," she said.

The radio on her hip went off noisily.

"Emergency, code orange. Komodo dragon exhibit," a female voice said.

Another emergency code? What was going on? Zane began to wonder if he was just having a bad dream. This just couldn't be happening.

#

Zane, Emmaline and Lettie ran to the conservation center that housed the zoo's most notorious resident, Budiman the Komodo dragon.

Beth Malone, a reptile specialist, stood like her feet were stuck in glue in front of the plate glass separating visitors from the Komodo dragon. Zane remembered having met her in the new employee orientation when he had started.

Tears were streaming down her face, and one hand clutched the radio.

Out of the corner of his eye he saw the monitor lizard backing out of the feeding area, its golden-grey tail whipping from side to side on the rock floor. The man being pulled across the floor, his stomach in the beast's jaws, was either dead or unconscious. He recognized the doughy face of Randy Womack as his head skittered across the ground.

"Oh my God," Lettie said, and buried her face into Zane's jacket.

Two men emerged from the feeding area, holding a piece of plywood taller and wider than them. Behind that he could see Doug, the assistant reptile curator, with a long-handled pitchfork-like tool.

Beth's mouth was twisted in agony, but her eyes never moved off of the dragon. "They're not going to get him away from Budiman 'til he's had his fill," she said, as Zane steered Lettie back out of the exhibit. Emmaline stayed behind, not seeming to notice they had left, but Zane was done protecting her at least for the time being. If she wanted to watch a lizard eat a man, more power to her. And sweet dreams later tonight, he thought. Let her tell Peter why she couldn't sleep.

Lettie threw up the soda she had drunk at Cap's on the grass outside.

"What the fuck are you doing here?" Virgil asked. Randy's crony was wearing his usual uniform of wrinkled trousers and stained blue shirt. He walked straight up to them and stood so close that tiny bits of saliva splattered on Zane's cheeks. "You had something to do with this, didn't you?"

Virgil was a few inches shorter than Zane's six feet, and weighed in at close to two hundred pounds. Zane held his ground, twitching a little as he sized Virgil up. He was more than ready to feel his fist on this man's jaw. Lettie shifted uneasily to the side, not sure if she should try to intervene, or how she actually would do it.

"I just got here, Virgil. With my sister and Emmaline."

"Awfully suspicious timing, asshole. I oughta take you into a citizen's arrest until the police arrive."

"I'd like to see you try."

Virgil reached his hand in his back pocket. Did he have a gun? Zane's fight-or-flight instinct took over, and he swung hard, striking Virgil's fleshy cheek and jowl with a right cross. Virgil stumbled to the right, almost tumbling over. His hand flew out of his back pocket, dropping his mobile phone on the grass right where Lettie had just thrown up. He looked shocked.

"You better not have broken my phone, Clearwater," he said. He picked the phone up and wiped it on his pants. "If you did, you're going to pay for it. I just upgraded."

"I thought…oh never mind," Zane said.

Emmaline came out of the conservation center and walked straight to Zane.

"I need your arms around me," she whispered, and held her arms out for a hug. He couldn't resist. He felt an electric jolt when her head rested on his chest, his heart hammering against his ribs so that he was sure she could feel it. He leaned into her, his body tingling wherever they touched, realizing, more fully than ever before, that despite everything he was still in love with her.

CHAPTER SEVENTEEN

Zane and Lettie followed the staff and others who had been in the reptile exhibit area to the Nature's Attic theater for questioning. It felt like one of those goofy British murder mysteries his mother had watched sometimes, where a detective with a funny accent gathered all the suspects in one room and tried to reconstruct the crime.

"We just want to ask you a few questions, here on the spot," the dark-haired uniformed policeman told them as he shepherded them into the theater seats. On the raised dais, three spotlights shone down on an empty podium. On the floor next to the stage, Detective Old Spice sat at a folding table.

"Doesn't the Tulsa police have more than one detective?" Zane asked, regretting the sarcasm as soon as it came out of his mouth.

"And I was just wondering if there was any kind of mysterious death where you weren't involved," he replied, not smiling.

Zane settled into the chair opposite him and motioned for Lettie to take the seat next to him. She still looked shocked and pale.

"Nasty business, huh, darling? I'm really sorry you had to see something like that," Old Spice said to Lettie.

She sniffled and nodded.

"So, I've been hearing that Mr. Womack won't exactly be missed around the zoo. Not a popular character, I gather."

"And you've realized that he's the one who fired me, I suppose."

Old Spice looked at his notebook for a moment and nodded. "That was the same day of the fire, huh?"

Zane gave a short nod. He knew cops didn't generally believe in coincidences. He brought out his cell phone and showed him the text messages he thought were from Randy.

"Interesting," Old Spice said, writing a few notes in his book. "And you came from home?"

Zane told him about Cap Fager and their visit to his bar.

"You didn't know about her relationship with him?"

Lettie rolled her eyes. "Obviously not. We hardly knew anything about her, don't you think?"

"You've had a lot of surprises this week," he acknowledged. "Look, we're going to check out your story. There's cameras all over this place so we should be able to find out what time you got here. But I've got to say, it's not too often when one person is involved in two different homicide investigations in one week."

Lettie gasped.

"Homicide?" Zane said.

"Your mother's death is being treated as a homicide now, Zane. You knew that didn't you?"

"I guess not exactly...I don't know," he said.

"And Randy Womack. That lizard didn't slit his throat, I guarantee you that. Some person did, and then shoved him in the enclosure. It was a pretty big statement, if you ask me. Someone had a big beef with that guy."

"He was with me the whole time!" Lettie cried out. "We've

been together all day." She started sobbing with big hiccups. A uniformed cop behind the detective stepped forward and handed her a tissue. Lettie pressed it into her eyes and Zane put his arm around her and drew her close. They waited a few minutes for the tears to stop, and when they didn't, Old Spice closed the notebook.

"Best take your sister home, Zane. We'll talk again another time."

Zane felt like a pit of dread opened up in his stomach, like he was falling through a big black hole. Blood roared and rushed in his ears, somehow producing a sour taste in the back of his mouth. His grip tightened on Lettie's shoulder, and he felt both hands start trembling. He made a show of fumbling for his keys in his pocket so they wouldn't notice.

He just hoped the next time Old Spice came to talk to him, he didn't come with handcuffs and an arrest warrant.

\#

Magnolia was getting groceries out of the trunk of her car when Zane pulled the truck into the space next to her. She gave him and Lettie a bright, wide smile that only faltered slightly when she saw Lettie's puffy eyes and tear-stained cheeks.

She tucked one bag in the crook of her arm and Zane grabbed the second one.

"Let me bring you two dinner tonight," she said. "I was going to make brisket in the slow cooker."

Thinking it would cheer up Lettie to have company—and maybe himself too—Zane agreed and they settled on a time. He drifted behind her as he carried two of her grocery bags, and stifled a yawn, not wanting to give Magnolia the impression he was anything but looking forward to having dinner with her. But the reality was he could barely keep his eyes open.

His whole body felt leaden and slow. He just wanted to shut his eyes and sink into the velvety blackness so close he felt like he could touch it.

He had become the shiny, metal ball in one of those old pinball machines they had at the mall arcade. Flung around, bouncing off walls only to rebound from another barrier, flashing lights and bells going off. Everything was bright and loud and unpredictable and out of his control. On top of that, he felt like a failure. It seemed like he could barely give his sister any semblance of a normal life. How would he take care of her for the next four years?

He just wanted to crawl into bed and never come out.

He woke up hours later to hear Lettie greeting Magnolia at the apartment door. The smell of spiced beef floated into the bedroom, and his stomach growled in response.

"I wasn't sure if you had plates and all that," Magnolia said, setting a big paper bag full of dishes and more on the kitchen counter next to the crockpot she'd also brought. She started unpacking the bag, and Lettie set the table.

"Anything I can do to help?" Zane asked, standing uncertainly by the table.

"Nope," Magnolia said with a pretty smile. "Just sit back and relax."

Zane sat down and watched her as she went to work, filling the plates with delicious smelling beef, a green salad with bright red cherry tomatoes and mashed potatoes. Finally she brought the plates to the table and set them in front of him and Lettie.

"It's still hot," she said.

Zane was surprised how hungry he was. After the morning's terrible events, the desire for sleep had trumped hunger all afternoon. But now that he smelled food he was famished. He took a bite of the brisket and felt his taste buds come alive.

"Oh wow," he said. He didn't say much more as he cleaned the plate, then looked up to find Magnolia smiling at him.

"I'm sorry," he said sheepishly. "I guess I was hungrier than I thought."

Magnolia's smile widened. "Nice to have someone enjoy my cooking," she said. "And there's dessert too."

"You're a great cook," Lettie said. Their mother cooked maybe two or three times a year, but mostly Lettie and Zane fended for themselves with frozen meals or peanut butter and jelly sandwiches.

Magnolia removed foil from a casserole dish of apple cobbler and set it on the table. It was still warm and smelled heavenly.

Zane ate a forkful of cobbler and then another and another. Magnolia talked about her job as a bookkeeper for a company that made some kind of industrial fasteners out by the Port of Catoosa, her family in Arkansas and how much she liked horseback riding. She had a horse in Arkansas but hardly ever got the chance to ride in Tulsa. Zane listened and added in a few "wows" and "uh-huhs" but mainly focused on the delicious dessert, while Lettie peppered her with questions about horses. The only time she'd ridden a horse was at the pony ride at the Tulsa Zoo.

Almost as soon as Lettie mentioned the zoo, her mood shifted and she grew quiet.

"Did you hear that one of the zoo employees was attacked by the Komodo dragon today?" Magnolia said.

Zane filled her in on his past employment there and the fact that he and Lettie were there when it happened.

"Oh, I'm sorry I brought it up," she said. "I had no idea." She closed her eyes and took a deep breath.

"It's okay, Magnolia. It's fine. You've been...this has been a great meal."

She opened her eyes. "I usually pray before a meal, but you were so hungry I didn't want to stop you," she said.

Zane felt sheepish. "Sorry about that."

"It's all right. I think you needed to eat. But now, after hearing about what happened today, I'd like to pray for you two." She stretched out her hands to hold theirs. Zane wrapped his hand around hers; it felt warm, dry and fragile. His other hand held Lettie's. He'd expected her to roll her eyes but she seemed to really like Magnolia so she was resisting what must have been a strong urge. Prayer, like home-cooked meals, was a rare occurrence for them.

"Lord, protect my new friends Zane and Lettie, who are going through some hard times right now and keep them safe. Ease their minds and let them know that they can rest all of their troubles in you. Let them feel your presence in their lives. Amen."

"That was nice," Zane said. "Thank you."

Magnolia smiled and began clearing the empty dessert dishes. They washed up together, like a little family of three, repacked the dishes, and Zane told Lettie to work on her homework. She sat at the kitchen table doing a worksheet for history class, while he and Magnolia scrunched up on the couch, the television turned on low to some reality show. It was nice to have her as company on this night. He reached for her hand and she gave it to him, a little surprised but with a pretty smile. She leaned her head against his shoulder and they sat like that for a long time.

#

He was sifting through the trash can in his middle school lunch room, looking for food. Behind him, Lettie watched, her eyes hopeful. He could feel the waves of hunger coming off of her.

He heard someone laughing but he didn't care. He just kept

digging.

Zane opened his eyes and reached for the phone to check the time. 5:30 a.m.

He felt nearly crushed by the weight of responsibility. Lettie.

He got out of bed, trying to shake the dream out of his head, and went to the kitchen to take comfort in their store of food. No one was going hungry today.

Not today, a little voice said in his head. *But tomorrow?*

He made pancakes for Lettie and watched her bike off to school. He spent the morning in the apartment's parking lot, changing the truck's oil, and glad to be out of sight of the burnt trailer and the Majestic and Emmaline.

He thought about what Jeremiah would want his help with. He had to be running more than a small-time meth lab. He certainly didn't seem to be making it for his own personal use. His good dental health was plenty of evidence he did not indulge in the drug. He really was nothing like most of the meth cookers they showed on the news—the toothless, skinny worn out losers being arrested in front of some low-rent motel room they had set on fire, while child services carted their children off to some foster home. Or the woman who spent six hours trying to build a meth lab in a Walmart sporting goods aisle—they arrested her as she was mixing sulfuric acid with lighter fluid while families pushed shopping carts around her.

No, Jeremiah seemed to be more of a boss. Zane had to admit he felt some pride, thinking of this man, his father, as some kind of rich drug lord than some small-time criminal just trying to get high. He was working from a business model, not an addiction. He was making money by filling a demand.

One thing Zane had come to understand through his own addiction to alcohol and whatever else would get him high was that his addiction wasn't the fault of the people who made liquor. It was his own fault; something inside him that got triggered by alcohol and made him want more more more. So he wasn't going to judge Jeremiah or himself for making a living off of other people's problems. People did it all the time. The fact that Zane had his sister to take care of was enough of a reason for him to get in the truck and drive to meet his dad.

Zane pulled into the Reasor's parking lot a little before one and did a quick circle looking for Jeremiah's truck. Not seeing it, he parked at the end of an aisle in a spot with plenty of empty spots around it. He had two and a half hours until Lettie would be out of school, and while she was used to biking home from school alone he didn't want her to spend too much time by herself in the apartment. He was worried about her, with the violence of yesterday and the potential for more confrontation at school today.

He saw Jeremiah's truck turn into the parking lot and hesitate for just a moment until making a beeline for the parking space next to his.

Jeremiah lowered the passenger window on the truck and gestured for Zane to get in.

"So, you want to make some money?" Jeremiah grinned at him. His eyes were lit up like a fire burned within him.

"Yeah, of course," Zane said, feeling the hairs on the back of his neck rise. They definitely weren't going to buy a lottery ticket or do landscaping work. Jeremiah's fingers rat-tat-tatted on the truck's door in a fast rhythm. His whole body seemed to be vibrating. Zane thought he'd never seen the man so wound up, and this made him nervous about what was to come.

Zane cleared his throat. "But, you know I've got some heat on me, so I'm not sure I'm your man. Police were questioning me again yesterday. They think someone set that fire deliberately, so they're calling it murder. And my former boss, the guy who fired me. Well, he turned up dead yesterday."

Jeremiah eyes glinted with satisfaction. "He did, did he? I saw something on the internet about a death at the zoo yesterday. How did that happen, boy?"

"I didn't do it, if that's what you're asking," Zane said. "But the police probably think I did. Someone slit his throat and threw him in the cage with the Komodo dragon."

Jeremiah let out a big laugh, throwing his head back so it bounced against the truck headrest.

"Fucking karma," he said.

Zane didn't get anything too funny out of the situation. It was a ridiculous way to die, but he didn't find much amusement in the knowledge that the cops were probably considering him as suspect number one in a death penalty state.

"I mean, you had to enjoy it, just a little, right?" He punched Zane in the arm. "A little? I'm waiting for someone to put the video online."

"I'm not sorry he's gone, if that's what you mean," Zane said. Jeremiah's enthusiasm was unnerving him. "But I had my sister with me and Emmaline and it upset them both and it was pretty gruesome. And it's like someone set me up or something, texting me to be there."

"But you have an alibi, right? You were with your sister?"

Zane nodded.

"Then don't worry, son," Jeremiah said, pointing the truck into the 11th Street afternoon traffic.

They rode silently until they hit Apache Street, where Jeremiah made a right and pulled into a big empty parking lot for a strip mall with Mexican restaurants serving goat and menudo instead of the more familiar burritos and tacos. To the left was a bakery called

La Flor Panaderia, with a big white wedding cake in the window, and next door to that was a crowded little restaurant called *Guelagatza*. Zane had no idea how to pronounce it.

"You know how to handle a gun?" Jeremiah said, reaching into the extended cab of the truck to grab a blue and white duffle bag. Inside were two guns and boxes of ammunition.

"Sure," Zane said, a cold sweat popping out of his pores. He tucked it in the waistband of his jeans under his coat and they walked toward the restaurant.

Laughter and male voices speaking rapid-fire Spanish erupted from the restaurant, and he could smell fish and sweet corn from the breezeway outside the door. Yellow light streamed through the small portions of the plate glass windows that were not covered in a bright mural of a beach scene replete with a blonde mermaid, friendly octopus, menacing shark and playful dolphins.

Four dark-haired men sat in a turquoise laminated booth against the wall, underneath another mural, this one of a sunset desert scene with prickly cactus. The laughter and smiles faded slightly, replaced by curiosity and something slightly more sinister, as Zane walked through the door Jeremiah held open.

The smell of fish was much stronger inside. The scuffed floor looked dingy in the yellow light, and dust sat thickly along the baseboards. They walked past the men, now silent, through the narrow aisle toward a barrel-chested man with a thick mustache. He wiped his hands on the dingy white apron that covered an equally dingy white T-shirt, his face neutral instead of welcoming.

A white door swung open behind the register, and a slender woman walked past with a glance at Jeremiah and Zane, holding a platter of steaming food over her right shoulder. Wisps of black hair that escaped from her tight ponytail were glued to her high forehead by sweat.

The men at the table greeted her warmly, with a hunger that was for more than food. She was strikingly beautiful, with smooth olive skin, a straight nose and hollow cheekbones.

She bent down to rest the tray on a nearby table, and wiped her forehead with her arm before handing out the plates. The man at the cash register observed her for a moment, then returned his watchful gaze to Jeremiah. Zane wondered absently if she was his daughter or wife. Zane's nervousness seemed to have brought him heightened powers of observation. Colors seemed brighter, time seemed slower, every breath felt deliberate. He noticed a framed Scarface poster hanging behind the cashier station. A sure sign of gangsters operating out of this place, he thought. Every wannabe thug in juvie loved that movie.

"Where's Beto?" Jeremiah said to the man behind the cash register. The man behind the register flicked his eyes to the left and made a show of looking them both over from head to toe.

"I talk to him on the phone, he's coming," the man said. "You want something to drink?"

Jeremiah shook his head. Zane swallowed, his throat dry, but there was no way he would take anything if Jeremiah didn't.

"You got the shit?" the man said.

"I told Beto I would," Jeremiah said. "You his secretary or something?"

"Just curious," he said.

"You oughta watch that tendency," Jeremiah said, his eyes locked on the other man's in a game of stare down. Jeremiah won. The man pulled a white bar towel out of a metal canister full of murky water and wrung it out, and began wiping the counter.

The door opened and an ugly, squat, short Mexican walked in. He was in his late-thirties, wearing a dark wool coat that had long blond hairs on the shoulders and lapels and very shiny black shoes.

He gave Jeremiah a friendly smile.

"Hello, amigo!" he said, spreading his arms wide as if he was going to hug Jeremiah, but then stopping short. He spoke Spanish in low tones to the man behind the register, who nodded and went through the swinging door to the back of restaurant.

"Where are your fine sons?" Beto asked. "You have them wait outside?"

"They're busy. This here is Zane," Jeremiah said, pointing to him. "He's with me."

"Okay, okay, Zane, nice to meet you," he said. "You men hungry? Carlos's daughter cooks a great turtle soup here. Makes you strong." He thumped his chest for emphasis.

"Let's just do the business. You got the money?"

"Yes, yes, amigo," he said. "Not on me, but I have it. Carlos is bringing it from the back."

The four men at the table had stopped eating. They were paying attention to the conversation. Zane saw the bulge of a gun on the hip of the man sitting with his back to them. The woman had disappeared.

Beto took a few steps to the counter and rested his hand on it. "You got the stuff?"

"In the truck. You give me the money, we'll stroll on out of here and get the stuff out of truck. Easy as herding chickens."

The barrel-chested man came out holding with two hands a red and white drawstring bag, the kind used to carry sports gear.

Two of the men at the table got up and stepped out into the parking lot and looked around, then came back in and nodded at Beto.

Beto opened the drawstring bag as Carlos kept a tight hold on it. Beto waved Jeremiah over to look inside.

"Surely there is no need to count," Beto said. "We have done so much business together."

Jeremiah dug into the bag, pulling a stack of bills from the bottom and examining them. He nodded and put it back, then walked to the parking lot, with Zane, Beto and Carlos and two of the men following closely behind.

Jeremiah slowly pulled a ring of keys out of his jacket pocket, then unlocked the metal tool box in the bed of his truck and pulled out a grey plastic storage bin, the kind people use to store Christmas decorations or miscellaneous crap in their garages.

Beto popped it open, took out a rock and snorted it up his nose. He shook his head as if to clear it as the methamphetamine hit his system, then resealed the container.

"Always good doing business with you," he said, gesturing to Carlos to hand over the red and white bag of cash. He did so, as Beto lifted the meth out of the truck. Jeremiah handed the cash to Zane, who clutched it to his stomach. It was heavier than he thought it would be. The four men moved as a unit back to the restaurant.

"I half expected that daughter to be out here waiting to ambush us," Jeremiah said. "You've got to be ready for anything with these people."

Zane fought for control of his breath. His body felt white-hot, and he was covered in a skin-soaking sweat. He slid into the truck seat and laid the gun on the rubber floor mat.

"You did all right," Jeremiah said. "Better than Clyde did his first time out."

"Why didn't you bring them?"

"Well, now, I guess it's no real secret that Clyde's gotten a little too dependent on the product. And Link is, what do you call it? His enabler. I wanted to see how you did with this transaction, maybe talk to you about bringing you in."

"Yeah," Zane said. "But I told you I got a lot of heat on me right now."

"You think I don't know what that feels like? Try having thousands of people think you raped and killed two little girls."

There it was, Zane thought. The million dollar question. He swallowed hard, feeling his heart thump in his chest. It wasn't possible, couldn't be possible that his father did this awful thing. A jury acquitted him. But he still had to ask.

"But you didn't do it, right?"

"Yep, just like you," Jeremiah said with no hesitation. "Presumed guilty until proven innocent."

"I told you I don't really remember what happened the night of the fire," Zane said. He wanted his father to tell him this was all right, that it did not mean he lit the fire that killed his mother.

"Well, here's the thing about the night those little girls died. I had smoked so much weed and drunk so much beer I don't remember what happened neither. I woke up in a cave in the hills with an empty twelve-pack of cheap beer."

Zane looked out the window while he let the information, with its horrifying similarities to his own situation, sink in. A man in a dirty barn coat waved at them from a tractor on the side of the road. The air in the truck was stifling. He lowered the window a crack and closed his eyes as cool air hit his face. Jeremiah glanced at him.

"But fuck, you've just got to believe in yourself, don't you? I mean, why would I want to do something like that to two little Campfire girls? A lot of folks in Sallisaw, who knew me growing up, didn't believe it at all. They still think that the sheriff was just pinning it on me because I was an Indian. There was a lot of that kind of discrimination shit going on then."

Zane opened his eyes. The thought of his father being

discriminated against because he was an Indian made him angry. People were so ready to give up on one another. No, worse than that, they were looking for excuses to write people off. But that wasn't what he was doing today. Zane knew that he was looking for reasons to hold on.

"But you don't know for sure?" Zane's voice was hoarse.

Jeremiah grimaced and shook his head.

"They made a big deal about how I had blood on my jacket, and I didn't know how it got there. Thing was, though, back then they were just starting to know how to do all that DNA testing they show on TV now, so they couldn't say one way or another if it was my blood or what. And my lawyer told me that sheriff was such a shitty detective he didn't even preserve the evidence right."

Zane looked down at his hands, which were resting palm down on his thighs. If you inherit your eye color, your hair color and the shape of your ears from your parents, doesn't it follow that you inherit other things too? he thought. Alcoholism runs in families; violence and anger could be just as easily passed down. Was this why his mother kept the identity of his father (and herself) a secret? Did she hope that keeping him away from the influence of his father might stop the inevitable? But it didn't. In fact, Zane felt more angry with his mother than ever. Here before him was his father, the source of half of his DNA, the building blocks of Zane's personality. And he had the same experience as Zane: a forgotten night, a violent crime, a series of accusations.

He slumped in the seat and pressed his palms to his eyes. Could he have just been born this way? So it was all pre-determined and he was fated to his actions?

What an amazing rush. A flash of freedom that sunk into his skin and into his bones. He closed his eyes and concentrated on this new narrative for his life and his problems. He felt connected to his roots, to the world. What can you do, he thought. It's just genetics.

Jeremiah's voice broke into his thoughts. "Anyway, son, I think if you want to make some money so you can go back and finish welding school, then this is one way you can do it a lot faster than washing vomit and spilt soda pop off the sidewalk at the zoo. Work for me for a few months, until things cool down, then you'll have some money in your pocket and you can decide what you want to do. Selling meth is a pretty shitty career choice, but it might be okay as a part time job, you get what I'm saying?"

The money was definitely tempting, though he knew that his buddies in AA wouldn't think too highly of the choice. And even though he wasn't sure he actually trusted Jeremiah, Zane had faith in his own ability to protect himself...and Lettie. He'd keep her clear of all of this. He wouldn't even let Jeremiah know where they were living. And he'd make some money to help keep them from living in the truck and eating from dumpsters.

"Let's do it," Zane said. Jeremiah clapped him on the back, smiling like a proud parent.

"That's it, boy. You've got to seize the opportunity. *Carpe diem.* You ever heard that expression? It means seize the day. You only live once. You got to play the best hand with the cards you're dealt, and that's exactly what you're doing. I'm proud of you."

Zane felt warm with pleasure. *Carpe diem.* Maybe it was time to make a stand with Emmaline as well.

CHAPTER EIGHTEEN

His wallet fat with the five hundred dollars Jeremiah gave him, Zane bought a seven dollar ticket into the zoo. He wanted to surprise Emmaline, tell her how he felt about her and that he wanted her to be with him, for real. No more fuck-buddies. Time for the real thing.

He'd texted Magnolia and asked her if she could check on Lettie when she got home from work, and she'd agreed. It wasn't ideal, but he'd do better with Lettie in the future, once he got this stuff with Emmaline sorted out. It felt important to do it right away, before she left to go to Oklahoma City with this Hollywood producer who had to be just using her, as far as Zane could tell.

Maybe Emmaline's casualness about their relationship was because he hadn't made his feelings clear. Maybe she thought he liked things just the way they were and had no idea how much he wanted her. Loved her. Had always loved her. God, when he saw that text that she was in danger—he felt like the air was being squeezed out of his lungs. All he wanted today was to save her. That drive to the zoo crystallized his feelings for her, made them more real and more important than ever. And his father's words: *Carpe diem.* Why not act today? Why not enjoy the pleasures of having her in his life as soon as he could? He imagined her falling into his arms like she did yesterday, this time with her lips on his, her body pressed against him out of desire not fear. Why should he wait another day for that?

She sat on a ledge outside the glass door of the event center, talking to her pageant dress client Keysha who wore a bright and shiny red puffer jacket over slim jeans and cowboy boots.

"We've got to think visually for Oklahoma City," Emmaline said. "What's the stuff that gets on reality shows? Fighting obviously works, we've seen that."

"I'm not doing anything undignified," Keysha said. "But maybe something like a practical joke."

"Or sabotage of some kind," Emmaline. "Everyone loves to hate a villain. What if you replaced someone's hairspray with spray adhesive?"

She looked up and saw Zane.

"Zane, what are you doing here?"

"I came by to talk to you," he said. Keysha looked up from her phone and gave him a quick smile.

"I wish you'd called. Me and Keysha are just having a little strategy session for Oklahoma City tomorrow."

Keysha slumped against the back of the bench and stretched her long legs out. Zane kept his eyes trained on Emmaline, hoping Keysha would get the idea he wanted to talk to her alone. But she was oblivious.

"Spray adhesive in the hair is pretty damaging, Emmaline," she wrapped a lock of her own hair around her index finger as if to show how precious it was. "I'm not doing that. But what if it were that hair paint instead, like in orange or blue? She'd spray it on and instead wind up with blue hair!"

"I like it," Emmaline said, obviously intending to continue her conversation with Keysha while Zane stood there waiting. "But one spray and the jig is up. What about telling her some really bad news, like her pet died or something, right before the show?"

"That's just mean," Keysha said, crinkling her eyebrows together.

Zane rubbed the back of his neck and took a deep breath. "Em, let's go somewhere and talk," he said.

This got Keysha's attention. She tilted her head to the side, the dangly stars and moons in her earrings laying on her shoulder. She stood up and said, "I've got to call my mom anyway." She walked away from them, tapping her phone then pressing it to her ear.

"Peter says it is all about who is more outrageous on these shows," Emmaline said.

"Yeah, about Peter," Zane said. "I think you should stop seeing him."

Emmaline's face tightened. "Oh, Zane." She patted the bench seat next to her. "Come sit down."

Zane felt himself swaying back and forth on his feet but he didn't want to sit. He tried to calm himself down by planting his feet on the cement and looking directly in her eyes. But all he saw in them was door after door slamming in his face. *Carpe diem*, he told himself. Finish what you started, even if you already know the ending.

"You know I love you. I don't want anything bad to happen to you. The other day, when I thought you were in trouble, it was so clear to me."

"I know, Zane. I love you too." She grabbed his hand and he squeezed hers hard.

"No, I mean I *love* you," he said. "Not just like friends."

Her face melted into a mixture of pity and pleasure.

"I know, Zane. Part of me has known that for a long time," she said.

"I think it is time for us to bring it out in the open. I want you to be my girlfriend, not just my friend with benefits. I don't want to see you with another man. This Peter, I'm sure he's using you, Em."

"Maybe I'm using him too," she said. Her voice was low and flat and her eyes were calculating and cold. Still, he pressed on, hoping to shatter the ice forming with his warmth.

"But I want you to be with me," he said. His voice was pleading now. He didn't care.

She hesitated, her hand fluttering off wooden slats of the park bench as though she thought about touching him then changed her mind.

"Oh, Zane. I just don't feel the same way you do. I thought you understood that. We have this long history and this deep friendship. But we don't have the spark, you know?" Her eyes sought his for understanding and agreement.

He understood what she was saying. She meant she didn't have the spark, he thought. He had it; she didn't. Tears filled his eyes.

Slow footsteps on crunchy leaves sounded behind them. "My mom said that some girl in Florida broke out in hives when someone put pepper spray all along the inside of her gown," Keysha said.

Zane didn't move. Emmaline shook her head, as Keysha caught a glimpse of Zane's face in profile. She closed her mouth with a click of teeth and turned back around.

Zane flicked the tear off his cheek with his thumb. He had his answer. Now he had to find the strength not to beg.

"I've got to go," he said, his boots crunching on dead leaves. He didn't look at Emmaline, though he could feel her eyes on him as he rushed by Keysha. His ears ached for the sound of Em's footsteps behind him, her voice calling for him to stay. But she sat on the bench, watching him leave.

#

Zane flipped through the television's six working channels on an endless loop, unable to concentrate on the images flickering on the screen. Lettie was sprawled on the couch doing her homework, and he could still smell the spaghetti and meat sauce from the dinner he'd made for the two of them. The cool weather outside should have been the final component for a cozy evening at home, but he felt lost and uneasy, the skin on his neck and arms itchy despite being covered in a thin layer of sweat. He thought about turning the heat down but Lettie had been complaining it was too cold.

Lettie had printed out a picture of their mother at school and taped it to the wall next to the television. He'd taken the photo on her birthday last year. In it, she sat in her recliner hunched over, but with a beaming smile, a store-bought cake in her hands with one candle, already blown out. Zane only vaguely remembered the celebration. He remembered her as mainly unhappy, scowling, complaining and smoking, but here was a moment when she looked happy. Was that possible? It must have been taken in the days before Arno Jackson and his threats, perhaps when she thought she was still safe and hidden from her past life in her trailer in the Majestic.

She wouldn't have been surprised at all by Emmaline's reaction today. "That girl's always trying to go above her raising," Sherri had said many times. "She's always thought sunshine came out of her ass instead of shit, and she's only gotten worse after she got her college degree." Zane learned a long time ago not to talk about Emmaline to his mother.

Two sharp raps on the door. They didn't sound like the soft

taps he'd come to expect from Magnolia. He looked through the peephole and got a fish eye's view of Detective Old Spice.

He unlocked the door. Old Spice stood alone on the cement step, wearing a red jacket, its stand-up collar zipped up to his neck. His left hand was shoved in his jacket pocket, his right hung at his side, empty. He looked pale and tired.

"Hi," Zane said, stepping back. "What's going on?" He was embarrassed to hear his voice had trembled when he spoke. But the timing of the visit, the look on the detective's face…he didn't need Lettie's tarot cards to tell him something bad was coming.

"Can I come in?" he said, looking over Zane's shoulder and spotting Lettie, who watched curiously. "Hi Lettie."

"You must get a lot of overtime. You work some long hours," Zane said, leading him into the apartment to the couch, where Lettie coiled into a ball to make room for them next to her. Zane clicked the thrift store television onto mute.

"Long hours are part of it," he said, settling uneasily on the edge of the sofa cushion. "Algebra?" he asked, looking at Lettie's notebook filled with equations.

"Yup," she said, rolling her eyes. "I hate it."

"My son had a real mind for math. He always said it was a language he understood better than English. It was right around when he got to algebra that he realized he knew more about it than his old man."

"How old's your son?" Lettie asked.

"He's, uh, thirty, I think. Spends all his time making video games now, out in California."

There was a stretch of uncomfortable silence.

"Look, I shouldn't really be here," the detective said. "Tomorrow, we're going to get an arrest warrant for you, Zane, for the death of your mother and for Arno Jackson."

By the time his words registered in Zane's head, Lettie let out a long, ragged "no." And then she sprang to her feet and pummeled Old Spice with her fists. He grabbed her forearms and held them tight.

"Stop, Lettie," Zane said.

Zane felt helpless and alone. The detective was watching him with a mixture of pity and wariness. He probably wished he hadn't come here, alone, to deliver this news. Lettie looked terrified—but whether it was at the thought of her brother as a murderer or the possibility of him going to jail and leaving her in foster care, he could only guess.

Zane wanted nothing more than a shot of whiskey, then another.

Enough alcohol and he could forget he cared. But here and now, sober and sitting on the couch, his sister's future in his hands, he cared way too much.

What the fuck was this detective doing here anyway?

"I wanted to let you get things with Lettie in order," he said. "The captain would be pissed if he knew I came here tonight. But I think you deserve the chance to set things right, without involving child protective services. Maybe Lettie can stay with the Perrymans. Or did you find any of your mother's family?"

Zane jerked his mind back to the conversation. "Yeah," he said. "We met our grandmother, Verda."

"I'm not going to live in Okmulgee!" Lettie said. "This is crazy. Zane didn't set that fire, I know he didn't. Because I didn't go to that thrift store like I said. I didn't want to go to that sleepover. I was going to hide in the bushes and wait until you and Mom fell asleep and then come back in and go to bed. I saw Zane leave, then this other man came. I guess that was Arno Jackson. I gave up on my plan then and biked to the sleepover. I made up the thrift store thing."

"Lettie, is that true?" Zane asked.

"Yes!"

"Why didn't you tell us this before?"

"I don't know," she said.

Old Spice closed his eyes briefly, as though doing mental calculations of some kind. "Lettie, I know you want to help your brother. But there are serious penalties for lying to us about things like this, so I want you to think real hard about it," he said. "You sleep on it tonight and tomorrow if you want, you come to the station with Zane and make an official statement."

"I'm not lying!" she said.

"Zane, I may have made a mistake here, but I wanted to give you chance to take care of things with your sister. I've got a little sister myself. Our parents died when we were young and our aunt and uncle raised us. I looked after her fiercely. I can see you feel the same way about Lettie. I want you to have time to wrap things up right."

In one smooth movement, he stood up and walked to the door. He looked back at them, said a curt goodbye and walked out quickly, as if he regretted the whole visit and wanted to put it behind him as quickly as possible. The door shut with a loud click, echoing off the nearly bare walls of the apartment.

Sherri smiled at him from the wall next to the television, where a washed-up celebrity was trying to make her comeback through a ballroom dancing competition.

Zane hugged Lettie tight, as if he could keep her in this moment instead of facing whatever would come tomorrow.

Once Lettie was asleep, Zane walked a few steps out of the apartment and sat on the curb. The night was still and cold, his breath visible in the muted light of the quarter moon in the clear sky. It felt good to be outside, no ceiling overhead or walls closing him in. He pulled out the cell phone and called his father.

"Speak."

"It's Zane."

Zane heard ice clinking against glass and the sound of Jeremiah swallowing.

"What's going on?" He gave the word "on" a special emphasis, dragging the "n" sound out for a few beats.

"They're going to arrest me tomorrow." Zane felt his voice break on the word "arrest" but he hoped Jeremiah missed it.

Jeremiah was silent for a moment, then let out a long breath.

"Tough break. I was afraid that might happen," Jeremiah said. "You got a lawyer?"

Hopelessness hit him like a stone as he thought about the public defender who represented him in juvenile court. She was a bony woman in her mid-twenties, with stringy brown hair, who told him he was just her third case since graduating from law school. When he asked her if she won the first two cases, she changed the subject. She urged him to plead guilty and even now he suspected it was so she wouldn't have to go through the work of a trial. Was that the best he could expect this time around, with so much at stake? The death penalty hanging over his head?

"No, I don't have a lawyer. I'll take the one they appoint me, I guess."

"The guy who defended me, back in the day, he's still doing law. You could look him up. His name's Pete Hackett."

"I don't have any money to pay him," Zane said.

"I guess you don't," Jeremiah said. "Now, he did my case for free but that was a career-building move for him, if you know what I mean. Representing a bastard like me got his name in the papers and on television. Your case, I don't know if he'd take that on for free. He might be a fancy pants lawyer making big bucks now."

Zane fiddled with the thick black sole of his work boot he'd bought for welding school. Steel-toe for safety, all leather so they wouldn't melt with the heat, and no laces to catch a spark. Those boots cost him a hundred and twenty-five dollars and he'd worn them too much to take them back to the store for a refund. Maybe he could sell them, along with his welding equipment, to one of the other students, just to get some of his cash back.

"So, let me think about how maybe I can help you. So this is what you want to do, huh? Turn yourself in?"

Zane let out a sharp laugh. "I don't want to do it. I have to do it, don't I? What I'd like to do is run as far as I can, as fast as I can."

"It's an option, you know. You always have choices in this life. They may be lousy choices, but you got choices."

"They've made up their minds. I know if I let them arrest me then I'm practically already convicted. You did it—you hid away and then when they did find you, you were acquitted."

"Was a long time ago," Jeremiah said. "Things were different too. Lots of folks out here did not believe I was guilty, and the Cherokees gave me their kind of religious sanctuary. You're a little more on your own than I was."

Jeremiah stopped talking and took another drink. A truck roared by, its engine a wall of sound, and Zane waited for the noise to fade. Blue light from the television glowed from the apartment window across from him. Those people probably had no worries tonight. They could watch the news and hear about the crimes and the murders and robberies and maybe even the fire his mother died in, and they could shake their heads and say "ain't that terrible" and go to bed and never think about it again. Not him.

"What about Lettie?" Zane said.

"Sometimes, you just gotta think about yourself first. A man's gotta take care of himself first. Only then can he protect others."

Zane looked up at the sliver of moon, his eyes straining to see the dark outline of a full orb. He remembered as a little boy telling his mother he could see the full moon, even though only half was lit up. She told him she didn't know what he was talking about, that all there was in the night sky was the half moon. That he couldn't possibly see the full moon yet because it wasn't there. He remembered trying to explain it to her, until he saw the smile around her eyes and realized she was teasing him.

"You got a lot to think about, Zane. Now, listen, you get a good's night sleep tonight, well, as good as you can. I know you feel like you're all alone, but you've got me and Link and Clyde. And when you wake up in the morning, if you need my help, you just call. You hear what I'm saying?"

Zane said good night and laid the phone on the curb next to him. He took a deep breath, then another, trying to fill his lungs with fresh air to dissolve the cold, hard ball of anxiety growing deep inside.

#

"I'm not much of a housekeeper," Verda said, opening the front door of her little pink house to welcome Zane and Lettie. "I don't like to throw things away very much."

She just delivered the understatement of the century, Zane thought, as he followed Verda and Lettie into the house. Their movement kicked up dust bunnies and sprinkled particles in the air. Zane fought the urge to sneeze.

He'd never seen a house like it. The living room was completely full of stuff. Towers of boxes and bags extended to the ceiling like skyscrapers, with just a small footpath between them. His shoulders brushed against boxes and plastic storage containers and magazines and cereal boxes stacked in neat rows on either side. It smelled like lavender air freshener and coffee. She led them into the kitchen, where the footpath opened into a wider space holding a burnished oak table stacked with newspapers and books and loose paper and mail. There were two chairs at the table, and a rocking chair next to the white gas range, its top hidden by more stacks of boxes and grocery bags and junk mail.

Lettie set her duffle bag on top of a black trash bag stuffed with something soft, like pillows. It let out a little sigh of air with the weight of her bag, full of clothes and shoes. She'd brought just enough to get by until the Perrymans came back from Oklahoma City.

Verda got around surprisingly well in the crowded house with her cane, possessing a grace born out of long practice navigating her personal labyrinth. Zane wondered how the house hadn't been condemned as a fire hazard. A white and orange calico cat slunk into the room and slalomed between Zane's legs.

"Since Osbert died, I haven't quite gone through his belongings. And I have my collectibles that I just can't seem to part ways with. Anyway, Lettie, let me show you to the guest room."

Zane didn't see anything he would call a "collectible" in the house. It all looked like junk.

Lettie gave Zane a murderous look as she followed Verda into a dark hallway. The only way Zane had been able to get her to Okmulgee had been by promising she could skip school until the Perrymans got back from Emmaline's latest stepping stone in her reality television career.

If there were pictures of Sherri on the wall, they'd long been hidden by stacks of crap. The sheer volume was overwhelming and intriguing; you wouldn't so much look through it as you would excavate it like an archaeological dig. It was hard to believe that all this had been collected only since Verda's husband died three years before.

"So, I gave the bail bonds man a check already. He will come get you out a few hours after you turn yourself in." Verda squinted at him, leaning on her cane.

"That's the plan, but it may take longer. I'm not sure. That's why I wanted Lettie to stay here, in case they have me spend the night in jail."

"Do you want a sandwich or anything? For the road?"

Zane wasn't hungry at all. His stomach was in knots and his mouth was so dry he felt like any food would turn to dust on contact.

Lettie flung herself against him, her chest heaving with sobs against his. He kissed the top of her head and held her tight, hoping she couldn't smell the vodka on his breath. If she did, she chose to ignore it.

"Let's just go away, as far as we can," she whispered. "To Mexico."

"Can't do it, little sis," he said. "This is the best thing. And we'll get through this."

They hugged for a few minutes more, until Zane gently separated himself from her. Verda stepped in and put her hand on Lettie's shoulders.

"It's going to be all right, pretty girl," she said to Lettie. Zane pulled his phone out of his jeans pocket and handed it to Lettie.

"Why don't you hold on to this for me?" he said. "It's paid up through the month." She took it from him with resignation.

Lingering wouldn't help make leaving easier, Zane thought, but turning away from Lettie felt nearly impossible. The only thing that helped move his feet toward the door was the thought that he was doing the right thing for her, leaving her with Verda, even though they'd known her for less than a week. But it was clear to Zane that she'd decided to love them as family and that she was glad to have them in her life, even with all of the trouble and sadness they brought her. Maybe because she'd lived with so much sadness for so long, she was grateful for whatever scraps of love they brought her.

He followed the narrow footpath back to the front door and left without looking back.

CHAPTER NINETEEN

It took about forty minutes to drive from Okmulgee to Tulsa, where Zane was expected to show up at the 11th Street police station and turn himself in for arson and murder.

Zane passed the entrance to the north US 75, with its bigger white letters spelling out TULSA on green metal. Instead, he drove another two hundred yards and turned left onto the south US 75, toward Henryetta, and ultimately Sallisaw.

He woke up that morning knowing he would not be going to the 11th Street Police Station after dropping Lettie off, or ever if he could help it. He was going to his father to learn how to disappear.

It took surprisingly few words to explain to his father why he was coming to Sallisaw. In fact, it was almost like Jeremiah knew he was going to call all along; as though he'd given him the burner phone for just this reason. Was it a long-dormant father and son connection? Or just a side benefit of having a father who was a professional criminal? Zane wasn't sure. But he was sure that his father, who was known for escaping the long arm of the law for weeks and weeks during the state's biggest manhunt, would know how to help him hide.

He tried to concentrate on his driving, but his mind kept

drifting back to what would be going through Lettie's mind once she learned that he'd run instead of turning himself in. Would she think he was guilty? Or would she continue to believe in his innocence? But how could she continue to believe in him when he'd left her with a grandmother she'd just met in a house so filled with stuff that there was no room to breathe?

He glanced in the rearview mirror and saw a black and white cop car coming up fast on the right. His heart pounded blood so fast he felt light-headed. They'd come to find him. He eyed the speedometer and saw he was going eighty miles per hour. If he got pulled over for speeding now, it would be all over. He eased his foot off the gas and held his breath for three long seconds until the black and white pulled alongside him then passed him. Zane slowed down even more, letting the distance grow between them. They weren't coming to find him yet. No one even knew he wasn't going to show up yet—they wouldn't realize it for a few hours. He took a deep breath, trying to slow his heartbeat down like he did the truck's engine.

He pulled off the highway and into a truck stop at the next exit. When he took his hands off the wheel to shift into park and turn the engine off, he realized he'd been gripping it so hard that his short nails had dug crescent moons into his palms. He slumped against the seat and closed his eyes.

His mind was whirling. This was just the beginning. In fact, it was the warm-up. He could still change his mind, turn the car around and pull into the police station. Let them book him, take his fingerprints, his photo, fill out paperwork.

No. That wasn't how it was going to happen. He was going to take care of himself first. He'd hide out for a while, and eventually the search would cool down. Maybe they would start looking at other suspects. They'd find out more about Arno Jackson. Maybe

Arno set the fire. Zane just needed to wait it out. Maybe once things calmed down a little, he could start doing his own investigating. He could try to clear his name himself, just like people did in the movies. He imagined briefly going to the police with evidence that he was innocent. Then, just as fast, the thought came that he might find evidence that he did do it. He chased it out of his mind.

He was going to miss Lettie like crazy. He already did. He wondered what she was doing, and imagined her laying out her crystals and her candles, working on a spell to give him strength.

He thought about going into the truck stop, maybe to get some beer to calm his nerves. But then he realized that there were cameras everywhere—and he didn't want to leave any traces that he was here. He'd probably already left enough of a trace by just parking here. Some camera probably got his license plate already. Panicked, he started the truck and backed out so quickly that he nearly hit a skinny trucker on his way to the pay-as-you-go showers, carrying a raggedy blue towel and a plastic grocery bag with bottles of shampoo. The man slapped the side of the truck as Zane put it in drive and zoomed out of the lot.

#

An hour later, Zane parked behind Jeremiah's truck on the sloping dirt shoulder of a two-lane highway about fifteen minutes outside of Sallisaw. Link got out of his dad's truck and took Zane's keys from him. Zane lifted a black trash bag of clothes and shoes and some cookies and snacks he'd taken from the apartment and threw it in the bed of Jeremiah's truck. Amazing how you could whittle down your possessions to the bare necessities if you were forced to. He felt wild, like anything could happen.

A flock of plump wild turkeys scratched for nuts on the side of the highway, their dark wings outlined in bright bands of white. One strutted toward them, his red beard quivering as he gobbled the turkey equivalent of "You lookin' at me?"

Zane slid into the seat Link had occupied in Jeremiah's truck, still warm from his body heat.

"It ain't gonna be easy," Jeremiah said. "This ain't no luxury cabin or nothing."

"I get that."

"I got you some stuff you're going to need," Jeremiah said, pointing at a bag from a camping store. "Solar battery charger, lantern, some of them cowboy books. We'll come by and check on you from time to time, and you'll have the cell phone I gave you for emergencies. The thing is you're gonna get lonely and bored. They didn't come up with that phrase cabin fever for nothing. No internet, but I got you a radio too, that way you can hear the news from time to time, know what's going on the outside world. Just make up some kind of routine for yourself, something you do to fill the day, so you can structure your time."

Jeremiah pulled the truck onto the highway and Zane watched as Link drove his truck in the opposite direction. No time for second-guessing.

"Actually, living by yourself out in the hills like this, well, it's sort of like prison in the way you're isolated. You live on your terms. But better than prison because of course you're free to go outside and all that. But both prison and living out here, they give you a lot of time to think. You want to make that time as constructive as you can."

Jeremiah slowed down for a stop sign at an empty crossroads. Thick black power lines stretched along tall wooden poles like a parallel highway for energy currents.

"You got a plan for how long you're going to do this, son?"

"Til they quit looking for me, I guess."

"Police can be real bloodhounds, boy, they don't give up real easy. Might be longer than you think."

#

After a sharp turn onto a gravel road, Zane saw the outlines of a crude log cabin built in the middle of a thick grove of oak and hickory trees. The trees grew close together, their bare branches intertwining and blocking out light as effectively as they might have had they been covered in leaves in summer.

A set of rickety wooden stairs creaked under his feet as he followed Jeremiah to the door. The cabin was so small you could see it all from the door. Nothing had been done to ready it for his arrival. A double bed without sheets covering its blue and white mattress was against the wall, some pillows and a horse blanket thrown sloppily on top.

Jeremiah lit the lantern and its warm glow filled the room. The air was damp and cold.

"There's some wood out back already chopped, but probably only enough for one or two weeks. You'll want to be careful with how often you have a fire anyway, not to draw too much attention if anyone's out here hunting. But this shouldn't be the first place they look for you. Link's gonna leave your truck somewhere out by Durant so it'll look like you were heading south."

After Jeremiah left, Zane wrapped himself in the blanket and sat on the bed. There wasn't much wood, and maybe finding some more should be his first order of business.

The deep silence of the cabin was broken by a clap of thunder. Zane went to the window and saw the sky was covered in a thick blanket of dark clouds. A storm was coming. Rain spattered onto the window. He'd look for wood tomorrow.

He walked the perimeter of the cabin. A shelf on the wall near the fireplace held a small stack of old books, covered in a thin layer of dust. A field guide to birds, another to reptiles and snakes, and a couple paperback novels by Louis L'Amour. He opened one and started reading, trying not to think too much about where he was, and what he was doing.

CHAPTER TWENTY

The cell phone Zane had given Lettie rang with a call from a Tulsa number she didn't recognize.

"Hello?"

A male voice said, "Is this Lettie?"

"Yes."

"This is Detective Pastor. Remember, I was at your apartment last night. I'm looking for Zane."

"I thought he was with you," she said.

"He never showed up at the station," Pastor said.

It was a long time before she spoke, and when she did finally get the words out, her voice was shaky and small. "He dropped me off at our grandmother's in Okmulgee this morning. I haven't seen him since," Lettie said.

"You don't know where he is?" Pastor sounded more than skeptical.

"He didn't tell me anything other than he was going back to Tulsa," she said. "He gave me his phone." She sounded lost, and he took pity on her.

"OK. Well, if you hear from him, you give me a call right away, Lettie. OK? It's for his own good."

She hung up the phone without agreeing. Verda, sitting in the rocking chair in the kitchen, a pot of soup simmering on the stove next to her, raised her eyebrows.

"So he didn't show up?" she said.

"He didn't show up," Lettie repeated robotically.

"Here we go on another rollercoaster ride," Verda said. "Did you bring your tarot cards, Lettie?"

"Of course."

"Let's have a reading then," Verda said.

#

"Think about your question, but don't tell me," Lettie said. "Shuffle the cards."

Verda shuffled the tarot cards like a professional, bending them into a waterfall of backflips.

Lettie took the shuffled cards and cut the deck, then spread the cards out in a long fan on the kitchen table. She'd had to clear a space by setting stacks of *Good Housekeeping* magazine on the floor.

Verda selected three cards and lined them up, while Lettie smoothed the rest back into a neat deck. Something had to be orderly in this chaotic home.

"The first card is the magician," Lettie said. "This is the card for the situation. A fresh breeze is blowing. Bringing a creative solution. The magician is casting a spell in this card - this means he's in control of the situation."

She turned over the next card and smiled.

"This is a great card to have with the magician. The fool. It's in the action position. It means people will help you accomplish your goals. It also means there is no blueprint for what is happening. It's just being made up as you go along. It's about uncertainty and how comfortable you are with it."

"Now for the outcome," Lettie said. Boosted by the positive nature of the cards so far, she turned it over and her face fell to see a drawing of a man hanging upside down, his ankle tied to a tree branch and his head nearly touching the ground. His eyes were open and his hands were behind his back. A faint halo glimmered around his head.

"The hanged man," Verda read off of the card.

Lettie opened her book of tarot card meanings and read out loud. "In the future position, the hanged man foretells of a coming battle and warns you not to be aggressive. The best victories are battles that are avoided, not won."

"It doesn't mean Zane is going to lose," Verda said. "Usually these cards that look negative, they have positive meanings too."

"Absolutely," Lettie agreed. "See, down here it says to use helpless situations to study and learn. These kinds of predicaments release you from the obligations and responsibility of being in control."

"Ain't none of us in control in this situation," Verda said. "It's pretty much in God's hands now."

"And maybe Zane's," Lettie said. "So do you believe in God?"

"Of course I do, sweetie. Born and raised Presbyterian and still make it to church on Sundays unless there's ice on the roads."

"And you like tarot card readings?"

"I think they're harmless enough and fun," Verda said. "Though this one wasn't as fun as I'd hoped. Maybe I should have asked if I'd win next time I went to the casino."

"What did you ask?"

Verda put the three cards she'd drawn face down on top of the pile. "I asked if Zane was going to prison for these crimes. And I wouldn't rightly say they gave us much of an answer, would you?"

CHAPTER TWENTY-ONE

Zane woke up with the sun shining in his eyes through a tear in the dirty white curtains on an east-facing window. The air was chilly and damp and the cabin smelled musty, but it had stopped raining sometime ago. The silence was broken only by the rise and fall of bird songs.

Remembering his father's advice to bring structure in his days, he decided to go for a morning run and get a sense of the terrain. He hadn't run a mile since juvie, but it seemed like a good time to start up again.

He could also use the run to scout around for more firewood. The task sparked a small, buried memory of reading somewhere that the best wood for fires were the dry, dead limbs still on trees Maybe something one of the counselors at had juvie told him, or maybe something he had learned at the Boy Scout orientation he'd gone to, hoping to join along with his friend Brian. He had not known that it cost eleven dollars for the handbook and another fifty for the uniform. He had come home with the pamphlet and his mom had just dismissed the idea like she did everything that required money, like field trips or sports teams or birthday parties.

The wind was sharp, and the sun played hide and seek behind

leftover storm clouds moving steadily across the sky.

He took a deep breath of wet-smelling air and took off running. His sneakers made soft squishes into the dense, damp layer of leaves and loam and old vines. Boulders popped up between the trees, covered with moss and vines and little pools of rainwater. He flushed a plump grey rabbit out of some underbrush onto the trail in front of him.

He followed the narrow, barely-there trail as it veered to the left, away from the road, and through mud, rock and shrubs to the top of a knoll. The forest teemed with life. Every plant and creature seemed to be getting ready for winter. The squirrels hung from the branches of the many hickory trees, bounding across their slender limbs, harvesting nuts.

The forest opened into a grassy meadow, and Zane became very aware how visible he was standing alone in the clearing. He saw a flash of blue in the trees behind him, and heard a rustling in the tall grass. His heart started pounding. Was someone watching him? He slowed down to a walk, panting a little, and scanned the horizon. He saw no one, only a shadow of movement behind one of the thick oak trees.

He waited, counting slowly to thirty. No further movement. He skirted the meadow and headed back for the cabin. Probably hunters. But still, he had to be careful. He had to be invisible.

He laid low at the cabin the rest of the morning, waiting until the sun was high and golden to go to the little brook he'd seen on his run to try to catch a fish with the old pole and hooks left in the cabin.

Zane walked along the brook until he found a pool by a deep undercut bank in the shade of overhanging bushes. He squatted and dropped his line, the grub worm at the end of the hook sinking slowly. The fish must have been hungry, because he quickly had five little trout to eat for lunch.

Heading back to the cabin, he scrambled over a rock ledge, placing his left hand in a crevice for balance while he held the fishing pole and basket of trout in the other hand.

An immediate pulse of pain made him drop the pole and fish, and he slid partway down the ledge, tearing his jeans. He pulled his hand back to see two puncture wounds seeping blood. A quick and menacing rattle, like nothing he'd ever heard before, beat like a fast drum in his ears. He never saw the snake; it recoiled and vanished like a magician's handkerchief.

Zane tried to think what to do. He couldn't go to the hospital.

"*Utsanati* wishes humans well in general," a man's voice said behind him. "The snake didn't want to do you harm, but you startled him as he sunbathed in this last of the autumn's light."

Too numb with shock to be surprised by the presence of another person, Zane held his hand up and turned to look behind him. He saw an old man, stooped so that he was barely as tall as a child, with a weathered brown face, and long grey braids. Compassion and kindness spilled out of his brown eyes, and something else. Recognition, perhaps. Zane thought of the man who had given him the rock at the powwow all those years ago. Could this be the same person?

"Should I suck the venom out or something?" Zane was beginning to panic as his hand quickly swelled and the pain intensified.

The man spat tobacco juice and saliva into his palm and rubbed it on the bite in four circular motions. He blew warm breath onto Zane's hand, then began to sing in a low, plaintive voice.

"*Dûnu 'wa, dûnu 'wa, dûnu 'wa, dûnu 'wa, dûnu 'wa, dûnu 'wa.* Listen! Ha! It is only a common frog which has passed by and bit you. *Dayuha, dayuha, dayuha, dayuha, dayuha.* Listen! Ha! It is

221

only an *Usu ˮgi* which has passed by and bit you."

The pain slinked backwards as the man rested on his haunches.

"Do I know you?" Zane asked.

"I know your spirit," the man said. "And you know mine."

"Are you Cherokee?"

The man stood up. "Yes. My name is Ernest Buckskin. Can you walk? You must come with me to my home. You need to rest and you need more medicine."

Zane realized he couldn't tell the man his real name, and frantically tried to think of one to give him. He finally settled on the name of one of his buddies from welding school. "I'm Charlie," he said.

"Nice to meet you, Charlie." The man's eyes twinkled like they shared a joke. "Now come with me."

#

Zane woke up with the moon rising behind the trees, as big as a Halloween pumpkin and just as orange. Cool wind danced across his face and the stars glittered in a dark blue sky.

He lay on a bed of pine boughs, the dead limbs of another tree criss-crossing above him and resting on a boulder. His throat was dry, but when he tried to sit up, his hand and arm felt as heavy as a thousand pounds and throbbed with pain.

Outside the crude shelter, Zane saw a figure move, a long grey braid glinting in the moonlight. Ernest brought a cold metal cup to Zane's lips and told him to drink. It was a bitter tea, but Zane's throat was so dry he swallowed it quickly and with relief.

He must have fallen back asleep, because the next time he opened his eyes it was as the sky lightened and a round red sun rose on the horizon.

Ernest kneeled beside Zane, and scooped water out of a bowl.

Zane opened his mouth, eager for a drink, but instead he let it dribble onto his head and chest. Zane's skin felt so hot he expected the water to sizzle on contact. The man sprinkled water on him three more times, chanting something quietly, then pressing some beads into Zane's hand and leaving him to sleep some more amid chattering of nuthatches and songbirds.

Zane woke up again, the sun low and soft yellow white in the west. Ernest sat on the ground to his right, his back against the boulder. Zane watched him as he sat there, silently, his legs crossed, back straight, and eyes staring straight ahead. He seemed very relaxed.

"I ought to thank you for taking care of me," Zane said.

The man blinked, and turned clear kind eyes on Zane's. "It is what anyone would do."

Zane tried to sit up, but was immediately dizzy and nauseous.

"Slowly, slowly," Ernest said. "First roll on your side." Zane did so, his view changing from a roof of tree branches and blue sky to a view of flat earth and a boulder a few feet away. He stayed in that position for a few moments, then pushed himself to sit up. Leaves fell from his hair. His right arm was covered in a greenish paste, and swollen. A wave of pain hit, and Zane bit his lip in response.

"Your body has fought hard for life," he said. "I wasn't sure you were going to make it the first night."

"First night? How many nights has it been?"

"Three days since you were scratched by the brier," he said.

"You mean bit by the snake," Zane said. The last three days may be hazy, but he remembered that detail very clearly.

"In Cherokee culture, we take great pains not to offend supernatural beings or *ada'wehi*, like the rattlesnake. If the unfortunate incident happens, like it happened to you, we say you were scratched by a brier."

Zane looked at the man's face, a web of deep, fine wrinkles spreading over his cheeks and forehead, sparse grey stubble on his jawline and chin. His eyes were clear green, and he had the grace and fluid movement of a cat.

"Is that awful smell me?" Zane asked.

The man laughed and nodded.

#

With quite a bit of effort and several rest stops, the man helped Zane walk back to the brook. He must have known the terrain very well, for he zeroed in on a perfect spot for bathing—a large, still pool, leaves like lily pads floating on top. Zane stripped off his clothes. They felt heavy and caked with sweat. He waded into the cold water, willing himself to keep moving so as not to embarrass himself in front of the man, who probably bathed in icy cold water all the time. He glanced over to see what Ernest was doing, and saw him standing on the bank, fiddling with some beads on a chain and muttering under his breath.

Zane took a deep breath and plunged himself under. He came up shivering but exhilarated, the sun now low in the sky and glaring in his eyes.

"Three more times," Ernest said. "For good luck, as you might say."

Zane did as he was told, and on his last time, he stayed under longer, opening his eyes and looking through the cloudy water at the minnows swimming around him. He wondered if that green paste on his hand was tasty to them.

He popped to the surface and Ernest held up a heavy blue and grey wool blanket as a gesture for him to come out of the water. He rubbed the last of the green paste off of his puffy arm and hand, and walked in a shivering daze to Ernest, who dried him like a father might dry a baby after a bath. He felt renewed, clean, even reborn.

#

He spent that night by the stream, just as he used to sleep by the river in Tulsa when things got to be too much with his mother. The sound of water moving over rocks lulled him into thinking that he had gone back in time to the days before the fire had changed everything. Would he do things differently, he wondered, if he could go back to that time but with the full knowledge of his mother's secrets? Would he be kinder to her? Would he insist that she tell him the truth about his father?

Zane dreamt that night of following a crow as it flew silently through long, empty corridors of a vast building. The tips of its long wings grazed the walls as it slowed for sharp turns into more hallways. As he ran behind the crow, the light grew dimmer and dimmer until they were nearly in darkness. With a screech, the crow landed on the floor in front of an open door.

Heart beating fast, Zane looked in the door and saw Lettie, tied up and gagged on the floor, her eyes pleading for help.

#

Zane woke up and sensed he was alone. Perhaps Ernest had gone to check the animal traps or to fish. He sat up with some difficulty, his calves and hamstrings sore from the exertion of walking to the brook the day before. He was still wrapped in the blanket; his clothes were damp and draped over rocks. The chilly night air had not helped them dry. He put on his boots and wrapped the blanket tight around him and set off for the cabin. He had to get in touch with Lettie, even if it meant he couldn't use that burner phone again. As he tramped back to the cabin, slightly disoriented, he planned it out. He would go back to the cabin, grab the phone and some clothes, and hike closer to the campground. If he didn't find a pay phone, then he'd use the burner phone to call her, then throw it in the lake and try to find a place to buy a new one.

Back at the cabin, he got dressed in fresh jeans and two flannel shirts to make up for the loss of his coat, which was still too soaking wet to be of any warmth. But the phone was nowhere to be found. After ten minutes of searching, he gave up, assuming some campers and hunters came upon the cabin while he was gone, found it unlocked and took the phone. Luckily, they hadn't seen his wallet, buried in the messy sheets crumpled on the bed. He still had the money from his father.

He walked over to the campground, empty and forlorn given the cold weather and the fact it was the middle of the week during the school year. He found a pay phone by the showers and loaded it with all the change he had in his pockets, then dialed his old mobile number. He'd wake up Lettie, but that was okay. He just wanted to know she was all right.

A man answered the phone.

"Hi, who's this?" Zane said.

"Don't you recognize your dad's voice, son?"

"Jeremiah?"

"Me and you, we got a little problem," Jeremiah said.

"Where's Lettie?"

"She's right here," he said. "Say hi to your brother, Lettie."

"Zane, he's crazy. He killed…" Her words were abruptly cut off, like someone grabbed the phone from her. The next voice he heard was Jeremiah's.

"Aw, I hate that word crazy," Jeremiah said. "Link, will you show her what I think of that word?" Zane heard a smack of flesh on flesh and Lettie's howling cry. He fought the onslaught of black rage by gripping the phone and slowing his breathing. Getting upset wasn't going to solve anything now, he thought. But he should have known better than to have introduced Lettie to Jeremiah and his violent brood. He should have kept her a secret.

"Now, Zane, me and the boys came by to find you at the cabin yesterday but you weren't there. We did take your phone though. What a piece of luck that you called this morning. Saves us some time."

A red truck came barreling down the driveway toward Zane. He recognized Clyde at the wheel.

Clyde leaned over and popped the passenger door open.

"Get in."

CHAPTER TWENTY-TWO

After driving in silence for what seemed like hours but was probably only ten minutes, Clyde slowed down alongside tall fence of evergreen shrubbery, thick and dense as a concrete wall. He turned in a small opening adjacent to a beaten metal mailbox leaning forward on a crooked wooden post. He floored it up a steep dirt incline, branches scraping against the sides of the truck, like the sound of fingernails on a chalkboard.

At the top of the hill sat a clapboard house no larger than the cabin he'd been staying in. The roof sagged. A blue plastic tarp covered the front window, and the siding was so worn that only remnants of white paint remained on the grey, weathered wood.

Jeremiah's truck was parked in front of a wooden shed in even worse shape than the house.

"Is Lettie here?" Zane demanded.

Clyde just shrugged. His eyes were glassy.

There was something so menacing about the house that Zane shivered. Overgrown vines choked the foundation, and no light came from the windows. A broken children's slide lay on its side on the ground. The rusted frame of an old bicycle leaned against the wall.

The door creaked open and Link stood there, unsmiling. Clyde suddenly had a gun in his hand, and waved Zane out of the truck and to the porch.

Inside the smell of decay and death was strong, but Zane was so relieved to see Lettie he barely noticed it. She sat on the floor, silver duct tape over her mouth, her hands tied to an old-fashioned radiator that was bolted to the wooden floor. Her red and white pajamas were covered in a brown dust and she was shaking, either from cold or fear.

He started to rush to her, but Link blocked him. "Not so fast," he said, pushing on Zane's still-swollen arm and making it pulse with pain. Zane tried to stay expressionless but tears leapt to his eyes in instant response to the pain.

"You going to cry?" Link said, laughing.

"You see now that I gave you the good cabin?" Jeremiah said, his arms wide as he looked around the rundown space. "Not that I didn't see you turn your nose up at it when I first took you there."

Zane filled his lungs deeply, drinking the air as though it would give him courage.

"Why do you have Lettie, Jeremiah?"

Jeremiah just shrugged, the way people did to imply they were powerless against fate.

"I got to thinking about your situation —where the weak links were for you. Your weakest link here is your sister. She's very smart, that girl. She reminds me of her mother. She's got the same eyes and damn near the same smile. When you brought her to my house in Sallisaw, I thought I was dreaming. I thought I'd been taken back in time and was seeing your mother at eighteen again."

Lettie kept looking at the floor, her shoulders trembling. Zane felt like someone poured ice water on his stomach. Had Jeremiah done something to Lettie already? Had he hurt her? He tried to stay calm as he scanned her clothes for rips and tears and her arms for bruises. He saw none.

Jeremiah rocked from heel to toe on his worn cowboy boots, hooking a thumb in his belt loop. He's enjoying this, Zane thought, the anger rising in him again. But a simple calculation of odds made him simmer down. Three against one. Three armed men against one unarmed and injured man. Not the time to start a battle. He had to wait for his chance.

"Anyway, I just wanted to talk with her. I wanted to make sure she didn't see nothing that night that could, you know, incriminate you. I just wanted to find out where the weaknesses were. You have to do that, son. You have to look for the weaknesses."

Jeremiah crossed to Lettie and put his hand on the top of her head. She raised her eyes to Zane's and whimpered.

"Little Lettie here told us something downright interesting today during our little interview. Seems she did see something that night."

"Lettie, what did you see?" Zane blinked rapidly. He was frozen to the spot. Did she see him? Had she known all this time that he set the fire? Did she know her brother to be a murderer but kept it quiet?

"I'll talk for her, cuz she's a little tied up right now," Jeremiah said, laughing at his own lame joke. Lettie made grunting noises and shook her head rapidly at him, her eyes pleading.

"When Link and Clyde and me went to talk to her last night, she told us she'd seen Link before. Said she recognized him from being at the trailer park the day of the fire."

"Wait, what?" Zane shook his head, not comprehending. "She never told me she saw anyone."

"Guess she didn't remember it herself until she saw good ole

Link here again. Then it clicked into place for her."

"What was Link doing there the night of the fire?" Zane figured out the answer before he even finished asking the question.

"He was looking to buy property, weren't you, Link?" Jeremiah laughed and Link and Clyde joined in.

"Yeah, that's it. Me and my partner, Arno Jackson, looking for some investment property in some ratty trailer park."

Zane's eyes darted between the men and Lettie. His hands curled into fists.

"Did you set that fire, Link?"

"Hell, no," Link said. "I just drove the truck that night. And took care of the witness."

"I miss poor ole Arno," Clyde said. "Wish he hadn't gotten all soft that night and tried to warn Lily what was coming. He just wasn't smart enough to play both sides, but he certainly tried. Greedy little fucker."

Zane whirled to face Jeremiah. "You did it, didn't you? You fucking killed my mother!"

As he said it, he felt a ten thousand pound weight lift from his shoulders. If Jeremiah set the fire, that meant he wasn't responsible for it. Zane's knees nearly buckled from the sheer relief. He didn't set the fire that killed his mother.

"Bitch hid my son from me, all these years. She stole you from me," Jeremiah said. "Can you imagine how I felt when Arno first came to me with your picture? A man should know his son. And a son should know his father. It ain't right what she did."

Zane was reeling from the news, the sharp relief in knowing his own innocence, the horror at learning what his father did, and his fear at the situation he and Lettie were now in. And this strange, confusing warmth he felt to hear Jeremiah refer to him as his son. It wasn't right what his mother did, but how did it justify killing her?

She should have told him who his father was. He had a right to know this. He could have protected her. She kept this terrible secret from him, left him with nothing but a fake story about a Cherokee father who died on a rafting trip. While the real deal was sitting in Sallisaw this whole time, wanting to know his son and ultimately ready to take the ugliest, most brutal path to bring him into his life.

"Where's Verda?" Zane said.

"The old lady? She's probably at the police station reporting that Lettie's gone missing in the night, I'd guess. She don't hear so good, you know. Anyway, seems to me like you've got some choices to make here, Zane."

"Yeah?" Zane worked his jaw back and forth, trying to control his overwhelming desire to plant his fist on Jeremiah's face. He just wanted to lash out at all of them, at his mother, at the whole fucked-up situation.

"First off, is your sister here. I never had daughters and I'm damn glad of it because I just do not get how their minds work. Your mother never taught Lettie her proper place in this world."

Lettie raised her head sharply, the fear in her eyes replaced by anger and contempt. Zane was relieved to see the change in her; she was a strong girl and a survivor.

"I'm sure—" Zane said, stopping when Jeremiah raised his hand as a warning.

"I'm not done talking," he said.

"I don't see how your sister fits into our little puzzle too well. Now, you and me, we are blood and I think we can come to an understanding. But it just don't seem like your sister here would keep her mouth shut for too long with her big brother accused of murder," Jeremiah said. "And it just don't seem like you would go along real easy with her just disappearing, if you know what I mean. So my boys and I worked out a little plan here. I have to credit Clyde for coming up with it. I'll say one thing for that meth, boy, at least it gets your mind working a little bit even if half the shit you say is crazy."

Clyde stopped pacing for a moment and smiled at the half-baked compliment.

"It's like an initiation into the family," Clyde said. "You do this one thing, and then you'll be our full blood brother."

"Do what?" Zane said.

"We'll get to that," Jeremiah said.

The low, rumble and cough of a diesel engine floated in from the road. Clyde peeled back part of the blue tarp covering the front window and looked outside.

"She's here," he said.

"Well, we got to get going," Jeremiah said. "We'll continue this conversation later."

Jeremiah bent down in front of Lettie and stroked her hair. She tried to move her head out of his reach, but he cupped her face in his hands and held her still.

"Maybe we'll teach you a little bit of manners first," he said.

"Leave her alone!" Zane said, moving toward them until Link's body blocked him. He was holding a dirty white rag. Zane smelled some sort of alcohol or chemical, he couldn't place.

"Night night," he said, and covered Zane's nose and mouth with the cloth before Zane could even resist. He breathed in a sweet, flowery alcohol scent and fell to the floor.

CHAPTER TWENTY-THREE

Zane woke up in darkness, his throat and eyes burning and his lungs heavy and hard to inflate. He flexed his arms and legs and realized he was now tied up. He could smell vomit and hear labored breathing next to him. Lettie.

The sound of a diesel engine roared, as eighteen wheels skipped and screamed over asphalt at seventy miles an hour. We must be in a truck, he thought.

He laid there for what seemed like hours but may have only been minutes. Lettie hadn't woken up yet, but her breathing comforted him. At least she was still alive. At least he was alive.

The truck hit a pothole and his head slammed against the side of the cab. He figured they must be in the sleeping area behind the driver. He knew it well from playing in it while Emmaline's dad worked on his truck in the front yard.

Zane tried to say, "Lettie" but his voice was hoarse and cracked. He tried to swallow to wet his throat but his mouth was too dry.

"Lettie?" he croaked.

His sister didn't respond. He rolled to his side and inched closer to her, finally getting his chin onto her neck. It felt warm. Her shoulders rose and fell against his cheek.

He said her name again but she didn't move.

The pleated privacy curtains slid open by a crack, and terrified, he squinted at the bright daylight illuminating the truck's cab and dashboard. He automatically tried to bring his hands to his eyes to shield them but realized again that he was bound.

The driver downshifted and slowed, and Zane felt the truck arc to the right. They were exiting the highway. Icy shards of fear shot through him. This man—his father—was going to kill him and Lettie. What had he been thinking, to trust this man he barely knew, that his mother had changed her name and turned her back on her family to get away from? He had a brief moment where he wondered if he was having a nightmare, but the pitching and rolling of the truck brought him back to the here and now.

He'd never get married. Never have children. He wouldn't see tomorrow. He swallowed a sob, worried any sound would alert them that he was awake. He wanted to be conscious for whatever happened next. Life seemed so sweet and precious. Magnolia's face flashed in his mind, pretty and kind and full of promise. He thought of her praying before dinner, and recited the Lord's Prayer in his head.

The truck came to a stop.

"What are you doing?" a woman's voice said.

"I've got to get some gas, Susan," Jeremiah said with contempt. "Didn't you notice the fucking fuel gauge on empty? Or you too busy trying to stuff rocks up your nose that you don't give a fuck? You stay here, and holler if they wake up."

Zane heard the door open and shut, and the sound of boots on the ground, walking away from them. The woman's breathing quickened, and he heard the sound of cloth on cloth as she shifted in her seat. A few more moments passed, then the curtains clattered open. He saw the pretty face of the woman they'd seen at Jeremiah's house, the one who had just gotten out of prison and was trying to take her daughter home.

"Wake up," she said, her hair grazing his face. Her hand grasped Zane's shoulder and shook. He blinked and her face was just a few inches away, a Swiss Army knife in her hand.

"You've got to get out of here," she said. "He's going to kill you."

She stuck the knife blade under the zip tie and yanked it up. His hands popped free. She handed him the knife and he cut through his ankle ties, then Lettie's.

"Wake up, Lettie," he said, shaking her, then slapping her face. Her eyes flickered open but did not focus, then she rolled over and vomited.

"Why are you doing this?" he asked the woman.

"I don't want no part in murder," she said.

"Where is Jeremiah?"

"Out there somewhere," she said.

Zane thought about the times he was with Emmaline's dad when he refilled the truck. Trucks have huge fuel tanks, usually one on each side of the cab. Depending on how far Jeremiah was planning on traveling, it could take up to twenty minutes to fill the truck up, even with the high-speed pumps.

He only had one choice that he could see. Drive the truck out of there. Em's dad had taught him the basics, but he hadn't done it in a long time.

His head pounding and his hand throbbing, he crawled over the gearshift and into the driver's seat, and studied the dashboard.

"Wait," the woman said. "You need to hit me and push me out of the truck. He can't know I helped you."

"I can't...wait a minute..." Zane said, still looking at the dashboard and not sure he didn't need her to drive the thing.

"Hurry, he's coming!" she said. She put her hand on the door handle, prepared to pull it on impact. "Do it!"

Zane had just formed a fist when Lettie knocked her on the side of the head with a small fire extinguisher she'd found in the back. The door flew open and the woman dropped onto the concrete with a thud. Her mouth fell open, revealing grey stumps where her teeth should have been. Meth mouth, they called it, when your teeth rotted out from doing too much meth. Clyde and Link popped out of their trucks parked by the store and diner, and ran to her, glancing warily around.

Zane put the transmission in second gear and pushed in the parking brake knobs. He eased up on the clutch, and the truck rolled forward a few inches with a whine of the brakes.

Lettie scrambled into the front seat and slammed the door. She looked out the passenger window and saw Jeremiah running alongside the truck, gun in hand.

"Go!"

Zane pressed the gas but nothing happened.

"Do you actually know how to drive this?" Lettie said.

"Sort of," Zane said.

Jeremiah jumped on the running board, gun pointed at Lettie's head.

"Not so fast," he said.

"Help! Help us!" Lettie shouted, but her voice couldn't carry over the rumbling of the truck engines and the noise from the highway. Jeremiah whacked her with the gun in his palm and she slumped against the seat unconscious again. Zane raised his hands from the wheel in surrender.

#

Zane was laying down next to Lettie and Susan, both still unconscious and now bound to the bed in the sleeper cab.

Jeremiah had strung him like a pig on a spit, with his arms stretched over his head and tied to a hook on the inner wall, and his feet secured in the same way.

They had had their chance to escape at the truck stop and it had failed. The other patrons were either so preoccupied with what soda they were going to buy or so inclined to stay out of someone else's business that only one person approached Link or Clyde as they lifted Susan back into the truck. The fuel attendant who had casually asked if he could help was easily brushed off when Link said the woman was his mother and had epilepsy. So much for good Samaritans, Zane thought.

Susan stirred and her eyes fluttered open, gazing first at the ceiling then turning to meet Zane's.

"Sorry," she whispered.

He shook his head, trying to show her it was okay.

"We tried."

"He's a sicko," she whispered.

Zane felt a chill run up his back even though the sleeper cab was toasty warm from their body heat and heater on full blast.

"What do you mean?"

"Lots of people in Sallisaw think he just got a bad rap for those Campfire girls' death all those years ago, but I've seen him do stuff that makes me pretty sure he murdered those girls and did a lot worse. He comes off kind of charming, you know, in a dangerous way, but the charm part, that's the act. I just play along, you know. I try to tell my girl Breanna to stay away from him and his rotten sons but she won't listen. So here I wind up stealing trucks and getting caught in this mess, all just trying to stay on his good side."

"I won't tell him you tried to help."

Susan sighed and readjusted herself, then shut her eyes.

"Tell him what you want," she said. "I think he's going to kill me anyway."

Zane wondered why she hadn't moved far away when she had had the chance, but then thought of his mother and her attempt at starting a new life. Sherri had almost made it work. He shut his eyes too, wanting to ask Susan more about Jeremiah and what he had planned, but worried that Lettie was listening and would be more scared than she probably already was.

The truck grumbled and rattled into a lower gear, and the brakes squealed with pressure. They were stopping.

Link and Clyde carried Lettie and Susan out of the truck, Lettie still unconscious and Susan pretending to be. Jeremiah cut the zip tie around Zane's feet and let him walk though his hands were still bound.

They were parked in what looked like an industrial park full of warehouses. It was deserted. There was no traffic, and the boxy buildings, loading docks and parking lots stood vacant. It seemed to be well past quitting time, and already dark enough for the street lights to flicker on. The silo of a cargo terminal loomed overhead.

A faint bark could have been a dog's warning or a man's cough, or Zane's imagination. A train announced its arrival somewhere in the distance with a whistle and shrieking of brakes.

"I don't like having to point a gun at you, son."

"So put it away," Zane said.

Jeremiah threw back his head and laughed.

"I ain't stupid, I just said I don't like it," he said. "Look, me and you, we gotta talk. You've got some decisions to make."

He stopped in front of a concrete wall at the opposite end of the loading dock where the truck was parked as though ready to unload. A bright light came on, and the loading dock door slowly cranked up. Clyde unlocked the cargo door of the trailer and they both stood staring for a moment inside the back of the truck.

"The boys aren't sure what to make of our new cargo," Jeremiah said.

"You must make a lot of crystal meth to fill that truck," Zane said.

"Aw, that ain't what we got in there," Jeremiah said. "We're expanding, you see. And really it's because of you. Hadn't realized there was good money to be made in the lizard smuggling world. But your former boss, what was his name...Rudy?"

"Randy," Zane said, struggling to make the connection between this maniac and his good ole boy, lazy-ass boss at the zoo.

"Randy, right. Randy told me all about his little side business importing these here endangered reptiles through the zoo. Amazing how much a man will tell you when he's bargaining—I mean begging—for his life."

Zane gasped and shuffled back a few steps. He felt like he'd been punched in the gut with an ice pick. "You killed Randy?"

Jeremiah nodded with satisfaction. "I thought you'd like that. No asshole is going to fire my son and get away with it."

"You sent the text about Emmaline," Zane said, not quite believing what he was hearing.

"I thought you'd want to see him getting tossed around like a piece of meat by that lizard. Genius, wasn't it?"

"Something like that." Zane was confused and horrified. This man was a monster. No wonder his mother tried to keep him away. It was probably the best, kindest thing she'd ever done, to try to raise him as far from Jeremiah as possible. She couldn't help that Zane had the man's blood coursing through his veins, but she could make sure he was raised outside of his influence. Otherwise he'd be just like Link and Clyde, monsters-in-the-making, apprentices destined for hell.

He understood why his mother kept him away from them. It

didn't make it right, but he understood what she tried to do. She thought she could change the course of his life by giving him a fresh start. But the pull of his violent heritage was too strong. She must have seen that. He thought about the sadness in her eyes, when she dropped him off at juvie, her resignation at his violent behavior. She must have been so disappointed when it hadn't been enough to shield him from his father.

"Anyway, the zoo was just a convenient location for him, but really all you need are some connections, a warehouse and transportation. Low barrier to entry, as they say."

Jeremiah gestured grandly at the boxy warehouse behind them. Link appeared from inside the truck, holding a wooden crate with red markings along the side Zane couldn't make out. Possibly not in English, but it was hard to tell from the quick glance.

"Look, son, it's time to make some choices here," Jeremiah said, clapping his hand on Zane's back and squeezing his shoulder. "Here's one way it could go. The police find your sister dead in your mother's trailer. She ran away from Verda's when she realized that you were going to be charged with her death, and she killed herself. In her suicide note, she says that she is the one who set fire to the trailer and she couldn't stand to see you going away for it."

"You can't kill Lettie!"

"Calm down, calm down. You've got to think about it with a clear head, son."

Zane fought against the zip ties, then tried to scissor kick Jeremiah, missing by a foot and falling hard on his right hip. He grimaced in pain as he tried to push himself up using his left hand, still tender and slightly swollen from the snake bite. He wasn't sure he physically had enough strength to take Jeremiah on.

"Oh, that pisses me off," Jeremiah said, kicking Zane in the stomach. "What are you trying to kick me for, boy? Is that respectful?" He kicked him again, and the air in Zane's lungs shot out in a big burst, leaving him gasping on the concrete sidewalk.

Link and Clyde hurried down the steps from the loading bay and picked Zane up by his arms. They half-carried, half-dragged him back up the steps and into the loading dock, where they zip-tied his legs once again and left him laying on the floor, his cheek pressed into the cold cement, covered in a light coating of sawdust. Icy sweat soaked his clothing from the inside out, leaving him shivering and weak.

"Now, let's go over your options," Jeremiah said. He scraped a metal folding chair across the floor and sat above Zane.

"How about you let us go and we call the cops?" Zane said.

Link and Clyde laughed along with Jeremiah.

"Not a very realistic option, now is it?" Jeremiah said.

"See, boy, option one is that we kill your sister and you. Make it look like a murder/suicide, with you as the crazy who killed his sister and mother. People'll say, oh, that Zane, he kept to himself, you know. Never did know what he was up to. Used to fight with his mother. Not surprised he just turned on them one day."

"Not a very good option," Link said.

"Thing is, we might also need to have a little fun with your sister before she dies. You know, teach her some manners. I love to watch the way a girl's attitude changes toward you when she's begging for her life. We'll make it so she starts begging us to take her out of her misery. If you're anything like me, you'll want to watch. Might be a little hard at first, but then you'll feel this power…this god-like power. A life in your hands. Then you and me, we can get on with our life together. Father and sons, just like it's supposed to be."

Zane kicked hard against the ties, but found no give. He remembered Jeremiah telling him on the phone that he always had choices. But what if the choices were terrible?

"Let's let him think about option two some more and go see how Susan and Lettie are doing."

Jeremiah and his sons filed into the office, leaving Zane on the floor.

He heard footsteps, the sound of a heavy blow and a grunt.

"Let go of me!" Susan said. He heard scuffling noises, a sob, and the sound of two more heavy blows. Then quiet.

"Lettie! Lettie! Are you OK?" he shouted.

He waited, hearing nothing but what sounded like furniture being pushed a small distance across a floor.

"Lettie! Answer me!"

Finally he heard her small voice echoing off the loading dock. "I'm OK," she said. "They took Susan."

Clyde strode back into the loading bay, buckling his belt. He kicked Zane in the stomach with his cowboy boot. "Shut the fuck up." He grabbed the roll of the duct tape, tore off a piece and slapped it onto Zane's mouth. He walked back out, the sound of his boots on the concrete loud and sharp.

Zane wasn't sure how much time had passed until he heard a pop and the sound of something heavy, like a body, hitting the floor. Susan was dead.

CHAPTER TWENTY-FOUR

"See, it's a carnal thing," Jeremiah said, sitting back in the metal folding chair above Zane. He cracked open a pistachio and popped the nut in his mouth, throwing the two half shells on the floor, eye-level with Zane.

"It's about satisfying your animal instincts. You don't just survive. You dominate. I would have taught you all this, boy, if your mama hadn't kept you from me. Women are put here on this earth to torment us—it started with Eve and has continued on for thousands of years. I was surprised as hell when Lily left me. I didn't think she had it in her to do something so independent. I looked for her for months. If I'd known she was pregnant, boy, you know I would have searched the ends of the earth for you."

Zane knew what he had to do. He made a muffled noise, trying to indicate that he wanted to talk through the duct tape.

"You got something to say?" Jeremiah said, popping another pistachio in his mouth and tossing the shells on the floor. He set down the convenience store bag of nuts and leaned over to rip off the duct tape. Cool air hit Zane's lips and he took a deep breath, blinking back the tear that threatened to fall down his cheek as he thought of what would happen.

"I guess option two, then," he said. "But you have to promise not to do anything to Lettie before."

"I don't have to promise you nothing," Jeremiah said.

#

Link cut the zipties around Zane's ankles and wrists and he stood up. He tossed a prescription bottle of Xanax in Zane's lap. The label said the prescription was for someone named Samuel Bullhorn. He wondered if he even existed.

"Get your sister to swallow these pills," Link said. "She'll go to sleep and won't care about nothing."

"Where is she?" Zane asked.

"In the trailer," Link said, pointing with his thumb at the gaping black hole backed up against the loading dock. "Take one of the flashlights," he said.

Zane grabbed a black and yellow rubber coated flash light and clicked it on, following its circle of light to the truck. He heard Link's footsteps behind him—they didn't trust him totally, he thought. Link had been told to supervise.

Lettie was still passed out, her hair spread in a tangled mess on the floor of the truck. Zane was careful to keep the light out of her eyes. He kneeled down and jostled her shoulder.

"Lettie, Lettie, wake up for a minute," he said. After a few shakes, she stirred and blinked her eyes open. She started to smile but then fear erased it from her face as she realized where she was.

"Swallow these, Lettie," he said. "They are some pills to make you sleep real good."

"I'm already sleepy," she said. "I want to go home."

"We've got to take a long trip," he said. "And they want to keep you tied up for it. Wouldn't you rather sleep?"

He looked at her helplessly, feeling Link breathing over his shoulder. He turned around and saw Link was holding a gun that Lettie could clearly see.

"I guess," she said. He helped her sit up, and she shut her eyes and opened her mouth. He poured the pills onto her tongue—there must have been twenty of them—and then put the water bottle to her lips. She drank thirstily.

He sat down next to her and she leaned her head on his shoulder. He felt nauseous and overwhelmed by her unwavering trust in him.

"She's out," Link said. "Help me load her in this crate." He kicked the splintery wood of a crate marked PELIGROSO. Zane's hands shook uncontrollably as he helped Link put the lid on the top. Link saw it and said, "I'll nail it shut, man. You did your part. Now you go on and tell Dad it's done."

CHAPTER TWENTY-FIVE

"Girls usually kill themselves with pills," Jeremiah said as they stood outside the bed of the truck.

Zane couldn't help but think of the crate as Lettie's coffin, and he put his hand on it as though to send her a message of comfort. All he needed was one mistake, one moment where Jeremiah let down his guard, and he would make the most of it. He worried about Lettie, waking up alone in that box, thinking she was going to die. Jeremiah's voice jolted him back to the present. He reminded himself to stay focused.

"Link and Clyde will put her and the suicide note we typed up in the woods behind that shitty trailer park you all lived in. And it ain't that I don't trust you, but you understand we're going to need to keep you with me for a while to make sure you don't back out."

"Can I see the note?"

Jeremiah looked sidewise at him. "What do you want to do that for?"

"See if it is believable. I know her better than you."

Jeremiah considered the question, then shook his head.

"Link has it anyway in his truck. It just says what we said it did before. She set the fire, she can't stand to see you go to jail and she doesn't deserve to live. That kind of stuff."

Jeremiah opened the truck doors and waited for Zane to slide in. Once Zane had shut the door, he got in himself and started the engine.

"It's about survival in this world, kid," Jeremiah said. "The Cherokees see it as two worlds. Death just means moving between the two worlds." Maybe that was true, Zane thought, but he couldn't reconcile Ernest Buckskin's simple, peaceful ways with those of his father. Hearing his father talk about Cherokee spirituality made him feel ill and angry.

Above, the cloud bank broke apart, and a full moon lit up the white buildings and warehouses like gigantic tombstones. A red glow from the taillights of Link's truck illuminated the cab, giving Jeremiah an eerie reddish-orange glow that faded as Link drove away carrying Lettie.

As they drove along the two-lane highway, Zane looked for landmarks to try to figure out where they were. They must have driven in that semi for three or four hours, which could put them any number of places within Oklahoma, Arkansas or Missouri. Maybe even Texas.

Suddenly, the three coyotes from the trailer park stepped into the highway. They walked with their noses close to the ground then the lead coyote stopped suddenly, directly in the middle of the dotted yellow line of the highway, and stared directly into the headlights. His eyes reflected back like two red neon lights.

Jeremiah hit the brakes and the truck screeched to a stop just inches from the coyote's nose.

Now, Zane told himself.

He lunged toward Jeremiah and grappled for the revolver attached to Jeremiah's left hip. He got it unclipped and slid it a few inches out of the holster before Jeremiah headbutted the top of his head and jolted him back.

Zane kept a hold on the gun handle as Jeremiah tried to pry his hand off. Zane felt weak and the fingers of his snake-bitten hand were stiff and fumbling. He took his eyes off of the gun and onto Jeremiah's face, studying the pattern of grey and black whiskers on his cheek for a split second. This was his father. Jeremiah started to swing his face toward Zane's, and before they could lock eyes, Zane raised his right hand and punched him in the face with every last bit of strength and pent-up anger he had. Jeremiah's head bounced against the head rest from the impact and his hand slipped.

Zane looped his swollen index finger around the trigger guard and palmed the grip. It slid out of the holster easy, and Jeremiah tried vainly to block it, a few seconds too late. Zane grasped it with both hands and pointed it at Jeremiah's face. The sound of the two of them gasping for air filled the cab. Zane stared into his father's eyes, looking for a sign—of what, he had no idea.

"I can't let my sister die like that," Zane said.

"It's probably already done, kid. She's already gone. So you kill me, what do you have left?"

"I gotta know I did everything I could to save her," Zane said. "You're a sick fuck. No wonder Mom kept me away from you."

Jeremiah's eyes were wild, like a wolf backed into a corner. Zane thought he saw sadness in there too.

"You wanna kill me? Then shoot me." Jeremiah knocked his fist against his skull. "Right here, in the head." He hit his chest with the palm of his hand. "Or the heart. That's how you do it, son."

Zane squeezed the trigger, and blood splattered the truck windows and his face and clothes. The coyotes sprang off of the road in unison and disappeared into the woods. The truck rolled forward as Jeremiah's body slumped down and his foot came off the brake. Zane yanked the emergency brake up and sat for a moment, looking out the window through the drops of blood, wondering if the coyotes were real.

#

The police, alerted by Zane's 911 call from Jeremiah's phone, stopped Link and Clyde outside of Tulsa and arrested them for kidnapping. Lettie was rushed to the emergency room where they pumped her stomach out. The doctors said it was a good thing they hadn't given her more pills. The police found a bottle of thirty more Xanax in the glove box, along with a gun and the kind of knife used to field dress a deer.

CHAPTER TWENTY-SIX

The funeral for Sherri Clearwater, also known as Lily Davis, was a simple graveside service at the Castles in the Sky cemetery north of Mohawk Park and the Tulsa Zoo. It had always seemed like a peaceful place to Zane, with its long folds of green grass and its vine-covered castle walls at the iron gate entrance. Zane had purchased one of the least expensive plots deep inside its gated enclave.

Only a few people turned out on that grey November morning besides Magnolia and Lettie who sat on either side of Zane, holding his hands in the funeral home's black Lincoln Continental. Cap came, wearing dark pants and a coat, without his wife, and pressed two hundred-dollar bills into Zane's hand when he shook it. Verda Davis, in a long sack dress and black orthopedic shoes, stood next to Zane and leaned on Lettie on her other side for support. Emmaline and her parents were there, and the detective. Zane forced himself to remember his name and call him Detective Pastor.

Zane had never been to a funeral before, but he knew that he should say something. On television, people gave speeches about the person who died, telling stories about them that made the mourners laugh and cry. He couldn't think of any good stories to share. It was all still so confusing, but one thing seemed clear. His mother had wanted desperately to start a new life when she had found out she was pregnant with him. And she was successful for twenty-six years.

"Mom, you did what you had to do to take care of Lettie and me. I know you did the best you could. We love you, and…" Zane faltered a bit, not sure what else to say. "Rest in peace."

Magnolia plucked a rose from the floral arrangement sent by the Perrymans and handed it to him. Two white guys about Zane's age sprang into action, lowering the casket slowly into the ground.

"Throw the rose on the casket for your mother to take with her," Magnolia whispered.

Zane looked at the pink rose, its petals still wound in a tight bud. The last thing he would give her. He held it for a few moments, not wanting to throw it in, wanting instead to prolong the moment.

Magnolia took a second flower and handed it to Lettie, who threw it in right away, tears streaming down her face.

"You should have told us," he whispered, thinking that maybe he could have protected her more. He tossed the rose in.

Magnolia walked back to the car with Lettie and Verda. Emmaline walked up and hugged him tightly.

"I'm so sorry about all of this," she said.

He wrapped his arms around her, curious to notice that her hair, which usually smelled intoxicating, today just smelled a little sweaty and like, well, hair. It was like she had been demoted from goddess to human. She was still pretty as ever, but her face was tight with worry and her eyes seemed sad.

"Did Lettie tell you the TV show cut me loose? They said I wasn't the right fit," she said.

"That's too bad," Zane said, and he meant it. He knew how much she wanted that, and she was talented and deserved success.

"But it was really Peter's wife who put an end to it. That's what the assistant producer James said, anyway. Peter's wife found out we were together, and she told him no way. And apparently she is part owner of the production company."

Zane wasn't sure what to say to this bit of news. He thought of the pain, the shame and embarrassment of seeing her in that QuikTrip that day, buying condoms, oblivious to the pain she was causing him. Oblivious to everything but what she wanted.

Emmaline reached for his hand and squeezed.

"I realize now how important you are to me. You're the one who has always loved me. And I tossed that away like it was nothing. I'm sorry."

Those eyes, deep brown and rimmed with dark long lashes, now brimming with tears that made them look like melting chocolate. A week ago, he would have melted right along with them, into a puddle at her feet, grateful for her sudden change of heart.

He glanced over to where Magnolia stood with her arms wrapped around Lettie, her head resting on top of his sister's and her eyes shut. Tears ran down her face too, but they weren't the manipulative tears of a woman trying to get back in his good graces. They were the genuine tears of someone who cared deeply about him and his sister and wanted to be there for them in their grief.

He squeezed Emmaline's hand and kissed her on the cheek. She tried to lean in for a full kiss on the lips but he held her back.

"I've got to go," he said, and turned toward Magnolia and Lettie and his new life.

THE END